WANT IT
A Wolfshead Whiskey Novel

ELISABETH BARRETT

Published in the United States by Elisabeth Barrett

Cover design: Okay Creations

Epub edition ISBN: 978-0-9910943-9-4

ISBN-13: 978-1-946988-02-7

ISBN-10: 1-946988-02-2

www.elisabethbarrett.com

COMPLETE BOOKLIST

Wolfshead Whiskey Series
Own It
Want It
Need It

West Coast Holiday Series
Christmas in Tahoe
New Year's in Napa
Rendezvous in Point Reyes

Return to Briarwood Series
Once and Again
The Best of Me
Anywhere You Are

Star Harbor Series
Deep Autumn Heat
Blaze of Winter
Long Simmering Spring
Slow Summer Burn

ACKNOWLEDGMENTS

Writing my Wolfshead Whiskey series has been an incredible experience, but it would not have been possible without the help of so many wonderful people. In particular, I'd like to thank Mark Hall, Cameron Wong at Sonoma County Distilling Company, the folks at Anchor Steam Brewery, and the team at St. George Spirits. I'd also like to thank Joan Swan, Marina Adair, Elicia Hyder, and Jessica Scott, who have given me so much support and guidance. Thank you also to Jina Yoo, Sue Sbardellati, Layla Reyne, Alyson Charles, Kirsten Weiss, Gayle Parness, Rachel Scheuring, and Kristina Wright. Major thanks to Erin Crum. And of course, thanks to Jennifer, Jonathan, and my family. Love you!

CHAPTER 1

Juliette Costa was going to murder her brothers.

Right after she rolled this hundred-pound wooden barrel across a deserted parking lot.

Uphill.

While wearing three-inch heels.

At midnight.

In the rain.

That afternoon, she'd gone to downtown Portland to follow up with two upscale restaurants, new clients of her family's Italian import business that she'd personally signed last week. She'd returned to the warehouse late, hoping to get some work done.

But as soon as she saw that damn barrel sitting inside the delivery bay, she kissed her plans for the evening arrivederci because she knew it belonged to the Phelans, owners of Wolfshead, the brewery and distillery next door.

It was sheer luck that the Phelans hadn't already come knocking. No doubt they hadn't yet realized their barrel was missing, but once they did, all hell would break loose.

Hiding it really wasn't an option given that it was four feet tall and three feet wide, and had a picture of a howling wolf's head burned into the side.

God, her brothers were idiots for thinking they could get away with this.

Or maybe *she* was the idiot for cleaning up their mess yet again.

But if she didn't, she knew exactly how it would all play out. One of the Phelans would march right up to their front door, her brothers would see it as a declaration of war, and things would escalate. There'd be yelling and posturing. Name-calling and threats. The cops might even show up again. Or worse—there'd be fighting. And as much as her brothers annoyed her, she loved them, and seeing them getting smacked down by the Phelans again would suck.

She finally reached the opening in the chain-link fence at the edge of the Phelans' parking lot. Where one lot ended and the other began there was a change in the coloration of the pavement.

Unfortunately, when that heavy barrel hit the lip of the Phelans' pavement, it gave a little skip and bounce. She stepped forward to catch it, and it rolled backward, right onto her left foot.

"*Sh*—" Biting back a string of swears that would have had her nonna rolling in her grave, Juliette clenched her fists against the throbbing pain and looked up at the wet sky, wishing like hell she were anywhere else.

Or that she could pick up the damn barrel, but it was way too heavy, not to mention too bulky, to handle.

Any one of the Phelans could have lifted it solo, no problem. There were seven of them—seven tall, bearded, lumberjacked-up guys. A hundred pounds would be nothing to men as big as them, but it was definitely bad form to ask them to come over and retrieve the property her brothers had stolen.

So she took a breath, blinked away the raindrops from her eyelashes, and kept on pushing.

The barrel was grinding on the concrete, but at least she was making decent time now, about sixty feet away from the Phelans' main building, and closing in fast. The old brick buildings—two on the double lot—must have been built sometime in the 1920s when Portland was still developing. There was a light on in one of the upper-level windows, probably on some kind of timer because there weren't any cars in the lot—she'd checked. Otherwise, the building was dark.

But when she rolled the barrel another foot, the perimeter lights flicked on, illuminating the chain-link fence, the wet pavement. And her.

Juliette went utterly still.

Crap. She'd forgotten about the security cameras.

Come morning, they'd see her on candid camera, but the barrel really needed to be off her family's property, pronto. So she kept going, shoving at the curved wood, her heels sliding on the rapidly slickening asphalt.

The rain didn't bother her—it always rained in Portland—but couldn't her idiot brothers have picked something lighter to filch? A couple of cases of beer would have done the trick. Or a box of those Wolfshead baseball caps that everyone seemed to be wearing.

Ugh, the fact that she was even thinking about what *else* they could have stolen meant she really needed to scrape that money together and get out of here, ASAP.

Just another few yards and she'd be home free. Damn, it was even brighter here with that big floodlight shining onto the door. But it didn't matter because she…was…there.

Yes!

She shoved the barrel up against the warehouse door and stepped away, satisfied.

Until the barrel started rolling back toward her.

Noooo.

Quickly, she stopped it with her hands. If only she could tip it upright, but nope. Still too heavy, and now wet, to boot. She'd either have to roll it around the side of the building—not an appealing option—or find something to wedge under it. Casting her gaze around, she saw a couple of pallets over by the garage door.

She shoved the barrel hard, ready to race over to the pallets and back before it rolled down the slope, when a deep voice sounded from directly behind her.

"Need some help with that?"

She whirled around to find Brody Phelan looking down at her with that unnervingly steady gaze of his.

"Brody," she breathed, right before the barrel smacked her in the back of the legs.

She pitched forward, bracing herself for the inevitable face-plant, but it never happened.

Because in the smoothest move ever, Brody caught her just above the elbows at the same time he stopped the barrel from rolling forward with one large booted foot. She hung suspended in his arms while her brain processed that (a) she hadn't hit the pavement; (b) the barrel hadn't crushed her; and (c) Brody Phelan really had the most beautiful eyes she'd ever seen, an unusual shade of moss green, framed with reddish-brown lashes, crinkle lines at the edges.

If she were in the market for a guy (which she wasn't) and he weren't a Phelan (which he was), Brody would be exactly her type. Six three, with a wide chest and even wider shoulders. Massive biceps that bulged under his long-sleeved button-down shirt. Strawberry-blond hair swept back from his face and curling behind his ears. A thick, neatly trimmed beard that was a slightly darker shade of red. Huge hands that wrapped fully around her upper arms despite the fact that she carried plenty of extra flesh there, not to mention in other places.

"Hello, Juliette," he said, gifting her with the full charm of his smile. "What brings you over to our neck of the woods this evening?"

As if he didn't know.

Juliette cleared her throat. "I seem to have found myself accidently in possession of your barrel."

"Accidental possession," he mused. "Is that what they're calling stealing these days?"

"Stealing is such an ugly word, don't you think?"

"I don't think your brother was thinking much of anything when he swiped it."

Brody wedged his foot under the barrel, fractionally tightened his grip, then hauled her upright without much effort. Except he didn't let go. The heat from his hands seeped through her jacket, making her all too aware of his nearness and strength.

Damn, the man was big. And he smelled delicious—spicy and slightly sweet, like burnt caramel.

"Which one?" She had to know.

"Gio," he told her. "But the others helped. Just waltzed right in while Dylan was taking his break. I was going to come over this afternoon to have a chat with them, but I got caught up in work."

Gio. No surprises there. Her middle brother had a huge chip on his shoulder, and usually acted as ringleader.

Once again, her brothers had put her in a terrible position, cleaning up their stupid messes when they did stupid things.

All because of this stupid feud.

It had been a long time brewing—since her family had immigrated from Italy fifty years ago and set up shop right next door to Wolfshead. Family lore had it that Paddy Phelan and Joseph Costa, her grandfather, had hated each other on sight. There was anger and distrust from the very first, stemming from a property line dispute that resulted in a decades-long lawsuit.

The Costas had ultimately prevailed, but that was only the beginning. The feud had continued through the next generation and the next, bitterness simmering. There weren't constant attacks, but the tension was always present. And then seven years ago Sal, her eldest brother, had inadvertently left some packing material on the Phelans' side of the lot. That had been the catalyst for the new wave of fighting. Old man Paddy had come over, right onto the Costas' property, and ripped Sal a new one. Just with words, of course, but it was awful.

Then Juliette's dad had defended Sal because *nobody* messed with a Costa. Paddy had upped the ante by calling the cops. Papa had retaliated by filing a police report for harassment, and just like that, the feud was back on in full force. Sabotage, restraining orders—you name it, both families had done it—which in her mind was just dumb. Paddy was dead now, another generation was in charge, and they all should have moved on.

But they hadn't. If she didn't already have plans to leave her family's company, what she'd seen over the past few months would have been enough to send her running from all the testosterone that fueled the fighting.

Now, Brody Phelan was a different story entirely. As Wolfshead's Chief Financial Officer, he had a cooler head than the others. Typically, he didn't start fights, but he almost always finished them, effectively and without bloodshed.

Last month the two families had a huge argument about a delivery mix-up. After the yelling and the threats, Brody had stepped in with a plea for calm. When that hadn't worked, he'd ended up whipping out draft copies of a lawsuit—one he promised to finalize and file if her family didn't toe the line.

Brody was smart. Very smart.

That alone made him dangerous. Add *sexy as hell* to the mix and he was lethal.

Luckily, she and Brody had come to an understanding of

sorts. In public, they were cool to each other. It was expected, after all, given that he was a Phelan and she was a Costa.

But behind the scenes, they had something…more. They weren't exactly friends, but they weren't enemies, either. He helped her out by corralling his family's more egregious behavior and doing what he could to keep her apprised of anything the Phelans were doing that would affect the Costas' interests, and she did the same for him.

He also flirted like crazy with her, which she took to be part of the game they played.

Truth be told, she liked him. Not that she would ever admit that to anyone.

"What?" he said, his lips curling up at the edges. "No thanks for saving your ass?"

She snorted. "You should be the one thanking me. After all, weren't you the one who told me that American oak barrels are hard to come by these days?" She narrowed her eyes. "Unless you're planning on pressing charges."

He let go of her arms, tipped the barrel up so it wouldn't roll, then turned back to face her. "What would you do in my position? Your brothers have engaged in a consistent pattern of harassment"—Juliette opened her mouth to refute that statement, then closed it when she saw the look he was giving her—"a consistent pattern of harassment against Wolfshead. Stealing anything is bad, but you're right—these barrels are hard to come by. We need them for aging our whiskey, and they don't come cheap. However," he continued, opening his hand in what she recognized was a gesture of peace, "you returned it right away, and in pretty decent shape. There seems no good reason to stir up any more trouble. So, no. I won't press charges."

"Excellent," she said, rubbing her hands together. Just as she'd hoped. Now for the wheeling and dealing. "What else do you have for me?"

"Ed caught Tony skulking around the Wolfshead van. Thinks he was trying to let the air out of the tires."

"Not cool. I'll speak with him if you promise to talk to Connor. He's been standing at the edge of the property line again." With his arms crossed. In silence.

"Ah." Brody nodded, understanding. "He's freaking out your

brothers."

"Big-time." Connor was immense—six seven with lots of tattoos. She'd never heard the man say a single word, but then again, his stare was pretty damn effective.

"I'll ask him to stop," Brody said.

"Great. Thanks."

"Anything else?"

"Yes. Portland Eats." A well-regarded local event that both Wolfshead and Costa Imports usually participated in, a foodie smorgasbord that included the best artisanal food and beverage purveyors in the area. This year, Wolfshead had generously offered to open up its lot and the surrounding block, which it also owned, for the event. Of course, Juliette had convinced her dad to follow suit, and then several other neighborhood places had joined in, including a cheese-making enterprise called MaaMoo and a chocolate maker named Gūd. They'd participated in the event last year too, in a different location, but there were complications in the form of Gio throwing down with Brody's cousin Dylan. Not a good scene. "My family is now realizing what they've signed up for and is trying to back out of hosting if your family is involved. But I think I can get them to agree if we're on opposite ends of the event. That would mean we'd move our booth down a bit, and so would you. Thoughts?"

"I think it should be fine, but let me check with Gabe. Unless you want to do the honors."

"No, you can handle it," she said.

Gabe was charming. *Too* charming. Of course she could deal with him, but she'd rather expend her energy on more important things than deflecting half-assed pickup lines.

Brody nodded. "I'll take care of it."

"Great." Juliette felt some of the tension in her chest unwind. The barrel was back, she'd secured her brothers' safety, and started managing the next set of issues. Time to stop fraternizing with her hot frenemy and head home. "It was nice doing business with you, as always. And really, I'm sorry about my brothers. They get carried away sometimes. Family honor and all that. So thank you for accepting the barrel back and for not making a federal case of it. You and I are good, right?"

"Not quite." He reached out a huge hand. "Give me your cell

phone."

She raised an eyebrow. "A two-year-old off-warranty cell phone is the going price of American oak barrels these days?"

"Not to keep," he said calmly. "To program in my number."

"And why would I want your number on my phone?"

He gave her a cocky grin. "So you can invite me out for coffee as a thank you for saving your ass tonight."

"No. No way. We had an agreement. This"—she gestured between them—"is just business. We do not get personal."

He cocked his head. "Says who?"

"Says both of us."

"Three years ago. Times change."

"Yes, but you don't. Unless you're forgetting your girlfriend," she shot back. "Blond hair. About this high." She held up her hand to a medium height. "You sucked face in the parking lot for twenty minutes two Friday nights ago before she drove away."

He gave her an unrepentant grin. "Spying on me again with a stopwatch, Costa?"

"PDA much, Phelan?"

Brody shrugged. "Yeah, well, we broke up, so I'm single again."

"Ooh, so tempting, but I'll pass."

"Come on. You know we'd be amazing together."

"Look, Brody," she said, hand on her hip, "I've been a buyer for years. And as a buyer, I've learned the hard way to steer clear of things that have an early expiration date."

"Meaning?"

"Meaning you don't do commitment."

"Who says?"

"Everyone. It's your thing. You date women for three weeks and then poof"—she snapped her fingers for emphasis—"you're gone."

He gave her a sly smile. "Maybe I just haven't found the right woman yet. Maybe I've been holding out for you."

She shook her head. "Nope. Sorry. I have three brothers who pull the same crap, so your voodoo mind tricks won't work on me. You can't just smile at me and toss some sweet-talk my way and expect me to jump into bed with you."

His eyes lit up. "So you've thought about jumping into bed

with me?"

This. Man. "You're completely wrong for me."

"Yeah? Take me out for coffee and tell me all about it."

She gave him a faux-sweet smile. "That would take a lot longer than just coffee."

"Then let's do dinner instead," he shot back. "I know a great Mexican place."

Without meaning to, she laughed out loud.

He looked incredibly pleased by her reaction, all sexy smugness, and God, he was tempting. So, *so* tempting. Then she remembered who he was. And who *she* was.

She shook her head. "I can't do dinner, either. Good night, Brody."

"Not just yet," he said. "I'm walking you to your car."

"I'll be okay."

"And I will make sure of that."

He was back to being business Brody—the one who didn't try to get into her pants—and she didn't much care to fight anymore. He'd be safe enough walking her.

"Fine," she tossed off, striding away. The wind was still blowing, but not as hard, and it was still raining, which didn't really matter because she was already drenched. Brody caught up to her in an instant, his long legs taking one stride for every two of hers.

"You're going straight home?"

He said it like a question, except it really wasn't. "Yes."

He made a noise of approval in his throat. *Great.* This was all she needed. Yet another person dictating what she should do with her life.

Except Brody hadn't struck her as the type to dictate. Rather, he would suggest and persuade…with everything in his arsenal.

And the man sure had a lot in his arsenal, this super-sexy giant of a man with big hands and probably an even bigger…

No. She should definitely not go there. Although her mind couldn't help it, which really wasn't ideal if they were going to keep this business-only. Which she wanted to do. No, *needed* to do.

She glanced up at him, as if he could guess what she was thinking. Of course he was smiling.

"Enjoying yourself?" she asked tartly.

"Kind of, yeah. Aren't you?"

"No," she lied.

He laughed, warm and low. "I like you, Juliette Costa. And I think you like me—even if you won't admit it." She opened her mouth to argue, but he beat her to the punch by changing the subject. "Tell me. Why do your brothers always send you to clean up their messes?"

"Why do your brothers always send *you*?" she countered, feeling more than off-kilter.

"I volunteer. Aren't you going to ask me why?" he prompted, when she didn't say anything in response.

"Because you're a sucker?"

"Hardly."

"Because you're a masochist?"

"Nope, though I'm beginning to think *you* are." He held out his hand and waggled his fingers. "Come on. Hand over that phone. So you can call the next time there's a problem."

"Right. You want me to call when I have 'a problem.'" She put the final two words in air quotes, just so he knew that she had his number.

"Hey, I'm just trying to help," he said, and she must have flashed him a doubtful look because he laughed. "How about I make this offer a little more enticing. You give me your phone for two seconds and I promise not to tell the rest of my family what happened today. And I'll delete the security footage. I swear."

And *there* was the wheeling-dealing Brody she knew.

Juliette bit her lip, hesitating. Having Brody's number on her phone was a bad idea, but the draw of preventing her idiot brothers from being pounded into the pavement was too enticing to resist. Besides, he could program it in, but that didn't mean she had to call him. Or even keep it. She could delete it as soon as she got home.

"Deal." Reluctantly, she reached into her pocket and handed it over, placing it into his warm hand.

Brody made quick work of adding his name and number to her contacts, then handed back her phone. "Call me."

She frowned and shoved the phone back in her pocket. "I won't."

"Then text me."

"I won't do that, either."

"You will when you're ready," he said. "And I'll be here when you do."

They finally crossed over into Costa territory and reached her car, a beaten-up Camry that had seen better days. She stuck her key into the door, then she turned and looked up at him, the rain misting around his head, catching in his beard.

Curiosity got the better of her. "So…why *do* you volunteer?"

"I like helping my family. Keeping everyone happy." He rested a big forearm against the roof, half trapping her between the car and his body, and leveled a heated gaze at her—filled with desire and promise. "And that includes you."

The intense desire shooting through her veins was shocking. Disconcerting.

Arousing.

Badbadbadbadbad.

"Coffee," he said, his voice low. "With me. This weekend. I'm serious, Juliette. We've been dancing around each other for way too long. I want to try this. See where it goes."

His voice. God, it was mesmerizing. And his mouth. Gah. Just thinking about what he could probably do with that and his hands and that beard and…*no*. Giving in to Brody would be an unmitigated disaster of the highest order.

"You always get what you want, don't you?" she asked, keeping her eyes trained on his, as if he might pounce if she broke the connection.

"Yeah," he said.

"Not this time."

"We both know that you'll eventually say yes." He said this with utter confidence. So arrogant. And also, unfortunately, so attractive.

"I already have enough men in my life," she informed him. Bossy, controlling, aggravating men.

"Maybe," he said, leaning in close enough for her to feel the heat emanating from his body, the strength pouring off him in waves. "But I guarantee you've never had a man like me."

She arched an eyebrow. "Is that right?"

"That's right," he said, moving forward a fraction more.

He'd been in her space before, but not like this. Never like this, edging toward the line she'd drawn years ago, way too close to that point of no return.

She lifted her hand to his shoulder, and he went very, very still. Like a statue, hard beneath her fingers. She couldn't resist trailing down the wall of muscle that was his chest. Holy hell he was solid. Lower she went, then lower still. His breath hitched, then held. Sexy man.

He leaned in even more, bent his head low enough so she could feel his warm breath on her face, and she knew he was about to kiss her. Insistently, she pressed on his sternum. A warning to stop.

He froze for a breathless moment while he watched her and she watched him. A complicated expression crossed his face…and then he stepped back.

"Another time," he said, his voice husky.

She gave him a tight smile. Not if she had anything to say about it.

CHAPTER 2

Brody woke up with a crick in his neck, his tongue feeling like cotton. Thin light streamed in from the window, and a draft blew in from the door to the hallway. Dragging himself upright on his couch, he swung his feet to the floor and blinked a couple of times to clear his vision.

He'd spent the night in his office. Again.

It was becoming a bad habit, one that he didn't seem to be able to break.

The past year had been hard—harder than he ever imagined it would be. His brothers and cousins wanted to distill whiskey because that had been their dads' dream. He got that. Hell, he more than got that—he wanted it as badly as they did, mostly because *they* wanted it, and it was his job to make it happen financially. Except some days he felt as if his family had their heads in the clouds and he was the only one with feet planted firmly on earth where running out of money was a daily reality.

Distilling was crazy expensive. Sure, they had money coming in from the brewery side, good money. But on the distillery side, nothing, zilch, nada. Actually, since the accident, they had negative money.

So he slept in his office. And devoted his life to his family. And didn't date anyone for more than a few weeks.

Although that was for a different reason altogether.

Jesus, he was tired. So fucking tired. He yawned again, feeling his neck crack.

He needed coffee, stat.

Just as he turned to his office door, two of his cousins came in, clearly in the throes of a heated argument.

"It wouldn't be that big a deal to do," one of them said. That was Gabe, bright red hair flashing as he gesticulated wildly.

"It would," the other man said. And that was Ed, definitely.

From a distance, sometimes Brody had trouble telling his cousin Ed and Ed's identical twin, Dylan, apart, but up close it was easy. While they looked almost exactly the same from their reddish-brown hair to their six-foot-four frames, there were critical differences. For one, Ed was perpetually serious. Dylan definitely wasn't, and it showed in everything from their mannerisms to their speech patterns to their hobbies. Case in point: Ed liked introspective sports, such as fly-fishing. Dylan liked flinging his body off high places—the more dangerous, the better. Ed was intense and quiet, more likely to hide out during parties than make small talk. Dylan would be comfortable talking to a wall.

"You wouldn't have to touch it," Gabe said. "I'd handle everything."

Ed shook his head. "I still say no."

Gabe rolled his blue eyes. At six one, he was the smallest of the Phelan men, but his outsize personality and charm definitely set him apart.

Gabe was their sales guy, and a great one at that. Unfortunately, he also fancied himself an idea man, but every time he tried to put one of his plans into action, things typically turned out badly, especially if there was a beautiful woman involved. "What is your issue?"

Ed crossed his arms over his chest and glared at his younger brother. "You. You are my issue. What happens if someone touches a valve? Or decides that they want to hang out at the top of the fermentation vat, breathes in the fumes, falls in, and drowns?"

"It's not going to happen. I'll be with everyone the whole time."

"Famous last words," Ed sneered.

"I'm serious," Gabe insisted.

"As serious as you were about last month's tasting event that went completely off the rails?"

At that, Gabe frowned. "I told Hailey that she wasn't allowed to go behind the bar."

Ed didn't look convinced. "Uh-huh. And I'm guessing that's what you told Trina, too?"

"I was busy."

"Yeah," Ed stated. "Busy banging Staci in the utility closet."

Gabe waved a hand as if none of that signified. "This is different. It would be official." He stopped to think for a moment, then his eyes lit up. "I've got it! People could sign a waiver."

Ed just groaned and shot Brody a pleading look.

"What's going on?" Brody asked, except he wasn't quite awake and his voice cracked with the remnants of sleep.

Gabe finally turned to him, and when he did, his eyes goggled. "Whoa, dude, what happened to you?"

"I just woke up." He scratched at his beard.

"That's probably why you look like shit." Gabe made a strange face. "And why you smell so rank. You're working way too much."

Brody gave him a sour look and rose, stripping off his shirt in the process. He had deodorant in his desk drawer and spare shirts, too, a remnant from his days as a junior investment banker where working all night wasn't just a possibility, it was practically expected.

Ed turned back to Gabe. "Why are you coming down on him? You could learn a thing or two from his work ethic."

"I work plenty," Gabe shot back.

Brody finished putting on his deodorant and pulled a fresh T-shirt over his head. "What do you guys need?" The sooner he got this argument sorted, the sooner he could get his coffee.

"Right," Gabe said, turning back to him. "I want to give tours."

"And I say no," Ed stated.

"It'd be the perfect way to do outreach, and maybe even earn us some extra cash as we launch the new whiskey," Gabe insisted.

Ed shook his head. "It'd be the perfect way to be slapped with a giant lawsuit!"

"Let's see if we can't come to some kind of compromise," Brody said, holding his hands out in a gesture of peace.

"What kind of compromise?" Ed asked, his voice filled with unease.

"The kind where both of you get what you want," Brody said.

"I agree with Gabe that tours would be a great idea. I've actually floated the idea by Aidan myself, and if Gabe wants to do them, I'm fine with that." Gabe smiled triumphantly at Ed. "But," Brody held up his hand and went on, "I also agree with Ed that the way our setup is now, it's just too dangerous. Having visitors walk on our production floor creates a whole lot of liability we can't afford."

Gabe nodded. "So what's your proposal?"

"That Ed comes up with a plan—railings, cordoned-off areas, whatever it takes to keep visitors away from the machinery but still allows our people to do their jobs. I want to hear from him what it would take for him to feel comfortable with this. Then I'll do a cost estimate. In the meantime, Gabe can propose a plan for how he expects the tours to be structured—the timing, days of the week, that kind of thing. I'll do a cost estimate for that, too. If I can square both of the proposals, we'll go forward. If not, we drop it. Agreed?"

His cousins looked warily at each other.

"Okay," Gabe said.

"If it'll get him off my back, fine," Ed said. "But I'm not compromising on safety."

"Understood," Brody said. "I'll expect to see your proposals in my inbox next week sometime. Are we good?"

Gabe nodded. "Yes."

"For now," Ed said.

Brody nodded. "If you're good, so am I."

"Yep. Good. And I gotta go to a meeting." Gabe glared at Ed. "A *work* meeting."

Ed gave him a look that said he didn't buy it, and then he also disappeared.

Duty done. Now, coffee. Before he made it even a step, his older cousin Aidan strode through the door. Aidan was a former professional baseball player, and although he was now CEO of Wolfshead, he hadn't let his body go to seed. He was the same height as Brody, but had about twenty pounds of pure muscle on him.

"Thanks for handling them," Aidan said, walking over to Brody's desk and idly thumbing through a stack of papers.

"You could have done the honors," Brody said drily.

Aidan pulled out a paper and examined it carefully. "Who says I didn't?"

"You already talked to them?"

"Sure. They came to me first."

"Then why were they still fighting when I got them?"

Aidan dropped the paper and smiled tightly. "Because I told them both to get the fuck out of my office and get to work." His sharp blue eyes raked him over. "Sleep here again?"

Brody scrubbed a hand over his face. "Yeah."

"Thought when I left here at eight last night you were going home right after."

"Too much work. Things have been bad since the accident."

Wolfshead had been doing well, really well…until one of the ricks holding up the aging barrels had collapsed, destroying ten of their first-run barrels of whiskey, worth tens of thousands of dollars. That alone was bad enough, but thanks to the way the government regulated whiskey, Wolfshead was still on the hook for the taxes. They had insurance against loss, but it wasn't going to be enough to cover what they owed. Brody had been working overtime to deal with the insurance issues on top of his other duties.

"I brought you this," Aidan said, holding out a stainless steel mug. "Emma got it for me, but I thought you'd need it more. It's Coava. Black. Go on, take it. I didn't touch it."

"You sure?"

"Wouldn't have offered if I weren't."

"Thanks." Brody took the proffered mug and drank deeply. There really was nothing like well-made coffee, and this was Portland so there was plenty around. Almost immediately, the warmth and the caffeine jolted him more fully awake.

Aidan nodded his approval. "Good. Come on. Walk with me? We'll get some fresh air, perk you up some more."

"Sure." Brody followed him out the door and down the second-floor hallway.

In times past, Aidan would have demanded, not asked. Also, Brody knew for a fact that Aidan took his coffee with cream, which meant this coffee had been for Brody all along.

Thank God for Emma. Since Aidan had reconnected with his ex-wife, he'd been happier overall. And when Aidan was happy, he was a better leader and a better friend.

The two of them walked down the metal staircase, through the empty tasting room, and out to the parking lot.

Last night's storm had given way to a clear, cool morning,

typical for Portland in early August. As the dry summer season came to an end and the rainy season came on, there'd be more and more one-off storms until the steady rains came in October.

Today, there wasn't much wind, but the rain had made all the aromas sharper and clearer. Brody breathed in deeply, catching a whiff of wet asphalt and brick.

Over in the far corner of the lot was a basketball hoop his dad had installed years ago. Growing up, he'd spent way too many hours playing ball there with his brothers and cousins. Now it was old and rusted. The whole property could use an overhaul—new hoop, new pavement, shoring up the foundations of the old brick warehouse buildings—but he didn't have the time or the money right now.

They reached the fence that separated their property from the Costas', a four-foot-high chain-link job that had seen better days. It, too, could stand to be replaced, but he knew the Costas wouldn't step up, and Brody wasn't about to take on that expense solo for Wolfshead.

Brody leaned back against the fence and took a long drag. "Thanks again for the coffee."

Aidan's mouth went tight. "I know what you're doing for this place. What you've always done. Kept us together even when we were falling apart."

Guilt flashed through him, slick and fast. "You kept everyone together. Not me. I was gone, remember?"

"Here's what I remember. I remember having to quit playing ball. I remember being angry all the fucking time. I remember fighting with Paddy and anyone else stupid or brave enough to come up against me. And then I remember you stepping up. I had to be here, but you didn't. You were making bank in Asia, living your dream. A year in, I was struggling. All it took was one phone call and you wrapped up things and came back. Took a huge burden off my shoulders when you did, even though I know it was hard for you. You made this company what it is today. Everyone listens to you. Respects you."

"They respect you, too."

"They don't respect me as much as they fear me."

Brody met Aidan's gaze. It had always been the two of them, working together. They were each the firstborn, and even though

Aidan was a year older than Brody, their dads were twins and their moms were like sisters. Their bond was unbreakable—they were more than cousins. They were brothers.

Even when there were secrets that almost destroyed them.

Those secrets had cost him years he'd never get back—years away from his family. From Portland. From this brotherhood he'd forged in childhood.

He did not want to think about that right now.

"I had some glitches filing the insurance paperwork last night," Brody said. "I worked them out, though."

"I trust you. And I also know that we have enough money to cover it if the insurance company doesn't pony up."

"If we're taking money from the brewery side to cover our distillery costs, it feels like robbing Peter to pay Paul."

"We knew that's how it was going to go. We expected this. As long as everything's out in the open and everyone knows the score, we'll be okay, right?" Aidan gave him a searching look.

Brody shook his head. "It's been five years." Five years since he'd come back to Wolfshead, and he wasn't any closer to fulfilling the promise he'd made to his family.

Before Brody had returned, against Paddy's wishes, his brothers and cousins had started making whiskey again. Paddy said they couldn't do it, that they wouldn't be profitable, that it was folly to follow in the footsteps of their fathers—Paddy's sons—who had died in a Jeep accident up near Mount Hood.

Paddy had run Wolfshead with an iron fist, so Brody's brothers and cousins had struggled for months until Brody had returned to run interference and taken over Wolfshead's financial operations.

"I thought it'd take at least five," Aidan said. "And we thought it could take longer. It doesn't matter. We're doing okay."

"I just want things settled," Brody said.

"So do I, but not at your expense. You're taking too much on yourself."

"I'm doing exactly what I need to do."

"You're still punishing yourself for something that wasn't your fault." They weren't talking about Paddy anymore, and both of them knew it. They were talking about Brody's dad, John Phelan.

"He lied to me."

"What else is news?" Aidan said with a snort. "He lied to everyone."

But it had been Brody who'd uncovered the truth. Brody who'd had to live with his secrets, who'd taken the brunt of his father's anger, who'd suffered for years in silence.

And it was Brody who'd left, first time he'd gotten the chance.

In-state tuition and a big scholarship had been too big a temptation to pass up going to the University of Oregon, which was in Eugene, a bit too close for comfort to Portland. Aidan was there, which made it bearable, but as soon as Brody graduated, he'd gotten as far away as he could.

His dad had been furious, demanding that he return to help him run the family business. Brody had refused outright, instead heading to New York City to take a job as an investment banker. Away from Portland, Brody had thrived. He'd worked hard. Earned a place at Wharton for business school.

And then taken off for Asia, where he'd traveled to a different city every week, a different country every month. He'd been everywhere, seen everything—the lights and the friends, the women and the work. Living free. Feeling alive away from the secrets, away from the shame.

Until the accident.

The night he found out his dad and uncle had been killed, he'd been out at a bar with his team in Jakarta, Indonesia. Amid the flowing alcohol, the hooting and hollering, he'd gotten a call from Aidan. *Our dads are dead,* he'd said.

Immediately, Brody had felt sadness—and a shocking sense of relief. He'd come home to bury his father and his uncle. Spent more than a day with his family for the first time in close to a decade. But it wasn't until Aidan called him a year later that he made the decision to return to Portland permanently.

Winding up his affairs in Asia took some time. He quit his job, tied up loose ends with his clients, and broke up with his then-girlfriend. He also gave up his spot at Wharton and instead enrolled at UC Berkeley's Haas School of Business, where he could do a weekend MBA program that would ensure he could devote most of his time to his family. It wasn't until he was packing up his things to ship them back to the States that he'd felt something else—a bone-deep emptiness he'd suppressed for years.

"He made a bad choice," Aidan said quietly. "We've all done that."

"What he did was way more than just a bad choice," he said, daring Aidan to contradict him.

Aidan put a hand on Brody's shoulder and squeezed. "You're right. But we're stronger now because of it." *Because you came home.*

At that moment, a car came screaming into the Costas' lot, dubstep blaring. One of the Costa brothers, no doubt. Sure enough, after parking the car and taking up one and a half spaces near the front entrance, Sal emerged, his lean body still moving to the music in his head.

"Fucking prick," Aidan muttered, shaking his head.

A few moments later, another car swerved into the parking lot going fifteen miles an hour faster than was safe. It screeched to a halt in the vicinity of a spot, also near the entrance, and two dark-haired men tumbled out, arguing about something unintelligible. The two younger brothers.

"Assholes." Aidan was pulling no punches this morning.

A third car pulled into the lot, this one moving at a more sedate speed, though accompanied by a constant squealing sound. Slowly, the car came to a stop, perfectly angled in a space farther away from the entrance and safely away from the other two cars.

A long leg emerged from the driver's-side door, followed by the rest of a deliciously decadent body that Brody hadn't been able to get out of his dreams.

Juliette Costa. He'd know that figure anywhere. Today she had on a fitted top that showed off every generous curve. Her skirt was looser but floated high above taut thighs and shapely calves stacked on top of stilettos. God, she was perfect, with more than enough flesh to keep a man of his size warm on those rainy, chilly Portland nights.

And the mouth on her? *Damn.* He loved her attitude, loved that she always said what she meant. And all those snarky comments she flung his way riled him up like nobody's business.

Their verbal sparring had reached a fever pitch last night, and he'd been so very close to kissing her. If she hadn't pushed him away, he would have. Still, he was making progress: she was starting to flirt back.

Juliette flipped her long dark hair over her shoulders and reached back into the car to pull out her handbag and a huge stack of papers, which she hugged against her chest. She slammed the car door shut with a generous hip before realizing that one of the edges of her skirt had ridden up. When she gave a little shimmy to shake it down, the globes of her ass jiggled beautifully and all the blood in his head rushed straight to parts south.

Jesus.

Beside him, Aidan said nothing.

Brody cleared his throat. "Hear that squealing? Her serpentine belt's about to go. Someone ought to tell her she'll ruin her engine."

"And get my ass kicked?" Aidan said with a snort. "No thanks."

"Don't tell me you're afraid of Juliette Costa."

Aidan gave him a look. "I'm not afraid of anyone except Emma, mostly because I love her and it would break me if she left me again." He nodded at Juliette. "But that one? Her tongue should be registered as a lethal weapon. You should have heard the shit she gave Gabe the other day when he asked her out."

"What?" Brody's knuckles went white around his mug at the thought of someone else making a play for Juliette. "What the hell was he thinking?"

"That's what I said," Aidan said, oblivious to Brody's anger. "It was a suicide mission, that's for sure, but he blew it anyway."

Brody both did and did not want to know what his idiot cousin had done. "How?" he gritted out.

"It was boneheaded, even for Gabe. He started out by insulting her family, mocking her ride, then moved on to praising her, ah...*assets.*"

"Fuck." Brody clenched his jaw. "I'm guessing she did not take that well."

"You got that right," Aidan said. "She was on him like a viper. I told Gabe he should have done it the other way around. You know, butter her up a little before telling her that her family was wack and her car was junk. Anyway, let's just say I didn't need to speak Italian to get the gist of what she called him. By the time she was done, Gabe looked like he was gonna hurl."

Served him right. Juliette could take care of herself, but he'd have to have a talk with Gabe anyway. Tell him to back off. Because if anyone was going to make a play for Juliette, it was going to be him.

As if suddenly conscious she had an audience, Juliette stopped and turned. When she spied them, she stiffened, then started walking in their direction.

"See ya," Aidan said quickly.

"Wait, you're leaving?" Brody asked.

But Aidan was already strolling briskly back across the parking lot toward the brewery. "Don't need another woman to kick my ass," he called back over his shoulder.

Chicken.

Brody turned back to face Juliette. Her swaying hips and attitude put a huge smile on his face. *Bring it.*

Most women fell all over him. Wanted him for what he could do for them—in work, in life, and in bed. Especially in bed. Usually, he was happy to oblige. He liked fixing problems and he definitely liked giving people what they wanted. And not to toot his own horn, but he was damned good at it.

Juliette, on the other hand, had made it abundantly clear that she did not need or want him or his help. He wasn't even sure she liked him all that much.

And maybe he *was* a masochist, because that only made him want her more.

Juliette stopped on her side of the fence and pointed at the building behind him. "Wolfshead's that way, stalker," she informed him.

He took a long drag of coffee before answering. "But the view's better this way."

Juliette narrowed her eyes. "Did you delete the security footage?"

"Did you delete my number?"

Her cheeks went pink—enough to let him know that she'd considered it. "No," she admitted.

Promising. "I deleted the security footage," he assured her. "As soon as I got back inside."

"Thank you. I…appreciate that." Her dark eyes, so expressive, darted to the ground, then back up at his face. "I'm going to have words with my brothers this morning."

"Let me know if you need any help."

Her gaze went steely. "I can handle them."

"Oh, I'll just bet you can," he said. Truth. She could probably handle anyone. Even him, and for some reason that riled him up even more. "You gonna call me?"

"Nope."

"But you could, you know. Anytime."

"Don't hold your breath," she said tartly. He barely caught her tiny smile before she spun on her heels and walked briskly back toward her warehouse.

Damn, the back of her looked as good as the front.

CHAPTER 3

"What were you thinking by stealing that barrel? What could possibly have been going through your minds when you took property that did not belong to you and brought it over here?"

Juliette stood in the Costas' loading bay with her hands on her hips, staring down her tall, handsome, sneaky-as-hell brothers.

Tony, younger than her by two years, looked guilty and miserable, his hazel eyes downcast, his hands thrust into the pockets of his skinny jeans. Even Sal, four years her senior, had the grace to look ashamed, his dark brown curls seeming to droop with the tongue-lashing he was receiving.

But Gio? Her middle brother, just a year older, stared back at her defiantly, brown eyes flashing, mouth a stark line. "Those Phelans," he spat. "They left our olives out in the sun. Olives must be treated with respect. They must not be —"

"Spare me the lecture," Juliette interjected. "First of all, they did *not* leave our olives in the sun. The delivery guy left them on their side of the parking lot, you didn't follow up, and they got ruined, so don't pin the blame on them. Next, theft is a crime. If the Phelans had decided to press charges, you'd be charged with a misdemeanor, which carries jail time!" She paused for a moment to let that sink in. Unfortunately, Gio still looked furious, so she went on. "And if you'd stolen a barrel full of whiskey instead of an empty one, it would have been a felony!"

"A felony?" Sal muttered, his dark eyebrows going together. "Really?"

"It has to do with the monetary value of what you stole," she told him. She'd looked it up on the internet when she'd gotten home last night.

"Next time," Gio promised grimly.

Juliette whirled on him. "Don't you even *think* about it! Guys, you put me in a terrible position. Not only did I have to clean up your mess, but they caught me in the act."

"What? Who?" That was Tony, always with the concern, and always too late. "Which one?"

She cleared her throat. "Brody."

"The suit," Gio sneered.

"Well, he wasn't wearing a suit last night," Juliette informed him. "And he was awfully nice to take that damn barrel back without calling the cops."

Sal, her protector, got a hard look on his face. "What'd he say to you? I swear to Christ, if he said anything to you, if he was inappropriate in *any* way, I will kill him." As if to punctuate that point, he smacked his fist into his waiting palm.

"Me too," Tony said, following suit.

"Will you relax?" Juliette said. "Nothing happened. I rolled the barrel over there, and he took it."

"And then what?" Gio said, suspicion lacing his voice.

"And then nothing." Not quite the truth, but no way in hell was she getting into it with these three. "I apologized on behalf of the family. He agreed to let it go, he walked me to my car, and I drove home." Her brothers were still staring. "What?"

"He looks at you," Sal said quietly.

"Yeah, well, they *all* look at me when I'm cleaning up after you yahoos."

Sal narrowed his eyes. "He looks at you different."

"With intent," Tony said.

"*Bad* intent," Gio added, his tone ominous. "I saw him hanging out at the fence this morning. Watching you."

"You're not going to do anything stupid, are you?" demanded Sal, as if it were already a done deal.

This, right here, was exactly why she had to get away. As usual, her brothers were turning everything back on her, making her seem like the weak and helpless one, even though she wasn't at all. Her head began to throb.

"Will you three knock it off?" she snapped. "First of all, stop treating me like you treated Regina. I can take care of myself. Second, this isn't even about me. This is about *you*. And when I say *you*, I specifically mean your stupid pranks. They're making me crazy. *You're* making me crazy. So quit it, because if I find out that you've done anything else—and I mean anything—to antagonize those Phelans, I swear on the Holy Mother that I will dock your pay for a month, and you know I can do it because I'm processing all the paychecks now. *Capisci?*"

Her brothers made some noncommittal noises she chose to believe were *yeses*.

"Now go." She flicked her hand dismissively. "Do something productive that doesn't involve screwing with our neighbors." Her brothers grumbled, but mercifully scattered.

Rubbing her forefingers on her aching temple, she walked back through the warehouse, headed for her office where she had some ibuprofen in her bag.

Her mother came out of the shadows where she'd obviously been listening and fell into step beside her on softly padded feet. "You were too hard on them."

"No, Ma. I was too soft."

"They're good boys. They're trying."

"Yeah, trying to drive me crazy," Juliette said.

They were at her office now, literally a closet off a side hallway she'd commandeered just because she needed some space of her own. Unfortunately, there was no window. Or door.

She found the bottle of medicine and shook two pills out into her hand and swallowed them dry, her throat convulsing as she choked them down, then turned back to her mother.

In her late fifties, Francesca Costa was small and beautiful with a trim figure and thick, naturally curly hair—dark, but for one thick streak of white that shot back from her temple. Juliette had the same hair, minus the white streak, although her mom's always seemed so smooth and elegant, while hers typically ran to frizz if she didn't keep it weighted down with extra length.

Their faces were similar—big eyes and small, pointed chins from the Gallo side of the family. But while her mom's eyes were a warm hazel green, Juliette had clearly gotten the Costa genes, because hers were so brown they were almost black.

She wished she'd inherited her mom's stick-straight figure like Sal, but nope. She'd gotten shafted on that, too. Her curves had always meant clothes shopping was a pain in her ass—or rather, done to accommodate said ass. Most of the time, she left everything to her cousin Lucy, who thankfully had a better sense for what would work for Juliette than she did herself.

Her mother ignored that. "They're trying to be *men*, Juliette."

"Well, they're not succeeding." Unless being men meant making messes, yelling a lot, and telling her what to do.

Despite the fact that she had a master's degree, they treated her like a kid who not only couldn't handle herself, but didn't understand the business. Perfect example? Last month she'd tried to get her dad to change over to a new software program that would help them better manage their customer base—software she'd learned and utilized when she did an internship at a winery. She'd gotten shot down before she'd even shown him a demo.

They didn't take her seriously, and on the off chance they actually used one of her ideas, they gave her zero credit or thought it must be a fluke. Yet she was the one who kept things motoring along at Costa Imports, handling everything from ordering to customer relations to event planning.

"They're trying to protect you," her mother tried one more time.

"I don't need protecting! Say something to them," Juliette begged.

"They won't listen to me," her mother said. This was true.

"Then get Papa to say something to them."

"Pfft. You know he won't." On that point, her mother was absolutely right. Umberto Costa would only encourage them to keep doing what they were doing. Unfortunately, in the Costa family, there was a double standard when it came to girls and boys. Which meant that her three brothers got away with murder, while she couldn't even sneeze without someone jumping down her throat. "I wish you would just let them feel like they're taking care of you." Then, more quietly, "I wish you hadn't said her name."

It always came back to Regina, didn't it?

Her perfect older sister. Who'd turned out not to be so perfect after all.

"I'm sorry," Juliette said, the only thing she could say when her mother was looking at her with that awful mixture of melancholy and regret that was always there, simmering underneath the surface.

Francesca gave a sad little shiver, then blinked rapidly a few times. When she met Juliette's gaze again, her eyes were clear. "By the way, are you coming to Aunt Violetta's tomorrow?"

This was her family's fourth attempt at matchmaking in three weeks, and dodging them was exhausting. "I can't."

Her mother frowned. "What do you mean you can't? This is exactly what you should be doing. A nice boy is going to be there, just for you. You're not getting any younger, you know. You're twenty-seven. I started having kids before I was twenty-five."

"People get married later these days, Ma. A *lot* later." She loathed these setups even more than her brothers' heavy-handedness.

Francesca waved off her protestations. "I have it on good authority that this boy is from a good family, with a good job. Italian, of course. A podiatrist, I think. Or a proctologist." She shrugged. "I can't remember."

"One looks at your feet," Juliette said. "The other looks at your—"

"It doesn't matter what he is," Francesca said sharply, giving Juliette a scandalized look. "You'll be there."

The very last thing she wanted was to meet the foot doctor. Or butt doctor. Or any kind of doctor if he was one of Aunt Violetta's picks. "I have to work."

"You can work on the weekend."

"I'll be doing that anyway," Juliette said. Never mind that her brothers didn't or that she'd much rather be working on her own projects. And honestly, spending every waking minute with her family was not good for her mental well-being.

She'd known this would be the deal when she came back to live in Portland after school. Her family lived together, worked together, and played together. What she hadn't counted on was how stifling it would be. Marriage, especially to someone of her family's choosing, would stifle her even more. They wanted her to marry someone like them—an Italian man devoted to his family who would be devoted to hers as well, a man who would keep her safe, whatever that meant. She was certain that a man like that would never understand what she wanted or how to give it to her.

Francesca frowned. "You're staying at your aunt's place for

practically nothing. The least you can do is show up when she invites you over."

Juliette bit her tongue, but she wanted to scream. To tell her mom that she was done, *finito.* Done with dealing with her family and the business and the fix-ups and the aggravation. That she desperately wanted to show her family she could stand on her own two feet by opening up her own business, preferably in a galaxy far, far away. But they'd smother her alive if she even breathed a hint of her plans before they were cemented.

To escape, she needed capital. To get capital, she needed a bulletproof plan, one that her parents couldn't poke holes in or list out all the reasons why it would never work, or why the family needed her, or how she couldn't possibly think of doing something different, *away* from them.

But until she got a plan, she'd be trapped here in an infinite loop, cleaning up after her brothers, while being continually managed and stifled and boxed into a tiny corner until she had no room left to breathe. Or married off to a nice Italian guy who'd give her lots of nice Italian babies, thereby starting the cycle anew.

She couldn't let that happen. She *wouldn't.*

"I have a lot of work to do, Ma," she said, mostly to get her mom to quit pestering her.

"Good thinking. Get it all done now so you'll be free tomorrow night," her mom said. "Make sure you get a blowout before you come over. You want your hair sleek and smooth. And get Lucy to help you with your clothes. Tell her nothing too sexy. Doctors like their women to be a little more demure."

Ugh, no. Just no.

Francesca left as soundlessly as she'd arrived, and as soon as she was gone, Juliette sank down into her little chair in her tiny, doorless office. A hollow sound came from the drafty hallway behind her. She sat there for a moment, wondering how she'd gotten trapped here. And how she was going to get out.

She bet Brody Phelan didn't want to get out. He loved his family. Loved his work. She couldn't get involved with anyone right now, least of all him.

Working with her family was slowly killing her. What she needed to do was to stop thinking about Brody and concentrate on the task at hand—figuring out how to follow her own dreams before anyone married her off…or found out what she had planned.

Things were quiet until Thursday evening. She'd dodged meeting the doctor at her aunt's place though she'd had to face her mother's wrath the next day at work (it turned out he'd been a podiatrist), her brothers had lain low, she'd moved the ball forward with those holiday orders, and she'd started working on their contribution for Portland Eats.

What she hadn't done was think about her future plans.

Juliette locked the warehouse door, then briskly walked herself across the deserted parking lot to her car. She was swimming in work—and barely keeping her head afloat as it was. But instead of staying in the empty building, she figured she'd drag herself home, fix something to eat, then keep on working.

Then start the whole thing again in the morning as if she weren't dying to break free. She wasn't sure how much longer she could keep this deception up, especially because the thought that this might be her life forever was seriously depressing to contemplate.

She got into her car, pulled on her seat belt, and shoved the key in the ignition. It sputtered a little, but after a few tries, the engine turned over.

And then she was off. Damn it, her car was still making that squealing sound.

Her stomach rumbled, almost as loud as the noise under the hood. Maybe she'd do takeout. She had little in her fridge—ironic given her family's business—and just thinking about what to make, heading to the grocery store to buy ingredients, then going home to a cold house and a colder stove gave her hives.

She was mulling over whether she was in the mood for Indian or Thai when the engine suddenly seized and the car gave an awful lurch, jerking her forward, then back. While it was still shuddering, she quickly turned the steering wheel to the right. Just before the electrical system completely died, she eased the car over to the curb where it came to rest with a juddering thud. There was zero power, so she pulled up the parking brake, wincing at the harsh sound as the gears ground into place.

Her heart was racing a mile a minute. Thank God she hadn't been on a major road when the engine had cut out.

But now she was in a seriously dark and deserted area close to Morrison Bridge, which itself wasn't that dangerous, at least not in the daytime, but was kind of a sketchy place to hang out at night.

Well, *crap.*

Quickly, she pulled out her cell phone. The power bar said she only had 9 percent power left, so she called her parents' landline, thinking they should be home, but no one picked up. Nor did either of her parents pick up on their cell phones. For a moment, she thought something was wrong, until she realized that her parents were at Aunt Violetta's again. Calling Aunt Violetta would lead to all sorts of other complications, so she called Gio. He picked up on the seventh ring.

"Whassaaaaaap?" he said, just like a '90s frat boy. There was raucous shouting in the background as Gio's friends repeated the ridiculous phrase.

"Where are you?"

"What?"

"Where. Are. You?" she yelled, her voice echoing into the crisp night air.

"Migration," he yelled back. A brewery in the Laurelhurst neighborhood where they sometimes went after work.

"Are you drunk?"

"Naw." He laughed.

"Gio—"

"Well, yeah. A little."

"But you only left work an hour ago."

"I'm just buzzed," he said, sounding sullen.

"Who's got your car keys?" she demanded.

"Nobody."

"Is Sal there?"

"Yeah, but—"

"Hand him the phone," Juliette said. "Now."

"It's Juliette," Gio said, his voice a bit muffled. He clearly had the phone up against his chest, but idiot that he was, he didn't realize she could hear every word.

Sal's voice came through, too, though even more muffled than Gio's. "I don't want to talk to her."

"Come on, man," Gio whined. "Get her off my back."

There was muted arguing, then a shuffling sound. Finally, Sal picked up.

"Whassaaaaaap?"

Ugh. Stupidity was contagious. And so was the alcohol, because it was clear that Sal was also drunk.

"How many did you have?" Juliette questioned.

"Two."

"And the one in your hand?"

"Makes three."

Juliette sighed. "Take Gio's car keys. You got me?"

"He's fine."

"He's not, and neither are you. Both of you take a car service home. And if you don't, I'm going to tell Mom that you screwed up the holiday orders."

Sal's voice edged into a whine. "But you already fixed those."

"And I can just unfix them if you do something dumb." She hated her brothers right now, but she also loved them more than life itself. "I'm serious, Sal. You drive that car, the flak you get from a DUI is going to look like sunshine and roses compared to what you'll get from me. Got it?"

"Loud and clear." He didn't sound so drunk anymore, and she wasn't at all sorry for killing his buzz. "So…you, um, want something else?"

"No." It wasn't as though Sal was going to come get her tonight. "Just be safe. Okay?"

"'Kay."

On a sigh, she hung up the phone. Seven percent juice. Quickly, she dialed Tony.

He picked up on the third ring.

"Yo." He sounded distracted and there were pings and beeps in the background, which probably meant he was playing video games again.

"Hey, Tony. My car broke down. Can you come get me?"

"Uh…where are you?"

"Almost to the bridge."

"Just go back to the warehouse and I'll pick you up later."

"How much later?" she questioned.

"Um…a couple hours?"

Read: midnight. "Come *on*, Tony."

More pings and beeps. "I'm busy."

"And I'm hungry. Can't you come get me now?"

"I'm in the middle of a *League of Legends* marathon session with Jax and we're about to do a map-wide rotational play."

"You're doing what with who?"

Tony sighed, clearly annoyed. "It's too complicated to explain. Go back to the warehouse. Oh, and while you're waiting could you do me a favor? I forgot to send that email to the distributor. You know, the one in Tuscany for that olive oil? I would do it now, but if I stop playing, I'll lose my killer position."

"Seriously?" Tony was bailing on helping her out *and* he wanted her to do his dirty work?

"Yeah, seriously. Also, you really need to keep your car in better shape. Monthly maintenance is the key to automobile longevity. I mean, if you can't take care of your car, you really shouldn't be driving."

"Like you should talk!" Tony hadn't gotten the oil checked on his vehicle for thirty thousand miles and the engine block had overheated and cracked.

"That was different. I was busy."

"Bull—"

"Shit. We're about to destroy an inhibitor. I gotta go. Bye!"

It took a full ten seconds for Juliette to realize her brother had just hung up on her.

Damn it.

She got out of her car and slammed the door shut. Five percent power left. Really, she needed a new phone. And a new family.

Guess she was heading back to the warehouse to catch up on email. All freaking night.

As if on cue, her stomach growled.

Okay, new plan. What the hell should she do? Maybe call her cousin Lucy to come get her? No. Lucy taught class on Thursday nights. Maybe install that ride-sharing app on her phone—the one she'd always been too skeeved out to do because the app wanted access to all her private information? Four percent power, and her charger was at home. Not gonna happen.

Juliette closed her eyes. This was a sign. Or a metaphor for how her life was literally powering down.

She was never getting out of here.

She'd be stuck until her dying day with her broken-down car and a crap phone, cleaning up messes and preventing her annoying brothers from doing ridiculous things, while she was trapped, desperate to live. Scratch that. Just desperate. And hungry. Really hungry.

Three percent power. The screen was dimmer now, the phone fading fast. She scrolled through her contacts, her final Hail Mary.

Which is when a contact for Sexy Neighbor popped up.

Brody. It had to be. *She* certainly hadn't tagged someone with that nickname, and it was just the sort of thing he'd do.

He'd told her to call him. Practically begged.

Before she could wimp out, she pressed his name, then his number. She took a deep breath…just before the outgoing message clicked on.

"You've reached Brody at Wolfshead," his deep voice said. "Leave a message and I'll get back to you soon."

She almost hung up, until she realized that he would see that she'd called anyway.

"Um, hi, Brody. This is Juliette. I—you—" She took a breath. "So my car broke down. I just thought I—" She was making a total mess of this. "You know what? Never mind. I'll figure it out."

Then she hung up, cheeks burning.

Two percent power and she was out of options. Guess it was walking back to the warehouse for her. Maybe she could crack open some of those olives—the ones that were left out in the sun. They couldn't be *that* bad, could they?

But a split second later, her phone rang. She picked it up fast.

"Juliette? Hey, it's Brody. Sorry. I was just in a meeting. What's going on?"

"Nothing, I'm sorry to bother you. Go back to your meeting."

"Juliette," he said, his voice patient. "You called and I know you wouldn't have done that unless you were desperate."

"My car broke down under the bridge and I don't have a ride and my phone's about to die," she blurted out.

"Stay put," he commanded. "I'll be there in five."

As soon as she hung up, her heart started beating a mile a minute.

Crap. Super-sexy, super-arrogant, super-charming Brody Phelan was coming to help her. This was…not good. She should call him back. Tell him not to come.

But when she went to call him back, her phone flickered, then powered off.

Gah! She panicked for a hot second before realizing she'd already sealed her fate. It would be okay. She could handle him, same as she always did.

A few minutes later, a vehicle rounded the corner, its headlights shining down the road. It pulled directly in front of her and stopped. The driver's side door opened, then one booted foot appeared, then a long, jean-clad leg.

Of course Brody looked amazing, his hair pushed back from his face, the collar of his leather jacket turned up against the chill.

"Are you okay?" were the first words out of his mouth. He actually looked concerned, which was…sweet.

"I'm fine," she said. "Seriously, you didn't have to pull yourself out of your meeting for this."

He stopped in front of her, studying her intently. "Not an issue. So what happened?"

"It's the engine. It just kind of—I don't know—seized up or something."

"Got it. Why don't you pop the hood for me?"

She pulled the latch from inside, and Brody opened the hood.

"You don't actually know what you're doing here, do you?"

Brody didn't say anything in response. "Ah," he said, reaching into the engine. "Serpentine belt broke."

"Wait, what?" She peered where he was poking. "You figured that out in two seconds?"

"Already knew it. It was pretty obvious from the squealing sound coming from your engine, and I guess it finally snapped. Would have told you the other day but we got caught up in, well, you know." He gave her a devastatingly gorgeous grin.

"Right." Sexy, witty banter that only seemed to happen when Brody was around.

Brody pulled out what looked like a broken skinny black belt.

"That's it? A dumb piece of rubber caused all this?" She gestured to the engine in frustration.

"Actually, these days serpentine belts—also known as

automotive belts—are made of high-tech EPDM."

"I'm sorry, what?"

"EPDM. Ethylene propylene diene monomer." He pointed to where pieces of the belt had rubbed away. "See this? It's made of chloroprene, and it doesn't wear as well. You get a new EPDM belt in there, it'll last tens of thousands of miles longer." He was saying something else about the place where it had cracked and talking about how important it was to ensure that all belts and gears were running well in the engine, but all she was thinking about was the fact that the belt looked absolutely minuscule in his huge hands.

"You sure seem to know a lot about this," she finally murmured.

"It's what I do."

"Fix cars?"

He gave a little shrug. "Among other things."

"I thought you were a finance guy," she said.

"I am, but I like cars, too." He peered at the belt again. "Look, I actually have this exact part. I could install it for you."

"So you have your own automotive association? A club where you fix people's cars when they need help?" The snark escaped before she could help it.

"Something like that," he said, smiling a little.

"What if I'm not a member?"

He raised an eyebrow suggestively. "You could be."

She crossed her arms over her chest, knowing exactly how his mind worked. "What's the price?"

"Hmm…." he said, stroking his beard and pretending to think. "As I recall, membership's pretty reasonable these days. I accept payment in kind. Say, coffee?"

"It's a little late for coffee tonight, don't you think?" she said, her voice arch.

"It's never too late for coffee," he shot back. "But I didn't mean tonight."

"When, then?"

"Saturday. And to sweeten the deal, I'm paying."

She smiled tightly. "Sure, Brody. If you can fix my car, I'm in for coffee on Saturday. But *I'm* paying." No way did she want to be in even more debt to him.

"Deal," he said. "Okay, lock up your car and we'll get going."

She did as he suggested, then allowed him to usher her toward his vehicle, a big, old-fashioned-looking truck. He opened the door for her, and she clambered inside.

Brody got in the driver's side and pulled on his seat belt. Then he turned to her and gave her a slow once-over. "You good?" he asked, his voice a low, sexy growl.

It was just two words. Two little words that could have meant nothing at all, but the way her body responded was definitely not nothing. A full-body shiver she couldn't control. The quickening of her breath. The warming of her cheeks.

"Yes," she bit out, even though she was beginning to think this was not good. Not good at all. She snapped on her seat belt with a decisive click. "We're just going to your place to get the part? Then you're driving me right back here and putting in the rubber thingy?"

"The automotive belt." He turned the key in the ignition, and the engine roared to life.

"Yes. That." The truck was big, but being alone with Brody in an enclosed area was an even less good idea than calling him in the first place. She'd have been better off heading back to the warehouse and forgetting about him and his growly voice and his big hands and sexy beard.

Brody swung the truck out onto the street, leaving her broken little sedan behind in the darkness.

"I'll install the part after I feed you and take you on a little detour."

She snapped her head to glare at him, imagining what kind of "detour" Brody Phelan wanted to take. And why did the suggestion give her such perverse pleasure? Not that she was going to let him know that.

"What makes you think I want to do either of those things?"

"Your stomach," he said, giving her a wink. "I heard it rumbling from my truck."

CHAPTER 4

"*This* is the detour?" Juliette's throaty voice sounded into the clear, dark night.

From his seat on top of a wooden bench on the grounds of the Pittock Mansion, Brody looked across the city of Portland laid out below him in the darkness, the twinkling streetlights an imperfect inverse of the starry sky. Far off in the distance stood the shadow of Mount Hood, looming large even in the black of night. He couldn't see it, but he knew it was there. It would always be there, a constant reminder of everything he lost and loved in this world.

Despite everything that had happened here, he'd never stopped loving Portland. The city had heart, it had soul, and most important, it had his family.

Juliette was peering over the railing in front of them, and Brody shifted his attention to her long dark hair curling down her back and her coat wrapped around her curved form, a sight as enticing as the city below them.

"Yeah," Brody told her. "This is the detour." When she turned back to him, he held out a carton of lamb vindaloo and a plastic fork. "And this is me feeding you. Come on, try some." He gave her a sly smile. "Unless you can't handle the heat."

She strode over to him. "I'm too hungry to fight with you right now," she said, taking the utensil from his hand and forking a generous bite into her mouth. "Mmm, good," she mumbled, before practically snatching the carton out of his hand and curling it protectively against her chest. "Mine."

He laughed as she dug in, then picked up another carton—this one of chicken tikka masala—and took a few mouthfuls.

And then she was close to him, her fork poised over the food, looking up at him with pleading eyes. "Knock yourself out," he said. She grinned and went to town.

He liked watching her eat a hell of a lot, and he especially liked that she didn't hold back. Just ate with no apologies, then sighed with pleasure when she was done. "Thank you," she said, helping him pack up the remainder when she'd eaten her fill. "That was delicious."

"Always like feeding someone who appreciates it," he said.

"I definitely do. Truth be told, I was actually hoping for Indian food tonight."

He took a mostly empty carton from her hand, deliberately letting his fingers brush against hers. "Yeah? Looks like I can read your mind."

She turned away then, as she typically did when things heated up between them, and cleared her throat. "I didn't know you could come here at night."

"You can if you know what you're doing," he told her. The mansion closed at night, but the grounds stayed open. All you had to do was park at the bottom of the driveway near the gate and walk up. Juliette leaned back against the rail, arms crossed over her chest.

"Do you come up here a lot?"

"Yeah."

"To escape?

"Everyone needs time away," he said, his tone neutral.

"From your family?"

"I come to clear my mind. I sit right here on this bench, look out over Portland, think about…well, everything, really. Sometimes I bring dinner. And I'm usually not alone."

She pressed her lips tightly together, then turned away and walked to the railing.

"What?" he asked.

She shook her head, her curls swaying with the movement. "Nothing."

He came off the bench and joined her. "Just ask what you want to ask."

"Is this your make-out spot?"

"Ha! No. You're the first person I've ever brought up here."

She tipped her head up to look at him. "I don't understand. You said you weren't alone…" She trailed off in confusion.

"Usually there's a crowd up here," he explained. "Tonight it's empty. We got lucky."

"Oh." She looked down, then back up again. "Well, it's beautiful."

"I'm very much into beauty. In any form." He stared directly into her gaze so there was no way she could mistake his meaning. She clearly didn't, because she did exactly what she always did—she changed topics.

"Is that why you have that beautiful truck? It looks vintage."

"Yeah, the Ford," he said. "But she's not mine. I built her for Connor."

"You…built her?" He could sense her confusion.

Brody nodded. "Restored her. Refurbished the engine. It's what I do."

Her mouth fell open a little. "I thought you were joking. About knowing about cars."

"Nope. Though I admit I just do insides, not outsides. Once I square all the mechanical stuff, I outsource everything else."

"How do you decide what cars you're going to work on?"

"The driver's needs. Connor's our chemist and he does a lot of woodworking in his free time, so he's always hauling around something heavy, hence the Ford truck. Finn, on the other hand, plays guitar and has a lot of gigs, so I hooked him up with a '67 Mustang hardtop that took me the better part of a year to restore."

"And you? What do you drive?"

"I restored a Camaro a few years ago, but I'll have to figure out what to do with her now that I just finished my baby."

"Your baby?"

"A 1968 Torino—a true American classic," Brody said with some satisfaction. "I found her in a neighbor's shed moldering away, the undercarriage rusted so bad I was afraid it'd drop out if I even breathed on her. Bought her for three hundred bucks and had to flatbed her to Mount Hood, where we have a cabin."

"Sounds like you got cheated out of three hundred bucks," she said with a little laugh.

He shook his head. "It was a steal. Guy didn't know what he

had. Or maybe he did, but he didn't want to put the work into her. I kept getting derailed on other projects, but I finally finished her up a month ago. She's still up at the cabin, but I'll get her back to the city soon."

"Aren't you afraid you'll ruin it, driving it around?"

"Cars are meant to be driven. Sure, I might put her away for a couple of months during the winter, but it's not even September yet. We have a month or two left before the heavy rains come. And in late spring, I'll take her out again, show her off."

"When did you get into this? *How* did you get into this?"

"I always loved cars. Took shop in middle school and just got hooked. Drove my mom crazy, all that grease on my clothes, issues of *Popular Mechanics* piled up on my bedside table, but she knew how much it meant to me so she just let me be."

"Your mom sounds cool."

"She is," Brody said with absolute certainty. "There was this old empty shed on the Mount Hood property. It took months, but she finally convinced my grandfather to let me use it. I made it into my own auto shop, tools on the wall and everything. I even had my own lift made out of a couple of concrete blocks. It was my refuge, you know?" One he still used.

"Was your dad into cars, too?"

"No," Brody said flatly. Then, realizing it had come out too harshly, provided a bit of color. "Dad and I really didn't get along much, so it was something I did solo. But I was never really alone. There are seven of us. Our dads were twins, our moms were tight— we were really one family. You can imagine how crazy it got when we were together, so eventually, each of us found our own thing. Over time, I realized that my excitement about cars was actually useful, which made it even more meaningful for me."

"I have to admit…I'm impressed."

"Don't be."

"Why not? I think it's great. You're talented."

"I have many, *many* other talents," he said, lips curling.

She lowered her gaze to his mouth, then looked away. "I'll just bet you do."

"What about you? What are your talents?"

"Giving my brothers hell."

"Seriously. Tell me something real. If not a talent, then what you like. I don't know that much about you."

"Um…" For the first time, Juliette genuinely looked uncomfortable. "I like Salt & Straw ice cream. Especially sea salt with caramel."

"C'mon. You can do better than that."

She let out a huff. "Okay. Let's see—I'm sartorially challenged."

"Meaning?"

"Meaning I have no taste in clothes."

He gave her a once up-and-down, noting the sweater that skimmed her every curve, the skirt that hit just above her knee, those sky-high heels she typically wore, her light calf-length coat. "You look great to me."

"That's because my cousin Lucy picked everything out. She's the one who deserves all the credit. If I'm left to my own devices it's not pretty."

"I think you'd look good wearing anything." Preferably nothing at all. "But I was looking for something a little more…personal."

"That's as personal as it's going to get between us."

He shrugged, disappointed she wasn't going to say more, but not about to show it. "Too bad. Mint?" She looked at the small open tin in his hand as if it might bite her. "Come on, woman, no ulterior motive. Just an after-dinner mint. Jesus, you are really suspicious."

She finally took one and murmured her thanks.

He popped a mint into his mouth and sucked on it thoughtfully. Strange. Getting intimate wasn't his thing, yet he wanted to hear more from her. Clearly, though, it wasn't in the cards. Not tonight, anyway.

He was about to suggest they head back down when she cleared her throat. "I have my own podcast."

Now they were getting somewhere. He suppressed a victory smile. "What's it called?"

"Passion on the Vine. It's a reference to grapes. I'm kind of into wine."

"And passion?"

"Not that kind, pervert," she tossed out with a laugh, jabbing a sharp elbow into his side. "The life's work kind."

"Tell me more."

She gripped the railing tightly before letting go. "I started doing it a couple of years ago because I was in a rut. Doing the same thing over and over again. Mostly, I wanted to talk about what I loved with people who weren't my family. People who got me."

She looked out to the city below. "It worked. Hearing others talk about their love of wine inspired me. And then I thought if I was so inspired, others might be, too. So I started recording my interviews—mostly regular folks to start, then a few local celebrities."

"That's incredible. And no one said no?"

She shook her head. "The first few interviews were hard to get, I admit. I mean, would you want to talk to some nobody?"

Brody shrugged. "It would depend on what I'd get out of it."

"Right, exactly," she said. "A lot of people felt like that and at least a dozen turned me down. Luckily, there were a few people who were willing to do an interview for a random unknown podcast. Because I was really local-centric, Portland kind of embraced it. These days, it's a lot easier for JC—that's my podcast name—to get interviews."

"Your family must love it."

"Actually, they hate it."

"Why?"

Her eyes darted left, then right, as if someone might be eavesdropping in the lilac bushes. "Because I dropped a swear word by accident one time and my mom said it was unladylike."

"Naughty girl. I like it. So you have a podcast where you interview people to talk about wine and swear, and this inspires you?"

She bit her lip, sexy as hell, and looked up at him. "Maybe. A little."

"To do what?"

"Ah, Brody," she said teasingly, "I can't tell you *all* my secrets."

He could feel her pulling away, and damned if he didn't want her to stay. To say more so he could find out what made this fascinating, stubborn, sharp-tongued woman tick. But she'd given him something valuable tonight. And he also understood the value of the long game. She'd tell him when she was ready.

"Are you ready to go? I still have that automotive belt to install, and it's getting late."

He turned away, but she caught his arm. "You're being so

nice."

She was looking up at him with those big eyes, lips parted, a sucker punch right to the gut. "I'm not always nice." Right now, he could think of a hundred *not* nice things he wanted to do with her.

For once, be a gentleman.

So instead of pulling her into his arms and kissing her senseless, he tugged her back toward the path, scooping up the rest of the food as he walked.

"Come on. Gotta go fix that car of yours."

Once they got back to her car, it took Brody only a moment to find the serpentine belt and the wrench he needed in the back of the truck. He handed it to a startled Juliette, who immediately frowned at him.

"Why didn't you tell me you had this part in your truck?" she demanded, her fist closed around the belt.

"Connor's truck," he corrected, head bent down as he loosened the tensioner.

"Connor's truck. Whatever. Why didn't you tell me you had this part in Connor's truck?" She waved the belt in his direction.

"Because then you wouldn't have let me buy you dinner."

She opened her mouth, then closed it again. "Seriously?"

He checked each pulley, making sure they were still operational. They were, so he reached out his hand. "The belt?" Wordlessly, she handed it over. "Thanks."

Holding the old and new belts side by side, he did a comparison. Perfect match. So he set the old belt aside and began running the new one. Satisfied the belt was properly run, he tightened the tensioner. "Try the engine," he told her.

She pressed her lips together but slid into the driver's seat and turned the engine. A moment later, it turned over, running smoothly once again. He eyeballed the belt. It looked to be on track so he shut the hood and wiped his hands on a clean rag.

"You really fixed it." She rose from the car seat, sounding surprised. "You fixed it and you fed me."

"I'd say that deserves a thank-you," he prompted.

She whirled on him. "How long?"

"How long what?"

"How long have you had that part? The automotive belt, I mean?"

He hesitated for a moment before speaking. "Two weeks ago Tuesday, day after I heard that squealing sound coming from your engine. Knew then what it was. Knew it was only a matter of time before it broke. So I had one ordered. I meant to tell you the other day at the fence, but I forgot."

Her eyes were wide when he finished. She stood there for a moment, frozen. Then she stepped forward and took his hand.

"Thank you, Brody," she said solemnly, looking up at him. "It really means a lot to me that you went out of your way to help."

A man could only take so much.

He squeezed her hand and tugged her into his arms.

And then he kissed her.

She made a noise of surprise in her throat. Then she moaned low, and all his plans for being gentle, for going slow and giving her time to get used to him, flew right out the window.

Because Juliette Costa was fucking delicious.

She tasted like spice and mint, and she was bold, too, sliding her tongue into his mouth as soon as she had the chance. Stroking it over his, tasting and exploring. Nothing turned him on more than a woman who went after what she wanted.

He got hard, right there, right then, and pulled her even closer so that she could feel how much she affected him. And hell, he seemed to affect her right back, because she moaned louder and grabbed the front of his jacket with one small fist. Except he wasn't going anywhere, because at that moment he knew she was his. All her fire, all her heat.

Now that he'd tasted her, knew how sweet she truly was, there was no going back. She was still kissing him just as ardently, and he realized that she must be as starved for it as he was.

She tilted her head, inviting him to deepen the kiss, and he accepted, taking her mouth the way he'd wanted to for so long. Amazing. He wanted more. He wanted everything.

All of a sudden she was out of his arms, eyes big, lips swollen, cheeks flushed. Completely edible.

"Wait. Wh-what are we doing?" She was cute when she was caught off guard. Vulnerable. Her pulse ticked rapidly at the base of her throat, her chest rising and falling with her breath.

"Finishing up our date. Don't tell me you didn't enjoy it."

"Oh, this isn't a date," she said.

"Sure was."

"Um, no, it wasn't. You picked me up by the side of the road."

"Yes," he said patiently. "And I also took you to my thinking spot where I fed you, we looked out over the city, and we talked about our families. Shared details about our lives. Held hands. Sounds like a date to me."

"This isn't a date," she repeated, saying the word *date* as if it were something distasteful.

He crossed his arms over his chest. "What's your problem with dates?"

"Nothing," she said a little too quickly. "Just not with—" She shook her head. "You know what? Never mind. Brody, thank you again. You fixed my car. You're an amazing kisser. Seriously. Amazing. And okay, I'm going to stop talking now. Good night."

If he thought she was flustered before when he was asking probing questions, her discomfort was now up to eleven. Fascinating.

"Good night! Bye!" She got into her car and actually started driving in reverse before slamming on the brakes and driving forward.

Brody grinned and walked to the truck with a swagger in his step. For the second time in an evening, he'd managed to do the impossible—rattle Juliette Costa.

And he couldn't wait to do it again.

CHAPTER 5

Saturday morning at 11:05, a knock sounded at Juliette's cottage door. Quickly, she walked over and opened it, grinning when she saw the smiling face of her cousin Lucia.

"Hey," Lucy said. "Did you finish your recording?"

"Yep," Juliette responded. "Just. Come on in."

"Cool."

Lucy and Juliette were first cousins—their moms were sisters—but the two of them looked nothing alike. Lucy was blonde where Juliette was dark, straight where she was curvy, and tall where she was short.

Today, Lucy was wearing black three-quarter-length yoga pants that only served to emphasize her lean strength, and a deep purple dolman-sleeved top that hugged her hips and bloused out around her torso. She wore absolutely zero makeup, and still managed to look completely put-together.

Lucy headed for the small kitchen right away.

"Are your parents home yet?" she called out to Lucy as she headed back to the living room. Her aunt and uncle typically went to the farmers' market on Saturday morning, which is exactly why she scheduled her podcast interviews during that time.

"Nope," Lucy said, and Juliette heard the fridge open. "They're hosting a party tonight so I think they have more errands than usual to run."

"Right." She'd almost forgotten about that. Her aunt and uncle's large Victorian-style house was where most of the family

48

congregated, owing not just to its size but its central location in the Laurelhurst neighborhood. Aunt Violetta just had one sister—Juliette's mom—but Uncle Leone had a big family that boasted five brothers and sisters, all of whom lived in the greater Portland area with their families.

When Juliette had lost her lease on her apartment three years ago, she'd needed something close to work but still affordable. Portland rental prices had only been increasing, and she'd found herself priced out of a lot of the convenient neighborhoods. Lucy's mom and dad had stepped up in a big way, offering her the use of their guest cottage on the back of their property for a modest price.

At the time, it seemed like a win-win for everyone. Juliette had gotten a great place to live, her parents had gotten the peace of mind that she was safe, and her aunt and uncle had gotten the satisfaction of helping family.

But over the years, things had started to chafe. For one, her family seemed to pop by unannounced all the time. And because Lucy's parents treated her like another daughter—which was wonderful and amazing but also completely stifling—there was little separation between work and home, though she desperately tried to make it so. And she had to hide the fact that she was still doing her podcasts, not to mention other things—like her dating life (nonexistent right now) and her future plans (too complicated to try to discuss).

"You're coming tonight, right?" Lucy was clearly rummaging around in the fridge now. "Ooh. Can I have an apple? I taught all morning and forgot to bring a snack."

"*Sei sempre il benvenuto*," Juliette called out. *You are always welcome.*

Lucy came out from the kitchen and smiled. "Thanks," she said around a mouthful of apple. "You're sweet to let me raid your fridge. Which I do every time I'm here."

"I wish I had more to feed you."

"This is perfect."

Actually, that was Lucy. Perfect. At least that's the way she appeared to most people.

She was smart and fit and owned her own yoga studio in Laurelhurst, the kind of neighborhood place that everyone crowded to in droves. And she was kind, a good daughter, and a really good friend.

But Lucy had a secret—one she rarely spoke about with family and never told outsiders: she was a cancer survivor. One of those terrible childhood cancers that for seven long years had robbed her of her hair, her friends, her *life*.

Lucy was one of the lucky ones. She'd recovered. Grown up and learned to live a typical life—except she was anything but typical. Since her recovery, she'd vowed to spend her days living life to the fullest. There was no time for negativity, no time for regrets. Her outlook was perpetually cheerful, and she never failed to find the good in everything and everyone, something Juliette found incredibly amazing.

"Seriously, though," Lucy said, sprawling onto a nearby sofa—a hand-me-down from her parents' den. "I need you to come to the party with me." She took another bite of apple. "Aunt Mattea is being weird."

Juliette narrowed her eyes. Aunt Mattea was Leone's older sister, and like everyone else in her family, was obsessed with seeing her kids married. She bragged—loudly and at length—about the significant others her sons and daughters had found, and wondered aloud why Lucy and Juliette, now past their primes in her mind, didn't follow suit. "Who got engaged this time?"

"Alfonzo." One of Lucy's cousins on her dad's side, a small, serious, dark-haired man in his early twenties. "And Angelina's going to be married in October, remember?" She made a face.

"Oh yeah. How could I forget? She's been even more bridezilla than usual lately." As soon as Angelina had gotten engaged half a year ago and chosen her bridal party, she had asked—no, demanded—that everyone go on a diet, including Lucy. So far, Lucy had ignored all of her edicts and convinced Juliette to do the same.

"Uh-huh," Lucy said, nodding. "She'll be there tonight too. Along with Joey. And his cell phone." Angelina's fiancé Joey was a perfectly nice guy, and honestly, she didn't mind it when people checked their cell phones, but Joey had taken it to a new level, barely looking up from the device when he was in company. Lucy thought it was ridiculous, and she agreed, but as far as Juliette was concerned, anyone who put up with Angelina could stare at a screen as much as he liked.

"Please?" Lucy begged.

"Promise me you won't leave my side the whole evening?"

"I promise," Lucy said solemnly, placing her hand over her heart. "And if I break my promise, may I buy a new pair of pants and forget to cut off the tag and walk around with said tag out all day with no one saying a single word about it, and only when I come home at the end of the day do I realize I've had it showing the entire time."

"All right, all right. I'll come. I'm sure my parents will be thrilled I'm there anyway."

Lucy shot her a grateful look. "Thanks. I owe you one." She finished the apple and rose to chuck the core into Juliette's compost bin.

"Eh, forget it. Say, you still hungry?"

Lucy was back in a flash. "Yes, but you don't have any more food," she said sadly. Her cousin exercised all the time, so she was always ravenous. A small price to pay for having a body like hers.

"Nope," Juliette said. "But if you give me a few minutes, we can go forage for something."

"Cool. I'll wait." Lucy sank back down onto the sofa. "Was it a good episode today?"

Lucy was one of the first people she'd interviewed for her podcast—and so far the only one she'd done in person. She'd been supportive from the start, something Juliette was grateful for.

Juliette swiveled her chair in Lucy's direction. "Definitely. My guest was John Mroz."

"The photographer!" she said with delight. "I love his stuff."

"I know. It was seeing that photograph of Mount Hood in your living room that inspired me to contact him. And get this—he's a fan of the show, too!"

"That's great, Juliette," Lucy said with genuine excitement. "So when are you going to get off your butt and work on your *own* passion?"

"When I get some money."

"Pfft. You have money."

"Not enough," Juliette said. "But I'm saving it up. Living below my means in the hopes that I can make it happen."

"You could make it happen now."

Juliette gave her a meaningful look. "Lucy, I live in your parents' guest house, I have no food in my fridge, and I never go out."

"You're also wearing clothing from your freshman year of college," Lucy informed her.

Juliette looked down at the red-and-green candy-cane-patterned leggings. "What? How can you tell?"

"I bought those for you as a Christmas present."

"I'm not saying that I don't have enough to live on, I just don't have enough to start my own business." Juliette rubbed her forehead and sighed. "If I wanted to do more of the same—wholesale and distribution—I'd be fine. I already have the relationships with the vendors, and warehouse space is easy to get. I'd just rent a place for cheap and call it good. But a high-end wine bar requires major connections and major money."

"I could lend you some."

"No." Juliette shook her head. "No way. You have to save it to expand your studio."

Lucy shrugged. "I can hold off. It's not like it has to be done right away."

"Your studio's bursting at the seams. I don't know that you can add any more classes without teaching 24-7, and that's not healthy for you. And you know I need to do this myself." Because even though Lucy's offer was incredibly generous, Juliette did not want her family's help. And that included her cousin.

Lucy's beautiful face was etched with understanding. "I get it."

"I wish *I* did," Juliette muttered. She barely knew where to start. "What do I need, I mean, aside from money and a plan?"

"Search me," Lucy said.

"Didn't you have, I don't know—a formal business plan or something?"

Lucy looked apologetic. "Nope. My parents just fronted me the money and I told them I'd pay them back. They trusted me when I told them the yoga studio would succeed."

"Right." Not only was Lucy an only child, but she had a hugely different relationship with her parents than Juliette did. Her parents didn't nag or smother. Maybe because they were just grateful she was alive after everything she'd been through. And of course her business had succeeded. She'd majored in physical therapy, and then gone on to get her yoga teaching certificate from one of the most famous instructors in the industry. Plus, she just had a way with people.

"It was different for me. I know that," Lucy said. "And I know how incredibly lucky I am. But to get investors, you definitely need a business plan. They're going to want to know the business is viable and it has a good ROI."

"ROI?"

"Return on investment," Lucy said. Lucy had minored in business. Smart Lucy.

"How do I start?"

"Ugh, I haven't done this in forever," Lucy said, her expression pained. "But I'll try to dig up some of my old books. Figure out if there's anything you can use. Cool?"

"Cool."

Lucy got a serious then. "You're going to make this work. I know you will," she said, her voice fierce. "And *when* you succeed and open up the most amazing wine bar in Portland, I'll be the first to congratulate you."

She held out her pinkie finger, and Juliette rose to link her pinkie finger with hers. Then squeezed, just enough so the other felt it.

They'd created the pinkie link during one of Juliette's visits to Lucy in the hospital where Lucy had been sequestered, sometimes for months at a time. Juliette had been chafing under the strictures of her male-dominated household, and Lucy had been so very lonely. They needed each other as more than friends or cousins. So they'd pledged to be real sisters forever.

Lucy looked up at her, and for the briefest moment, Juliette caught a glimpse of the fragile, broken child she had been.

Then she smiled and broken Lucy was gone, and the healthy, fit Lucy—the one everyone knew and loved—appeared once again. "You ready?"

"Yep. Let me just grab my cell." She reached over to the desk just as it started flashing. "Hang on." She scooped it up and peered at the screen.

It was a text from Brody.

You still owe me coffee.

"What is it?" Lucy asked. "Is everything okay?"

Juliette jerked her head up. "Oh, oh, yes. Just…hang on."

Before she could text him back, another text came in a second later.

Thinking of backing out?

No way.

Good. I'll pick you up at 2. What's your address?

He couldn't come here. Someone from her family would be sure to spot him, and then she'd be in even worse trouble. She texted back fast.

No—let's meet at Powell's on Hawthorne.

There was a long pause and then:

Okay. See you at 2 p.m.

She was about to text him back when Lucy's voice piped up from over her shoulder.

"Who's Sexy Neighbor?"

Juliette clasped her phone to her chest to hide the screen. "No one," she said quickly.

Lucy just gave her a look. The one that said *this is me you're talking to, remember?*

"Um…" she started, knowing she was turning bright red, then took a deep breath. She had to tell *someone*, and it may as well be Lucy. "His name's Brody."

"Brody who?"

"Phelan."

"Brody Phelan? Like of *the* Phelans?" Lucy looked impressed.

"The very one."

"Which one is he? The big one? No, wait, they're all big. The one with the beard? Oh, crap, they all have beards, too. And the hands. Ooh, those hands. Mmmm. Wait." She stopped, her eyes big. "Does your family know?"

"No one knows," Juliette snapped. "And no one will ever know."

Lucy eyed her. "Did you forget that we are Italian? In our family, everyone knows everything."

"I know," Juliette groaned, and leaned a hand on the counter.

"I'm not sure how you're going to keep this a secret, long-term," Lucy said, "but if anyone hears anything, it won't be from me. I'm not breathing a word." She pretended to lock up her mouth with an imaginary key.

Juliette wasn't happy about the secrets, but there wasn't a lot she could do or say right now. The cat—er, text—was out of the bag, and she'd have to face the consequences. Namely Lucy looking at her with an excited gleam in her eye.

She went back to her chair and flung herself in it. "Don't," she told her cousin.

"Don't what?" Lucy said, all big blue eyes and innocent expression.

"Don't think whatever it is that you're thinking. Don't try to romanticize this or make it all perfect and gushy."

"But it *is* perfect and gushy. Think about it," she said, clasping her hands together in front of her chest, "the two warring clans, one Irish, one Italian. The fighting brothers, the angry fathers, the two young lovers—"

"We are not two young lovers," Juliette ground out.

"Hmm, you're right," Lucy said, cocking her head and giving her a once-over. "Twenty-seven *is* kinda old."

Juliette pointed her finger in warning. "Don't even start." She got enough of that from her father, who frequently harangued her about her advanced age. "Besides, you're half a year older than I am!"

"Too true," Lucy said with an unconcerned laugh. "But we're not talking about me. We're talking about you. And Brody Phelan."

"So I'm going out with Brody. Big deal. I'm only doing it because I owe him."

"And why, exactly, do you owe him?" Lucy asked shrewdly.

She was just digging herself deeper and deeper. She settled for the barest sketch of truth.

"My car broke down and he fixed it." She left out the part about the kissing. And the liking it. "So you see, it's just payment of a debt," she continued. "No need to get all fancy."

Lucy gave her a look. "Um, *yeah* you need to get fancy."

"Not me."

"Juliette, seriously? Have you *seen* those men?"

"I have," she said, rising from her seat and pacing to the window. "Which is exactly why I'm not dressing up. We hate the Phelans, remember? I'm just paying him back for fixing my car." Not because she wanted to go out with him again.

"First of all, *I* care that you look adorable and you should, too. You've got a killer body, which you should flaunt. Why do you think I choose all those clingy fabrics for you to wear? If I had those curves, I'd show them off like crazy."

Juliette swung around and stared at her in disbelief, which Lucy clearly saw as Juliette's assent to go on.

"Second of all, you don't hate the Phelans and I certainly don't, either. I don't even know them. Aside from what you've told me, of course, and fixing your car sounds like a nice thing to do. Besides, I'm pretty sure it's just your father and brothers who hate them, and honestly, no offense, but the men in your family aren't that evolved," she said dismissively.

On that, they definitely both agreed.

"Finally, you can dress casually and still slay. Case in point." She rose and indicated her own outfit. Okay, Lucy was right about that. She definitely slayed in her attire and ballet flats, which looked cute *and* comfy.

"That's not fair," Juliette said, flinging out a hand in Lucy's direction. "You're paid to look that good."

"No, I am paid to lead people on journeys that will inspire them to be their best selves," Lucy corrected. "Part of which means looking this good. But I digress."

Oh, crap. Lucy was eyeing her again in that way she did when she was concocting a plan. Lord help her.

"All right. Your hair is amazing. No doubt about that. So you'll wear it down, natural. And we'll play up your eyes. You've got gorgeous eyes. And a banging body that we will dress to perfection. And by that I mean we will show off every curve."

"Seriously, Lucy. Please. I'm begging you."

Lucy grinned. "He's going to be the one begging when we're through."

"Oh God."

"He might be saying that, too," she said with a secret smile.

"You are killing me here," Juliette groaned.

Lucy pretended that she didn't hear her. "Okay, I happen to know that you have zero in your closet that will work because I picked out all your decent clothes and it's all business stuff and"— she looked in disgust at the Christmas leggings—"loungewear. So I'll tell you what we're going to do. You are going to take me to that new Korean place—the one with the spicy tofu soup—and you are going to feed me. Then we are going to raid my closet and find you something super cute to wear."

"But—" Juliette started, about to protest that none of Lucy's clothes would fit her, but the look on Lucy's face—the one that said *nothing* was going to get in the way of project Fix Up Juliette—stopped her from speaking.

"Hush." Lucy hooked her arm in Juliette's and dragged her toward the apartment door. "You just leave everything to me."

CHAPTER 6

After trying on way too many clothes, Juliette settled on a clingy navy jersey romper with a tie waist.

Or rather, Lucy had settled on it and insisted she wear it. Despite Lucy having about four inches of height on her, the bottom part of the romper came up a shade too high on her thighs for comfort. There were spaghetti straps on top, and to preserve some modesty, Juliette had thrown on a cardigan. She'd completed the outfit with a pair of gorgeous caramel-colored suede ankle boots— also Lucy's.

Lucy had also insisted on doing her hair (lots of volume) and makeup (smoky eyes and a neutral lip). It was more than she usually went for, but after Lucy had finished with her, she had to admit she looked pretty good.

Brody was already waiting outside on the sidewalk when she arrived at Powell's. She spotted him from half a block away wearing a leather jacket and a pair of dark sunglasses, the kind that made most people look as though they were trying too hard to be cool. On Brody they just looked right.

"Hi," she said, and as she approached, his jaw dropped open a little. "What?"

He composed himself fast. "Nothing. Nothing. Just, thanks for meeting me. I was worried you were going to bail."

"I always keep my promises," she told him.

"Noted."

They stood there in awkward silence for a moment. "So do

you want to go in?" she asked.

"Inside? I thought we were going to get coffee."

"You've never been to Powell's before, have you?"

"No—I don't really do bookstores. I mean, not since grad school."

"What? How can you call yourself a PDXer if you've never been to Powell's? We have to remedy this situation ASAP," she said, taking him by the crook of the elbow and propelling him toward the store entrance. "And just so you know, they serve coffee here. Delicious coffee. Which you would know if you'd ever bothered to go in. Here."

And then they were through the doors and inside.

Juliette had been here a thousand times, but tried to see the place through Brody's eyes—the concrete floor, the exposed ceiling, the utilitarian lighting, the thousands and thousands of books lining the shelves. It was bare-bones architecture, merely a warehouse, and it was usually crowded as hell, but there was magic on the shelves if you only knew where to look.

"It's huge," he said, looking around as she maneuvered him through the space.

"It's not as big as the one on Burnside," she told him, "but it's got a great selection."

"Of coffee?" he asked, sounding hopeful.

"Talk about a one-track mind. All right, Mr. Undercaffeinated. Coffee first."

They went to get their coffee at the kiosk, dark roast and good and hot. Juliette went to the coffee station where she proceeded to dump plenty of skim milk and sweetener into hers, the only way she liked to drink it.

"So do you want to check out some books while these cool off?" she asked over her shoulder.

Brody didn't answer, so she turned around. He was standing there, unmoving, breathing in the aroma from his cup.

"Um, Brody? You okay?"

"Yeah—just give me a sec. I'm about to inhale this and I figure I need at least the semblance of savoring first."

"Take all the time you need. No rush."

He took another few deep breaths, then tipped the cup to his lips and downed half of it in one long gulp.

"Whoa, Jesus, Brody, slow down!"

"Ah," he said with real contentment. "I needed that."

The coffee was actually singeing her fingers through the paper cup. "It's scalding hot! How did you not burn your mouth?"

"Destroyed my taste buds years ago when I was an investment banker. My record staying awake was forty-six hours, and I needed plenty of coffee for that." He took off his sunglasses, and it was then that she saw the shadows under his eyes.

"Late night again?" she asked sympathetically.

He nodded. "Yeah. Just trying to sort some tricky insurance issues out. Things have been…challenging…since the accident."

"Right." She'd found out about it from Brody the week after the rick collapsed. He'd been so calm about it, so collected. She doubted she would have had that much poise if they'd had an accident of that magnitude, but Brody had held it together remarkably well. Though she was starting to see the strain now.

"Everyone's being cool about it, but it's my responsibility. I mean, they rely on me to keep everything running financially. But I'll get it sorted. I always do. I'm ready now." He lifted the cup again, and at her alarmed look, he chuckled. "I'll sip the rest of it instead of gulping like a Neanderthal."

"I don't think Neanderthals drank sustainably farmed single-origin Venezuelan coffee."

"Probably not."

"Though it's probably wasted on you if you blew out your taste buds."

He took a more civilized sip of his coffee. "I still have some. I just miss the nuances in the flavor."

"Is that why you're the CFO? Because you can't taste the beer or the whiskey?" she teased.

"I like to think I'm the CFO because I have a degree in finance and I understand money." He shrugged. "I love drinking our beverages, but I don't have the artistry to create them. Besides, Finn and Connor have enough taste buds between them to keep everything running smoothly on that front."

Made sense to her. "So, do you want to look at some books?"

"Sure. Lead the way."

Coffees in hand, they walked over to the business section.

"Can you hold this for me?" she asked, holding out her

coffee cup.

"Sure. Hang on." He downed the rest of his in a long swallow, then tucked her cup inside his to hold.

"Thought you were going to sip, Neanderthal," she teased.

"I needed it bad," he admitted, then eyed hers. "Can I have yours too?"

"No way," she said. "I am going to drink every last drop, so don't even think about sneaking any." She turned to the shelves and began scanning, looking for something that actually might help her. Maybe this one. Or this. She gathered a few books in her arms.

Brody made a noise that sounded suspiciously like a gulp.

"Are you drinking my coffee?"

"If I were, I'd tell you it was disgusting." Another gulp. "What the hell did you put in here?"

"Sunshine and unicorns. And if it's so disgusting, then quit drinking it."

More gulping. "Seriously, it's awful."

"You suck at following directions," she informed him.

"Pretty much," he agreed way too cheerfully.

She swung around and peered into the cup. Completely empty. "Next time I'm going to put in double sweetener."

He smiled, completely unrepentant. "I'll probably still drink it. If I'm desperate enough, that is."

Rolling her eyes, she turned back to reach for another book. The small stack she had in her arms wobbled.

"Here," Brody said, reaching a hand out to take the top couple of books. "Let me hold those for you."

"After drinking all my coffee, it's the least you can do." She handed the rest of them over.

Ah, there was another promising volume, right on the bottom shelf. She bent over to reach it. This time, the sound she heard behind her wasn't a gulp, but a muffled groan.

The freaking romper, stretched across her ass. She could practically hear Lucy cackling.

She looked back over her shoulder. "What?" she challenged.

Brody cleared his throat. "Nothing." He looked at the top tome, then began to riffle through them. "*How to Write a Business Plan? Business Plans for the Complete Idiot? Start Your Business the Easy Way?* Something you're not telling me, Costa? Like maybe you're planning to expand?"

"Actually," she said carefully, "it'd be less of an expansion and more of a whole new venture."

"You don't say." He sounded interested. "What kind of venture?"

"I want to open a wine bar."

"Really? That's interesting." She could tell from his tone that he wasn't judging. Just listening and absorbing, trying to understand. "Is this a family thing?"

"It's a me thing," she said firmly. "My parents don't know. Don't even suspect I want to open up my own place. I don't think they'd be very happy, and they'll probably try to stop me." She turned to face him fully. "So you can't say anything. You swear?"

"I swear," he said, almost automatically, meeting her gaze. She stared at him for a moment, gauging his trustworthiness. There was truth in his eyes.

"Thank you," she said with a short nod.

"What kind of place would it be?" he asked.

"A high-end one, showcasing the best local and international vintages. One of those upscale but casual places where people want to stop by after work, meet up with friends before a night on the town. People can purchase bottles or cases if they want. And I want to serve food, like charcuterie plates and cheese and nuts and olives—light bites that pair well with wine."

"You've clearly thought a lot about this."

"I have," she agreed. "I mean, I do all the buying for my family business, and I feel like I can really leverage that knowledge into this space. Granted, I don't have a degree in business and I've never run my own company before, but I'm a quick learner."

"And you're smart."

For some reason, this pleased her more than anything else he'd ever said. "You think so?"

"Not even a question." For the longest moment, the two of them stood there, staring at each other until Juliette finally cleared her throat. "Anyway, to start a business, I need capital. I need investors. I need a business plan so prospective investors will take me seriously, and well, here we are."

"You don't need these books."

She gave a rueful laugh. "Um, yes, I do. I have degrees in

biology and oenology, not business. I wouldn't know where to start."

"How about with me? I could talk you through it, easy." He raised an eyebrow. "Unless you doubt my qualifications?"

"MBA from Berkeley? CFO of a multimillion-dollar company? I don't doubt them. If you're actually serious, I'd be a *complete idiot* to say no to your generous offer." She shoved the books back onto the shelf. "I guess this leaves only one teeny-tiny issue to discuss."

"Payment," he said with a grin.

"Of course." She crossed her arms over her chest and eyed him warily. "What do you want?"

"Dinner."

"Another date."

"Yes, another date," he said. "In exchange for me walking you through the steps to create a business plan that will get you exactly what you want in a fraction of the time it'll take you to read, distill, and regurgitate those books into a plan that an investor is going to throw money at. But I'll help you with it next week. Or you can waste months spinning your wheels…"

Oh, he was good. Sharp as a tack. "Deal. But no funny business."

"Maybe you'll want some funny business."

"I can guarantee I won't."

His eyes gleamed. "There's nothing I love more than a challenge." He pulled out his cell phone and scanned his calendar. "We'll have lunch to talk business plans. Is Tuesday okay?"

"Yes."

"As for dinner, it looks like I have time next Friday evening after work. I'll pick you up at seven thirty." He eyed her over his phone. "Your cousin pick out your outfit today?"

"Um, yes."

"Ask her to dress you on Friday. Tell her something sexy."

"Sure, I'll totally give her those instructions," she said in a tone that screamed *not*.

Brody just grinned at her.

"Well, now that that's settled, I guess my business here in this section done. What should we look at next?"

"Erotica?" he asked hopefully.

"I thought guys were more visual creatures."

"Some of us are more cerebral." He dropped his gaze to her lips. "Sometimes."

"Hmm. I have something that will really turn your crank."

He looked intrigued. "Go on."

She tilted her head, indicating that he should follow her. "I promise it'll get you all revved up."

"I like this." He ditched the now-empty coffee cups in a nearby trash can and caught up to her again quickly. "You are definitely speaking my language."

"Oh, I know I am," she said confidently, just as they arrived in the correct section. She held out her arms. "Here we are!"

When Brody realized they were in the automotive section, he laughed, loud and long. "I should punish you for getting me all riled up."

It was the way he said "punish" that got to her. More specifically, to her nipples and most definitely to her sex. Since when did a word from Brody get her all hot and bothered?

"And exactly how would you punish me?" she said, her voice breathless. She knew she was baiting him, but couldn't stop herself from doing it anyway.

Heat flared in his gaze. "You're playing with fire, you know that?"

"So are you."

The two of them stared at each other for a long moment. And then he stepped forward, speared his hands through her hair and kissed her.

Just like the first time, he was deliberate and very, very thorough, teasing her, making her want so much more than he was giving. He stroked with his mouth, his tongue, and even his teeth. It wasn't a fluke the first time—the man could kiss.

When he finally lifted his head, she was breathless and unbelievably aroused. Brody was pressed up against her, the proof of his own arousal poking her in the stomach.

"What was that?" she whispered.

"I don't know. But whatever it is, it's fucking fantastic." He bent down and kissed her again, deeper this time. His hands settled on her hips as he walked her backward up against the stacks. Her shoulder blades hit books as Brody swept his tongue against hers, touching, tasting, exploring. It felt good. Right. So did his big hands, now skimming up her sides, one coming to wrap around her back and pull her close, the other coming to rest high on her ribs, his big thumb settling just under her breast. She wanted him to touch her so very badly. Sweep his thumb up over her hardened nipple and make her moan.

She slipped a hand under his shirt, fingers playing over the hard ridges of his stomach, the gentle bulge of his pectoral. He was leanly muscled, but his wasn't a gym body. It was strength honed through use and honest work.

His thumb was rubbing a circle on her flesh, around and around in a dizzying pattern, making her want him to touch her in other, more intimate places. Just as she was about to take his hand and yank it up to cover her breast, Brody pulled away.

It was then that she realized two things: (a) they were in public, and (b) they weren't alone. An older woman with stick-straight hair and cat-eye glasses was halfway down the aisle, staring at the two of them with grave displeasure.

The woman cleared her throat. "Excuse me," she said in a nasty tone of voice. "If you are going to do that, would you please go outside?"

"Sorry," Juliette gasped, and then, completely horrified, she pried Brody's hands off her body, grabbed his arm, and tugged him into the next aisle. Her cheeks were burning. She could not believe she'd let him do that. That they'd almost been caught! "Ohmigod."

She turned around to look at him, and it was then she realized something.

Brody was laughing. Hard. Except silently, his big shoulders shaking with the effort to keep quiet.

"What's so funny?" she demanded.

"You," he said. "That lady. This. God, Juliette."

He was cracking up, and then *she* started cracking up, and trying to suppress the laughter so they wouldn't get in trouble yet again left her wheezing and snorting, which only made him laugh harder.

Finally, he wiped his eyes with his hands and reached for her, wrapping her up in his big arms and smiling down at her. "I haven't had that happen since college."

"Had what happen?"

"Get called out like that. The last time it happened, I was in my senior year working in the school library with my girlfriend. One thing led to another and needless to say, I got caught with my pants down by one of the librarians. Good thing the semester was almost over, since they banned both of us from the stacks after that."

She squinched up her face. "Ew."

"The point is, you make me feel young again. And that's something I haven't felt in a very long time."

"What are you talking about?" she said. "You are young."

"Thirty-one isn't young."

She shrugged. "Neither is twenty-seven. And for the record, I have never gotten caught in public doing…well, doing anything. Until now."

He grinned, a devastatingly wicked grin. "I like that I'm corrupting you."

"You're so not." She paused. "But I think we should skip the erotica section today."

"Yeah. Maybe self-help is safer?"

"God, no," she said. "That'll open a whole different can of worms."

"Humor?"

"I'm afraid you'll crack up again."

"I've got it," he said, giving her a small squeeze. "History."

"Sold."

CHAPTER 7

Hanging out in a bookstore with Juliette Costa was the best non-date Brody had ever had. It wasn't just that she was beautiful, or that whatever the hell she was wearing did incredible things for her ass. It was that she was real and funny and yeah, she did make him feel young again.

And he'd been feeling old for so very long.

They'd gone to history—boring, as advertised—then headed to poetry. That had been a grave mistake. Hearing Juliette read dirty limericks had them cracking up again, which meant more dirty looks.

So they'd gone back to the coffee kiosk where Juliette had procured him another coffee—black, of course—which he'd swallowed in only a few big gulps, much to Juliette's displeasure.

It was awesome.

Now he was waiting for her outside while she made her final purchases.

"Here," she said, thrusting a wrapped package in his direction.

"For me?"

"I thought you might like it," she said. "Go on, open it."

Carefully, he unwrapped the package, unsurprised to find a book—one on California car culture. Right up his alley. He flipped open the front cover, and there, on the inside, was an inscription:

"To Brody—" it said. "Thanks again for fixing my car." And she signed it "JC."

"Do you like it?" She was looking up at him almost shyly.

"Yeah," he said, stuck on the simple words and how much meaning there was behind them.

She nodded. "Cool. Well, I guess we're good, right?"

"We're good," he assured her. Really good.

"Great. I, um, had a good time. So I'll see you next week. Bye." She turned to leave, but he grabbed her by the arm before she even took a step.

"Wait a second."

She looked down at his hand gripping her arm, then back up at his face. "I have to get home, Brody," she said softly.

"I know." It's just that he didn't want her to leave. Not yet. "Did you walk?"

"Yes."

"I'll walk you home, then."

She stiffened, and he could actually see all that sweetness fading away. "That's not necessary."

"Definitely necessary."

Juliette shook her arm out of his grip. "What's the deal with you and walking me places? Don't you think I can handle myself?"

"Of course you can." She was one of the toughest people— man or woman—that he knew.

"Then why do you treat me like I can't?"

Brody shifted on his feet. Paused for a long moment, debating what to say. Finally, he opted for truth. "I had fun with you today. And I want to hang on to that for a little longer. Spend a bit more time before I get back to work."

She seemed to accept that answer. "Okay," she said softly. "But only to the corner." She turned and started walking up 37th Avenue.

"What do you mean, the corner?" he said, striding to catch up to her. "I'll walk you to your door."

She didn't look at him, but picked up the pace, the heels of her boots making a clicking sound on the sidewalk. "That's not a good idea."

"What's the matter? Afraid to be seen with me, Costa?" She didn't answer, but walked even faster, which told him that was *exactly* what she was afraid of. "Oh, come on. Really?"

Her face went red, but her voice was firm. "I live at my aunt's place. Well, not exactly at her place. At her guest cottage on the back of her property."

"There's no shame in that."

"I'm not ashamed. I mean, I pay rent and everything."

"Then what's the problem?"

"Nothing. Except for the fact that you're a Phelan. And just because you and I get along doesn't mean that the rest of my family likes you. At all."

Right. The feud. And honestly, this was a new one for him. He was used to having his name open doors in this town, not close them in his face.

"Why should it matter what your family says?"

She came up short, stopping right in the middle of the sidewalk, and whirled on him. "I can't believe you just said that to me, the man who lives, sleeps, eats, and breathes all things Phelan. I know you, Brody. You practically live at work. You don't go to sleep until the job is done. And you would do *anything* for Wolfshead. Are you seriously telling me it doesn't matter to you what your family says?"

Stunned at the truth of her statement, he didn't answer right away.

Her shoulders dropped, as if all the fight had gone out of her. "Look," she said, continuing on. "I had such a great time with you this afternoon and I don't want to spoil it. Let's just say goodbye here."

"Are we even a little bit close?"

"Another block. I live off Stark."

Brody checked his watch. It was almost five. "Is anyone home this time of day?"

"Well, no, but—"

"Let me walk you to your door, then."

He didn't tell her how lonely he'd been. How sex was sex, but he hadn't truly connected with a woman in forever because it was exhausting just to go through the motions. How fitful his sleep was. How literally the only bright parts of his week were working on his car—which he didn't have time to do anymore unless he actually took vacation days—or seeing her.

"Fine," she said tightly.

They reached the block, lined with well-maintained Victorian houses. Her aunt's house was almost directly in the middle of the block, no bigger or smaller than the properties on either side.

Juliette breathed an audible sigh of relief when she saw the driveway.

"No car," she told him. "They're not here."

"Good." He gave her a pointed look.

After a long pause, she jerked her head to the side of the house. "Come on." She led him through a gate into a small backyard with a few rosebushes, and a modest, one-story structure that took up most of the back side of the yard.

It was there she walked and unlocked the door, then turned back to him. "Thank you again for agreeing to help me with my business plan. I'll see you next week, like we talked about, okay?"

"You're right," he said.

"Frequently," she tossed back. "But about what?"

"What your family says does matter." More than she could possibly know. It was why he'd left—and ultimately, it was why he'd come home.

She reached out and grasped his forearm, squeezing gently. "I know, Brody," she said softly. He hated the pity in her gaze, wanted to see something else entirely. Something that would make him forget the past and focus only on the here and now, the things he could control.

"You know what else I know?" he said. "You like me. Come on. Admit it."

He'd meant to lighten the mood, but if anything, things got even more serious.

She looked away. "It's complicated."

"No, it's not." He cupped her jaw in his hand, tipping her face up to his. "It's a simple question with a simple answer."

Her gaze flickered, but she didn't break eye contact. "Yes, okay. I like you. Happy now?"

"Yeah," he said.

And then he took her mouth.

Brody kissed her deep and long, but not long enough. All too soon, he pulled back, then stood there, watching, assessing.

Juliette hitched in a breath, immediately missing the touch of his hand, the feel of his lips. This was a mistake—she knew it was, which is why she'd tried to ditch him before things got to this point. Except Brody was a hard man to ditch. And he was an exceptional kisser. "What are we doing?" she whispered.

He smiled, slow and deep. "Whatever you want."

This was how he was seducing her. Word by word, touch by touch, taste by taste.

Clever, persuasive Brody, offering just enough to tempt, giving her permission to take.

She never took. She was always the one waiting, watching, wishing as she stood on the sidelines.

She breathed in, inhaling his scent—coffee and books, and masculinity. She could practically see his mind whirring behind that deceptively mild smile, wondering how far she would take this, trying to deconstruct her own motivation even as she struggled to keep up with his.

He was whip-smart, dangerous. And unbelievably sexy.

This was unsafe. Unwise. But she wanted. Before her brain caught up with her body, Juliette grabbed him by the front of his shirt, pulled him inside, and slammed the door shut. Then she pushed him up against the door and kissed him.

The second she did, he groaned and wrapped his arms around her, one hand on her back, one in her hair. Emboldened, she stroked her tongue over his, rubbed her body up his solid one. If she was going to fall, she was going to go all the way.

She gripped his waist, hanging on for dear life, the feel of him making her heady. All that strength and power. All hers. She wanted to touch him everywhere. Finish what they'd started at Powell's.

There was no one watching now, so she took the opportunity to touch, sliding one hand up his side, loving the sensation of his muscles shifting as she traversed his torso.

More. She needed more. She went back down to get under his shirt and found bare skin. Beautiful. Giving herself some room to work, she smoothed her hands up his back, then around to his chest. Firm muscles, but with a light sprinkling of hair that tickled her fingertips. She slid the flat of one palm lower…lower…

Before she got as far as she wanted, he pushed off and spun her around so that she was the one up against the door.

"My turn," he said, kissing her, then burying his face in her neck.

"I wasn't done." She shoved at him, trying to get him to switch positions, but he captured both her wrists in his hand and raised them above her head, pressing them against the door. She wiggled against him, so he gave her some of his weight, and oh, she liked that. Way, way too much. Ditto when he gripped her jaw in his other hand.

Her cheeks were burning, and she was panting shallowly, completely turned on. And so was he, his rock-hard cock pressing into her hip.

"Brody," she breathed, right before he kissed her again, harder this time. She gave back as good as she got, showing him without words how turned on he was making her.

This made no sense. There was so much bad blood between their families, so much tension and strain between the two of them, but being in his arms, taking his mouth, his weight, his need, felt so very right.

"I want you," he murmured. "Tell me you want me, too."

"Yes," she said on a gasp, just as his mouth pressed against hers again.

God, he was good. A master, kissing her with just the right amount of heat and pressure.

He slid his hand around to cup her breast. "I love your curves," he said, stroking her nipple with his thumb through the thin, clingy fabric. She arched into him on a moan, her knees going weak with pleasure as he played, plumping and pinching, flicking and stroking. She was so primed and ready, when he wedged a leg between her thighs and pressed up against her sweet spot, her eyes rolled into the back of her head.

"I want to watch you fall apart," he said. "Just like this. You can do it, yeah?"

"Yeah," she breathed, by now seeing stars.

"Fast or slow?" he asked, then went to work before she had the chance to answer.

Fast. She went fast.

Just a minute with her rocking against him before she came apart with a glorious shudder and his name on her lips.

"Jesus, Juliette," he rasped. "That was fucking hot." He released her hands, and she started to crumple, but he caught her before she slid too far down the wall and kissed her mouth once, then twice. "Have dinner with me tonight."

"Dinner," she murmured, still flying high. Something tickled the back of her mind.

He brushed her lips with his again. "Please."

It was then she remembered. "Oh, crap. No. No dinner. My aunt and uncle are going to be home any minute. If they catch you here, I'll never hear the end of it." She started to panic, making little flailing motions with her hands.

She tried to wriggle away, but he held her still. "Settle down."

"You don't understand. I mean, they're having a party. A big one. Lots of people. Lots of…" She broke off, then shook her head. "You have to leave."

Immediately, he let her go. His gaze was guarded, his eyes shuttered. "Right. Leaving now."

"Wait, Brody, I—"

He was angry. She could see that. But everything was happening too fast. He was already grabbing the door handle, opening the door wide. Before she could stop him, he strode right out, head held high, not even bothering to hide himself. She almost called out but held her tongue. When he was safely through the garden—no sign of her aunt or uncle anywhere—she breathed a sigh of relief and slowly shut the door.

His reaction was understandable, but unexpected.

She thought that this was exactly what he wanted—a no-strings-attached fling with no promises that it was anything other than temporary. When it ended—and without a doubt it would end—they'd go their separate ways. He'd probably be thrilled that they'd kept it casual. Because when things got serious, people got hurt. And that destroyed everything.

CHAPTER 8

Brody took a sip of coffee and stared out his window. It was raining again, one of those barely-there last-gasp-of-summer sprinkles that grayed the sky and dampened the pavement. He'd seen rain all around the world—in Singapore where it came hard and fast, splattering along the steaming sidewalks and adding to the stifling humidity; in the jungles of Thailand, where it fell like a whisper, deepening the greens of the leaves; and in Hong Kong, where it pattered on the ground, darkening the city only to have the skyline emerge even more glittery and beautiful than before. But there was no rain like Portland rain.

No matter how far he traveled, he would always return here, to the city where he was born, where he now lived, where he would grow old, and eventually, after a hopefully long and productive life, where he would die.

His thoughts were dark these days, and it wasn't just how they were going to keep the distillery side of the business afloat. It was how he could keep his family from imploding at the slightest provocation. And also what the hell he thought he was doing with Juliette Costa.

He liked her. No, scratch that. He liked the women he slept with. What he had with Juliette was…more.

Thoughts of her pervaded his mind, had for a while, actually. He'd been thrilled when she'd finally flirted back, and look where that had ended up. With him, practically mauling her up against the door in her own house. And her dismissing him out of hand the moment they were through. Which had stung.

A knock on his office door had him turning.

His mom walked in, followed closely by Ulysses, the family's golden retriever, who was wagging his tail as he followed her in. Ulysses found his favorite spot near Brody's couch and curled up on the floor.

"Got a minute?" his mom asked.

At fifty-four, Fiona Phelan was still beautiful. She'd grown up on the Oregon coast and her style reflected that—minimal makeup, no fussy jewelry, and definitely no fancy clothes, which served her perfectly in her role as Wolfshead's accountant. Tall and slim, she favored snowboarding in winter and surfing in summer to keep in shape. Today she was wearing jeans and a roll-neck sweater. Her light red hair was pulled back into its typical tidy ponytail, highlighting the few strands of gray that she jokingly referred to as blond and refused to color.

She was natural. True. And very, very real, from the tiny pearl stud earrings—a sixteenth birthday gift from her own mother—to the attractive laugh lines bracketing her generous mouth. She'd always had a quiet temperament, but after her husband died she'd retreated even more into herself. Brody had hoped that his dad's death would give her some closure, maybe even allow her to find happiness with someone else, but she never dated. Didn't even go out, really, something that worried Brody.

But right now, what was worrying Brody more was the furrows between her brows, which had gotten a fraction deeper.

"What's up?" he asked.

"So you know how you wanted me to run the depreciation schedules for all of our fixed assets to help with your projections for next year? Something isn't jibing when I do the numbers. Can you take a look at it for me?"

"Sure."

He went to sit at his desk and motioned for her to put the laptop down in front of him. With a practiced eye, he skimmed the Excel spreadsheet his mom had prepared. "I think there's an error in percentages in cell N14. Twenty seems way too high."

His mom's eyebrows went up, and she peered in for a closer look at the equation he'd highlighted. "You're right! It shouldn't be twenty. It should be two!" Quickly, she reached over, deleted the extra zero, and clicked enter. When she scrolled down to the bottom of the column, she must have liked what she saw, because her shoulders relaxed. "That did it. I knew something was off."

"No problem. It was an easy fix."

She made a clucking sound of disappointment—in herself, no doubt. "Those spreadsheets are murder on my eyes," she muttered.

Brody pursed his lips but said nothing. His mom wasn't vain, but she was supposed to wear glasses when working at the computer. She wasn't wearing them now, so she'd probably left them at home…on purpose. He knew why. A couple of years ago, Brody had called her out on her squinting. It was then that she'd confessed she hated wearing them because they made her feel old.

Fiona had closed her laptop, but she was still hovering.

Brody cocked his head. "Anything else?"

"Yes."

For a long moment she didn't speak, not until he looked at her expectantly. "Well? What is it?"

"I'm…concerned about you," she said, her elegant hands grasped tightly in front of her. Shit. His mom wanted to *talk*, something he wasn't sure he could handle right now.

Brody frowned and busied himself by stacking up the insurance file folders on his desk. "I'm okay."

"No, Brody. You're not." Her voice was quiet, but insistent.

"How am I not okay?"

"I can't quite put my finger on what it is, exactly, but I know something's wrong. This isn't something that's just cropped up. It's something I've been noticing for a while."

"Nothing's wrong," he said curtly. "I'm fine. And even if I wasn't, I don't need you worrying about me."

"That's my job."

"I can take care of myself."

"I know." It was supposed to be a good thing, but she sounded so sad. "But it's not just Wolfshead's finances that you sort out, it's all the other issues that pop up. Aidan leans on you to do his dirty work. He should be the one keeping the peace, but because he is who he is, you're left to do it all. You break up fights, sort out issues. It can't all be you."

"Aidan helps more now. And so does Emma." Thank God for Emma.

"But who helps you?"

"I do."

"I understand. Believe me, I understand. So much has happened that's been outside of your control." She started ticking off on her fingers. "The price for the barrels increasing, the accident we had last month, Paddy giving you pushback on everything…"

"He was fiscally conservative."

"He was a stubborn old man who didn't like what your father and uncle wanted to do and chose to punish all of us over their choices. At least he let me stay on at Wolfshead. I think he felt bad about how your father treated me."

He and his mom were different people, but they were alike in this way—the two most important men in their lives had let them down, but nothing would come of bashing them.

"They're both dead"—in unison, Fiona and Brody made the sign of the cross—"and life goes on."

"That's right," she said, nodding. "Life goes on. Except you're not really living."

"I work. I spend time in my garage. I date."

"Pfft, you don't date."

"I have plenty of relationships."

"None that last."

"The same goes for you."

The brief look of surprise on his mom's face quickly morphed back to melancholy. "He really did a number on us, didn't he?"

He didn't have to ask whether his mom was talking about Paddy or his dad, because he already knew. "Yeah."

"I'm glad you came back. I wasn't sure you would, you know. I thought it might be too much…" She shook her head at some remembered pain. "Your dad was…"

A selfish asshole.

"…difficult," she finished. "Even when he was at his worst, I saw the strength in you, the determination to do things your own way, to follow your own path. And you did. You became a good man, the best man…but something's missing. The same thing that's missing in me. You're not really whole, and I know it's because of him."

"You should have left him."

"I thought about it," she admitted. "And some part of me wishes I had. But I knew I would be denying you the chance to be a family, to be close to your cousins. They're like brothers to you. It was what Christine and I always hoped for. You would have missed out on so much."

"Instead we suffered."

"I didn't know how bad it would be, especially toward the end." Fiona's voice was barely a whisper. "But what I do know is that it's over. He's been dead for six years, and yet you haven't gotten over it. It's time to move on." This, said more firmly.

Something in the vicinity of his heart cracked a little. As usual, she just wanted to see him happy, even when she herself was suffering. He gave her a gentle smile. "Thanks for the pep talk. Hoping you'll take some of your own advice."

"It's too late for me," she said tightly. "But it's not too late for you."

He rose, then wrapped his arm around her shoulder and kissed her on the top of the head. "It's not too late for you, either."

She'd suffered for so long, sometimes he forgot she was still a woman in her prime. And as much as the thought of his mom finding love was uncomfortable—he was her son, after all—more than anything, he wanted her to be happy. After what she'd been through, she deserved it.

She looked up at him, clear love shining in her eyes. "He didn't leave me with much, but the things he did leave me with are golden."

"Love you."

"Love you, too." Fiona let him embrace her for a long moment before she pulled away and picked up her laptop. "I'm going to go back and work on these numbers some more. I'll have it to you by the end of the day so you can work on those projections. But first, I'm going to take Ulysses for a quick walk. Hopefully he won't get too soaked."

Fiona whistled for Ulysses, who rose to his feet and padded over to her. "Come, boy." He did, following after her like a well-trained soldier.

When his mom was gone, Brody sank down once again in his desk chair. She was right—his father really did a number on them. She was damaged, and so was he. So were Connor and Finn, for that matter, although he doubted Connor would ever want to talk about it, and Finn was too busy playing rock star to worry about it. The groupies probably thought it was hot.

Not him.

Even after all this time, the specter of his dad still affected everything Brody did, everyone he touched. He'd never be whole, never have a normal relationship, because every time he came close, he'd see his father's face in his mind, taunting him.

Move on, his mom had said. As though it was so easy.

It wasn't. And he should know. He'd tried for years.

Moving on, getting close, finding love. Those things were easier said than done. Because no matter what he did or how much rain fell, his father's sins would never be washed away.

CHAPTER 9

The Alder Street Food Cart Pod was hopping the next Tuesday when Brody showed up just before noon. Hundreds of downtown workers swarmed the most popular trucks. Aromas of frying food, steaming vegetables, and roasting meat filled the air, mixing together in a mélange of odors that was uniquely Portland.

The city's street food game was strong, but Brody didn't often get to indulge—at least not the way he used to when he and his brothers and cousins would go out for drinks and end up at one of the late-night food carts, scarfing down greasy noodles or bulgogi at two in the morning after a long evening out.

It was a treat for Brody to be out of his office for lunch. Most days he wolfed down a protein bar or three at his desk between phone calls and meetings. But he'd promised Juliette help with her business plan, and that's exactly what he was going to deliver. They couldn't meet at her place—too risky, she'd said.

Fine with him. All that did was cement in his mind what they had—a decent business relationship with a bonus-for-now no-strings-attached physical relationship. She didn't want any more from him.

Clearly.

He spied her small, curvy form cutting through the crowd. Although she was wearing a conservative sheath dress, there was no way to hide her hourglass figure.

She pushed her hair back over her shoulders, and he caught his breath. She was gorgeous, and what made her even more attractive was that she didn't even realize how beautiful she was. Add in intelligence and an unwillingness to put up with his crap, and she was honestly the full package.

Except full packages didn't matter when there was no future.

She was still looking around, trying to spot him in the crowd, so he reached up a hand in greeting. Finally, she saw him and hurried over.

"Hi," she said. "Thanks for meeting me."

There was an awkward silence, where they just stood there, looking at each other for a long, uncomfortable moment.

Finally, Brody cleared his throat. "How was the party?"

"The party?" For a moment she looked confused. Then she understood. "Oh, yes. At my aunt's place. The usual. Way too much food, way too many people."

"Sorry."

"It's okay. It's what I expected. But I'm sorry you had to leave so fast. I—didn't want that. I really did want to have dinner with you."

"I had another engagement anyway." Truth. Even though he would have gladly broken it for her.

She actually looked disappointed. "Oh," she said, her voice soft. "Okay."

Now he actually felt guilty. Shit. He cleared his throat. "So what do you think?" he asked. "Food first, then work?"

She nodded. "Yes. I have a meeting at two, so I have a bit of time." She looked around. "This is crazy busy. Is it always this packed on weekdays?"

"Thought you called yourself a PDXer," he teased.

Juliette looked vaguely relieved that he was back to his usual self and gave an elegant little shrug. "I do, but I haven't been to the food carts in so long. I rarely get to go out for lunch, and today, I actually scheduled meetings downtown so I'd have an excuse to be here. I'm guessing you come here more frequently than I do."

"Early dinners mostly, especially if I'm having a late night."

"Does that mean you know what you want?"

"Yep. If I'm around for lunch, I always go to Nong's Khao Man Gai. They close early, so I'm usually too late to get it for dinner."

"What do they serve?"

"They only have one dish, and it's killer—garlic-and-ginger-infused chicken and rice."

"That sounds great."

Fifteen minutes later, to-go containers in hand, they strolled over to O'Bryant Square, a paved area perfect for a picnic, and found a spot on the crowded stone steps.

They sat close together, knees almost touching. He liked the intimacy, much more than he should.

Juliette, ever focused on food, had already opened up her container and was holding her face over it with an expression of pure bliss. "Oh my gosh. That smells so good!" She balanced the container on her knees, then closed her eyes and took another deep whiff.

"Wait until you taste it," he said with a smile, and tucked into his own plate of fragrant chicken and rice. It had been months since he'd had this dish, and it was just as delicious as he remembered, tender chicken perfectly seasoned with the right amount of spice and heat. Next to him, Juliette let out a little moan.

"Do you like it?"

"Are you kidding?" she said, another forkful halfway to her mouth. "This stuff is amazing." She popped it in and mumbled something about ambrosia.

"I wouldn't steer you wrong."

After a few minutes, Juliette put down her fork and sighed. "It's so good, but if I eat another bite, I'm going to burst. Would you like the rest?"

Brody shook his head. "No, thanks. Why don't you take it back to work and eat it for dinner? The meeting you're taking this afternoon probably means you'll be in for a long night. So, are you ready to talk business?"

Nodding, she tucked her closed container under her feet and turned to him expectantly.

"Good. I guess my first question is why do you need a business plan? Are you trying to attract investors? Get a loan? Or is this more for your own personal use?"

"For me first, definitely. I want to get a good sense of what the business will entail. I also hope to use it to attract investors. And—" She stopped. Bit her lip.

"And what?" he prompted.

"I need money and of course I want to attract an investor or two who will help me get things off the ground, but honestly, I need a business plan as much for my family as I do for me and outside investors. So they can see that this is a legitimate business and that I'm going to succeed. Otherwise, they won't take me seriously."

He got it. "All right. I agree that you definitely need a business plan. There are several sections to a typical plan. We'll keep it simple at first, and then when you get comfortable with the process and framework, we can add more. You'll want to have a summary that details the overall plan, your background and rationale for opening the business, your strategy, your basic marketing plan, and your financials."

"Hang on. I need a pen and paper for this." She reached into her handbag. "I came prepared. Just give me a minute, okay?"

"Sure. Take your time." He waited while she found what she was looking for, then repeated what he'd just said while she took notes.

"So you said this is simple. This really doesn't seem so simple to me."

"You're right," he said truthfully. "It seems simple, and it is—if you have a clear understanding of your business. If you don't, it's not simple at all, and this will be a good exercise for you to go through to figure that out. You need to do research to get a strong understanding of what building this business from scratch will entail, the market and your ultimate place within it, what kind of real estate you'll need, start-up costs, overhead costs, insurance…"

"Whoa, slow down," she said, her pen flying across the page. "I don't know how I'm going to figure all this stuff out."

"Don't worry," he said. "Because I will talk you through it, step by step."

Over the course of the next hour, Brody did as he said he would—walked her through each facet of the business plan step by step, giving her details about everything she needed to do to make the plan workable.

"Any questions?"

"Too many," she sighed. "This is going to be a huge amount of work."

"Yes," Brody said simply.

Juliette sat up straighter. "But I'm up for the challenge."

"I would expect nothing less from you."

She gave him a sidelong glance. "Let's hope your faith isn't misplaced."

"It's not. Gather your questions. I'm glad to answer them. Get something down on paper, and when you think you're ready to share, let me know. I can hook you up with Emma Crandall, Wolfshead's resident marketing expert. She has connections all over this city, and I bet she'll be able to help you out. And if the proposal is going to be as amazing as I think it is, then I'll set you up with a friend of mine—Mike Sutherland. He invests in restaurants in and around the Portland area. We can see if your project is something he'd be interested in pursuing. I trust his judgment, so even if it isn't something he wants to do, he would probably be able to give you some tips on how to make the plan even more attractive to other investors."

"You're being more than generous," she murmured.

"Yeah," he said, leaning back on his arms. "I am."

She nudged her knee with his. "Arrogant."

"You love it." Juliette's cheeks turned a little pink, giving him all the answer he needed. "Damn, you *do*."

"Yes, well, I like it when you're sweet, too."

"Sweet?" The word almost didn't come out, his throat was so tight.

"You didn't have to do this, Brody. Help me. Hook me up with your family and friends. It's okay." She gave him a gentle smile. "I like seeing this side of you."

Alarm bells went off in his head. He wasn't sweet.

"Of course I had to help you," he heard himself saying. "We had a deal, remember? Dinner in exchange for help with the plan."

She went completely still. "Was messing with me at my place part of the deal too?"

"No."

She spoke slowly and carefully. "What was it, then?"

"A bonus we both wanted."

She didn't toss a saucy comeback his way, but a strange expression flashed across her face, just for an instant. Almost immediately, she shuttered her gaze and looked away.

Part of him felt bad about what he was doing, but Juliette deserved to know the unvarnished truth. Better she know now what she was getting herself into with him—a whole lot of nothing.

Because yeah, he wanted her. But he didn't want anything permanent, and it was clear from the way she brushed him off the other day at her place that she didn't either. Sure, he'd been angry that she'd dismissed him, but that had faded fast when he realized she was only doing it to protect herself. Just like he did.

Abruptly, he rose. "I should go."

"Same." She put the pen and paper back into her bag and stood a bit more slowly.

"Will you make it to your meeting?"

She glanced at her watch. "Half an hour. Plenty of time."

"Good. So, I'll see you on Friday, I guess."

"Friday," she confirmed. "Thank you again for your help," she said, the words coming out sounding stilted. "I truly appreciate it. I'm sorry if I kept you longer than you anticipated. Goodbye, Brody." And then she simply turned and walked away.

He turned and did the same in the opposite direction, unable to suppress the feeling that he'd seriously fucked up with her.

And maybe, just maybe, that was for the best.

CHAPTER 10

If stubbornness were a degree, Juliette's dad would have a doctorate. Umberto Costa had been doing things his way for almost his entire life, and simply could not see that any other path made sense. No one could make him budge on anything, not even his own mother, may she rest in peace, who had lived with them until her death two years ago.

Right now he was standing in front of his desk, his fists clenched. He was a small but powerfully built man who was still in amazing shape at sixty-two. He had a bit of a belly, no doubt because he loved food as much as Juliette did and frequently indulged. His salt-and-pepper hair was thick and lush, and his face barely had any lines in it, a product of his Mediterranean heritage—except for that dangerously large vein currently throbbing in his forehead.

"No!" he shouted. "For the last time, we don't need any fancy software to keep track of our customers!"

Juliette took another deep breath and tried again. "I'm telling you we do need that software. Like, yesterday."

"Absolutely not!"

They'd been going at this for at least twenty minutes, and by now he was red in the face. If he hadn't done this a hundred times before, she'd be worried that he was going to have a stroke.

"As I was saying before you started yelling," she continued rationally, "our homemade spreadsheet is getting really unwieldy. I'm the only one who knows how to update it with the new orders, and it's too much for me to manage with everything else I'm doing."

"So stop updating it. There. Easy fix."

Juliette shot a glance over to Sal, who was slouched in one of the chairs on the far side of the room, his arms crossed over his chest, his face a blank. No help from that quarter. He hadn't wanted Juliette to bring up the software again at all, mostly because it was no skin off his back whether they had it or not. Besides, when it came to standing up to their father, Sal was a wimp.

Juliette's mom was also there, perched on another chair near the desk, watching the argument unfold with increasingly obvious nervousness.

In times past she would have folded, but now she wasn't backing down. Not this time.

"I can't just stop doing it," she explained. "If I did that, I'd have no way of keeping track of our orders and project upcoming revenue, not to mention all the dozens of other things I use the spreadsheet to do." Why was he not getting this?

"We don't need it. Everything I need is here," he said pointing at his head. "*This* is my computer spreadsheet."

She shook her head. "You've been focused on the purchasing, not the sales side. You have a handle on the relationships with our vendors, and that is great. But since we've expanded operations, I've added upward of fifty additional clients. There's no way I could remember even half of them if I didn't have them written down. We need all our contacts in one place." She gestured to the laptop with the demo. "Look how easy it is to use. And reasonably priced, too."

Her father made a rude noise, his way of telling her to pound sand. Unsurprising. Trying to get her dad to do something he didn't want was like trying to single-handedly budge an elephant.

"What if something happened to you? All that information would be lost, along with those relationships."

"Nothing's going to happen to me," he said, making a dismissive gesture.

"But what if something happens to *me*? Sal, Gio, and Tony don't do that work. I do. And if I leave—"

"Leave, ha!" her dad interjected. "Where are you going to go? This is your life. This is where you belong."

"I can't stay here forever, Dad. At some point I'm going to have to move on."

"What are you telling me? Are you telling me that you want to leave? Why would you want that?" He sounded incredulous. But before she could answer, his gaze dropped to her stomach. "Are you pregnant?"

Her mother gasped as Sal stood up, knocking the chair he was sitting in onto its back.

Juliette's jaw dropped. "What? No!"

But her dad wasn't listening. "Is it that Giaccalone boy? The one who was sniffing around you last year? I knew he was no good. Francesca, I told you he was no good!"

Her mother started crying.

"I'll kill him," Sal said. "I'll kill him with my bare hands."

"You're going to have to get in line," her father said. "Because I'm going to kill him first."

"Gio! Tony!" Sal was yelling. "Get the fuck in here! Juliette's got a bun in the oven and we're going to kill Rudy Giaccalone."

Oh my God, this was completely spiraling out of control.

"Stop it, both of you! It's not Rudy Giaccalone!" Juliette had gone out with him a year ago—mostly to appease her mother, who was friendly with his mother through church. A single date was all it had taken to realize that he was definitely not right for her. He'd actually told her that no wife of his would ever work, even though he himself had no discernable job and played video games all day. And he'd been way too handsy at the end of the evening. Disgusting. To this day, she and Lucy called him "octopus."

"Who is it then?" her father demanded, his face a bright shade of red, the vein in his forehead throbbing harder. "Who knocked you up?"

By this time Gio and Tony had raced into the room.

"What's going on? What's all the yelling about?" Tony asked.

"Juliette's knocked up."

"I'm not!" she said more forcefully, but no one was listening.

"Who're we gonna kill?" Gio asked, his expression murderous.

"Rudy Giaccalone."

"I never liked him," Tony said. "Those beady little eyes. And those hipster bowling shirts that look stupid on everyone."

"I'm going to call his father. Give him a piece of my mind," her father said. "Because if he thinks that his boy can come over and hurt my baby girl, he's got another thing coming."

"Jesus, Papa, please. Just calm down." At the rate he was going, he might actually have that stroke after all.

"Calm down? How can I calm down when you've been impregnated by a jackass who lives at home?"

"*I* live at home," Tony said, sounding affronted.

Enough was enough. "Will you listen to me?" she screamed. "For the last time. I am not pregnant!"

Her mom gasped again and this time, so did her father.

"So you're not pregnant," her dad said. "But you are sleeping with that Giaccalone boy?"

Juliette threw up her hands. "What is wrong with you? I try to have a conversation about something that would help me, help *us*, and first you jump to conclusions then grill me on who I am or am not sleeping with? Do you realize how crazy this is?"

"Why is this crazy?" her dad asked. "We care about you."

"This isn't caring. This is smothering. You're in my business all the time."

Her dad looked affronted. "You're my daughter! Everything you do is my business. Otherwise you'll end up like—" He broke off, but she knew what he wanted to say.

Regina.

Juliette looked over to her mother, who had her lips pressed together and was wringing her hands.

"Look what you did to your mother!" Umberto said.

Juliette swung back to her dad. "I didn't do anything. And as for being like Regina," she said clearly, making her dad flinch, "I'm not her. I was never her, and I'll never be her. But the way you're treating me is exactly what made her run." In the stunned silence that followed, she realized that her head had begun to ache with an intensity she could hardly bear. "I started this conversation because I need more sophisticated software than I currently have. You won't give me the authorization to buy it, which would make my life easier and the company run more smoothly."

"We don't need it," he ground out. "Things are fine the way they are."

And that, right there, was the problem. Things were not fine the way they were, only her father couldn't see that.

I can't live like this, she wanted to scream.

But instead, she quietly crossed the room to the door.

"You know what? You're right. We don't need new software. Sal can handle the orders from here on out."

"Now wait just a minute—" Sal began.

"Don't worry. You'll be great. I'll leave a thumb drive on your desk with the spreadsheet. Consider it a screw you very much for helping me out today."

"Juliette, I—"

"No," she said, making a slashing motion with her hand. "I don't want to hear it."

"Don't do anything stupid," Sal warned.

"I never do," she tossed back. "But then again, since you seem to think the worst of me, maybe I should start."

And she rushed out before the yelling started again.

This was how everything seemed to be ending lately.

She practically sprinted down the hallway, needing to get away. The walls of the warehouse felt as if they were closing in, and she started to trot, then to run. She burst out the side door, gasping for air, tears threatening to fall.

How did her family manage to do this every single time? Flip her words back on her and make her feel so small. She felt reduced, diminished. Like nothing.

She blinked up at the sky, trying desperately to hold it together. She wanted to scream, to cry, to smash something and have it burst into a million pieces.

The sky was cloudy, the air misty with rain. She was tired of fighting. Tired of arguing, of trying to change things that would never change.

Exhausted, she leaned back against the side of the warehouse and sank down until her butt touched her heels.

"Help," she whispered, burying her face in her knees. If there was ever a time she needed to be working on her own stuff, this was it.

She would leave work early. Go home. Start pulling together her business plan based on Brody's suggestions.

Ah, Brody. Everyone seemed to be disappointing her lately. He'd put her in her place quite effectively over lunch, making it crystal clear that he'd wanted nothing serious with her. She shouldn't be surprised. She'd known what kind of man he was from the very beginning. At least he was honest about it, and she couldn't fault him for being exactly who he was, especially since he was helping her out, to boot.

Besides, it was safer for both of them this way.

At that moment, her cell phone buzzed in her pocket. She pulled it out, only to see Hot Neighbor pop up on the screen. Frowning, she picked it up.

"Hello? Brody?"

"Hey. Are you okay?" His voice was low and soothing.

She pressed her palm against one eye, then the other. "Yes. Fine."

"You sure about that? You don't look so good."

Wait a minute… She peered around. "Where are you? Are you spying on me?"

"Not intentionally," he said slowly. "But I can see you on our video feed."

Quickly she scrambled to standing. "Jeez, stalker. Thanks for telling me I was on candid camera."

"Dylan set up a long-range feed," he said by way of explanation. "You look like you could use some company. Want me to come over?"

"Definitely not," she told him. "Everyone here has gone off the deep end. They'll probably shoot you on sight."

"So come over here. Meet you behind the distillery?"

"Sure. Okay." She could use a frenemy to talk to right now. Conscious that he was likely watching, she threw back her shoulders and tried to pull herself together. "Give me a few minutes. I'm going to walk around to the street."

The first thing Brody noticed when Juliette came around the corner was that her eyes were rimmed with red, as though she'd been crying or was desperately trying not to. That, and her expression. As if someone had given her a shiny new toy and then ripped it right out of her hands.

And that just gutted him.

"Hey," he said as she approached.

"Hey," she responded, and her lip trembled.

She wasn't ready to talk. He could see that, plain as day. So he did what he thought she needed. He opened his arms.

"C'mere," he said. To his great surprise, she actually came to him. He enveloped her in his arms and pulled her close. "Shh. It's okay." She wasn't crying. Not exactly. But she was shuddering and sniffling a bit. Then she said something unintelligible into his shirt.

Things must be really bad for feisty, fiery Juliette Costa to mumble her words. Or to take what he was offering. Soothingly, he stroked her back for a while until she seemed calmer. A car rolled down the street, but she didn't pick up her head to look.

Finally, when he thought she might be ready, he cupped the back of her head. "Want to tell me what happened?"

She shook her head into his chest. "It doesn't matter."

"It does if you're this upset about it."

"It's okay. I can handle it." This, also said into his chest.

"Is that why you threw yourself in my arms the moment I offered? 'Cause the Juliette I know would have told me to go fuck myself."

She turned her head to the side and her voice came out clearer. "I would never say that."

"Yeah, you're right. You would say something like, 'Is this a sneaky ploy to get me into bed? Because it sure as hell isn't going to work.'"

She laughed a little, then choked on it.

"Hey," he said, lifting her chin with his finger so he could look her in the eyes. "You can tell me. Whatever it is you can tell me. I swear I won't judge or make fun of you. I'll just listen."

For a long moment, she stared at him, then lowered her gaze. "I can usually take it. I mean, I've been doing it for so long. But for some reason, today really got to me."

"What happened?"

"It was so stupid. It always starts off like nothing. I wanted my dad to sign off on some new software that would make my life easier, but he refused."

"This wasn't the first time?"

"Try the fourth. I've tried everything—showing him the data, the financials, the benefits, but it's his way or the highway. It's been like that forever."

"I can relate." Paddy had been like that, bulldozing everything in his path, not caring about others' thoughts or ideas.

"Yeah." She frowned. "Except then it got a lot worse. Instead of keeping the discussion about the business, my family immediately turned around and made it personal. Things got completely out of control."

"I can relate to that, too."

She pulled back to look at him. "You don't understand, Brody. My family's Italian. We argue and we insult each other and…and we *swear*. Like, tons."

"Juliette," he said with infinite patience. "I'm Irish. All my family does is argue and insult each other and swear."

She laughed a little, then sniffled again. "You're right. I'm sure all families go through this kind of thing. It's just that we're dealing with a lot of baggage."

"Yeah?" He cupped her face gently. "What kind of baggage?"

Juliette paused for a long time, as if weighing what to tell him. "I think," she began slowly, "that out of everyone, you might get this."

"Try me."

When she next spoke, she fixed her gaze on a spot on the brick wall. "I had a sister."

"I know. Regina, right?" He'd known her growing up—she'd been a couple of years older than him—but she'd been in a car accident while she was in college. He didn't know the whole story, and as far as he knew, no one in his family did, either.

"It's not something we really talk about. Especially not with people outside the family. I loved her so much."

"I'm sorry." He knew all too well what it meant to have a person in your life one day and missing from it the next. "Tell me now. That is, if you want to share."

She took a deep breath. "Regina was the oldest—totally beautiful, witty, and smart, too. My parents had her young. She was seven years older than me, but she was my best friend. I wanted to be just like her—always laughing, quick with a joke. She graduated from high school a year early and went to college. She was going to be a nurse. She would have been a great one, because she was sweet, but underneath it all, she was tough as nails."

A silent tear squeezed from her duct and ran down her cheekbone. Another followed.

"She was doing great in college. Top grades, volunteered at

the hospital in her free time. And then she fell in love, but my parents didn't approve. Freddy wasn't the right kind of guy, they said, but that wasn't true at all. He wasn't Italian, but he was a nice guy, a good guy, and they were committed to each other, one hundred percent. Freddy asked my dad for permission to marry Regina. Dad said no. Gave every excuse in the book—too young, no money—but really, I think it was because he wasn't Catholic. Later, Regina and my dad had a big fight. He called her—well, he called her terrible names and said she was too irresponsible to know what she was doing with her life. She said he treated her like she was still a kid, and that she was leaving and never coming back. She got into a car—"

Juliette broke off, unable to continue. The tears were flowing freely now.

"They said it was her fault," she finally said. "That she blew the stop sign. Another driver hit her. He was injured. She was killed on impact. We didn't find out until they did the autopsy that she was eight weeks pregnant."

She swiped at her face with her palms.

"My parents were always a little crazy, but after that, they kind of lost all rationality. It became their mission to keep me on lockdown until they could transfer my care to a man of their choosing."

"You, but not your brothers."

"Exactly. I mean, I get it. They're very traditional, born in Italy, and I'm the only daughter they have left. After Regina died they became…different. And not a good different. I'm strong and smart. I can do things on my own, but they pretty much dismiss me out of hand. I should have shown them long ago what I can do, argued even harder, but instead I haven't stood my ground because I thought they'd feel like they were losing another daughter."

"You were strong to stay."

"I thought so, at least at first." She shook her head. "It's just been hard to watch the change happen. And it's hard to bear the brunt of it. If they were equal-opportunity controllers, I could understand, but they don't do the same thing with my brothers. If anything, they're even more lax than they were before. It didn't help them any. They always fought, but they started acting out even more. Anyway, yes, it's sexist, and yes, it's stupid, but it's them."

Juliette looked up at him, and he got another sucker punch to the gut. She'd been so brave, telling him all of this. And only she could look so beautiful having just cried her eyes out and told him the most devastating thing about her past.

"Thank you for telling me. And Juliette? No judgment. I swear."

"Thank you."

"I remember her."

Her brows went together. "You—do?"

"Yeah. Brown hair like yours. Like you said, sweet smile, but tough as nails. Mature, too. Broke up a fight between me and Aidan one time when we were going at it in the parking lot. Didn't even need to raise her voice."

Juliette nodded. "Sounds exactly like Regina."

"You got that from her."

"You think?" She looked up at him. Her look was so earnest and so fucking sad he almost couldn't speak.

"Yeah."

"Thanks, Brody. That really means a lot to me." She was quiet for a moment before she spoke again. "Thanks for talking me down. And I'm sorry that you're seeing me like this. I know this isn't part of the deal."

"The deal?"

"Yeah. The deal. The one where we flirt and maybe more, but it's not real. And then it's over and we go back to the way things were before. That deal."

He didn't like a lot of what she'd said, but it was too much to process right now after she'd just wrecked herself telling him shit about her family that was hard to say and hard to hear. Which made him feel like a coward, hiding from his own pathetic past and then taking it out on her without her even realizing why.

"I'm sorry I was such a dick to you at lunch."

Her eyes went huge, and then she shook her head. "You don't have to apologize."

"I don't?"

"No. You don't. In all the time I've known you, you've never pretended to be anyone but who you are."

"I don't think that's a compliment."

"Sure it is. You're honest. That's more than I can say for many people." She gave him a small smile, then pulled away and glanced at her watch. "I've been gone for a while. I'd better get back before they think something terrible has happened to me. If I don't, they'll probably send my brothers out after me. They'll find *your* brothers and cousins and, well, we both know what'll happen then."

"Right."

She cocked her head at him. "See you Friday?"

"Friday."

She nodded once, then walked away, quickly disappearing around the side of the distillery.

Shit.

Juliette had just rocked his world on its head. Because she'd shared a part of herself he doubted very much she'd shared with anyone else. And he'd liked it. A hell of a lot.

He'd dated scores of women. And not once had he ever cared enough to go deep, and he sure hadn't cared enough to comfort. That wasn't what they came to him for, anyway, and if they did, they found out pretty fast that he wasn't the right guy for that.

Slowly, Brody walked back to his office, replaying Juliette's words in his head. She'd laid some heavy stuff on him, but one thing she said stood out above everything else: *you've never pretended to be anyone but who you are.*

She'd called his bluff, stripped him bare. And he didn't much like the feeling one fucking bit, because he wasn't truly being honest—with her or with himself.

Which left the question: Who the hell was Brody Phelan?

A son, a brother, a cousin. A man who loved his family. A workaholic. A mechanic. An excellent lover, but one who never stuck around. A bastard who was lonely as fuck when the lights went out at night.

Because even surrounded by the people he loved, he was alone. And it was a loneliness of his own making. He'd filled it with work and cars and women, but it wasn't enough. It would never be enough because he wanted more.

What that "more" was, he wasn't yet certain. But he was starting to get an inkling of what that could be when he was with Juliette.

Something had shifted, and she was the reason. He didn't just want her in his bed, he wanted her in his life, but that wasn't him. That had never been him.

So why did he want that with her?

He'd thought he was done with these crises of faith. His dad was dead, Paddy was dead, and he'd finally returned to form at the helm of Wolfshead with Aidan at his side, leading the company out of the dark ages. He had way too much shit on his plate, shit that he promised he would deal with. And even though he was worried that he wouldn't be able to pull it off, that he wouldn't find a way to make the distillery arm profitable in the time frame he proposed, he knew that he had to because he never, ever broke any of his promises.

All of this meant he worked a hell of a lot. His life followed the same basic pattern.

He worked, he fucked, he drank, he worked some more. Sometimes he worked on his car. Lather, rinse, and repeat.

It used to be enough.

Now it wasn't. His mom was right. He hadn't moved on. There was something missing in his life. Something big.

And whatever the hell it was, he needed to figure it out, fast. Because if he didn't, he was going to end up doing something stupid with Juliette Costa. And that was the thing that worried him most of all.

CHAPTER 11

"What the hell is this?" Brody slapped the offending piece of paper down right in front of Gabe where he sat at one of the high tables in the tasting room. Oftentimes, a bunch of them would do takeout and have dinner together on Friday night as way to debrief and unwind. Tonight, Gabe was with Aidan, Emma, Connor, and Ed, eating Chinese food and drinking drafts from the tap.

Gabe swallowed the bite of the moo shu pork he'd been scarfing and looked up at him with guileless eyes. "It's a Portland Eats poster."

"I can read," Brody said sharply. "What I want to know is why this one says we're doing free tours?"

"Because we are," Gabe said, smiling broadly.

"Not until we had the proposals sorted, which we do not," Brody bit out. "And while I think we can manage them eventually, there's no way we'll have everything in place for Portland Eats. We can't just say we're going to do tours and things happen like that." He snapped his fingers for emphasis. "To start, we need to plan the safety features, get an engineer to sign off, and hire a construction crew to do the work."

Gabe smiled even bigger. "Done, done, and done."

"We also need permits," Ed pointed out.

"Already took care of it," Gabe said.

Brody leveled Gabe with his gaze. "How exactly did you do that on such a short time frame?"

"You know me," Gabe said with no small amount of swagger. "I can be incredibly persuasive."

"Yeah," Aidan mumbled. "With your dick."

Emma's long brown hair swayed as she jabbed him with her elbow. "Aidan!"

Aidan let out a noise of pure disgust. "Oh, come on. He clearly slept with someone to get those permits."

"I did not," Gabe said indignantly, eyes flickering with what seemed like actual chagrin. "Okay, well maybe there was some flirting. And the promise of a date. Where sex *might* have been implied." All at once, his swagger was back. He flashed a megawatt smile, the one that he used to charm his way into way too many panties. "What can I say? I'm good."

"Jesus." Connor, who'd been silently watching the interchange, shook his head and went back to his carton of fried rice.

Gabe let out a frustrated breath. "Look, all that matters is that I got our ducks in a row and our permits in place. By my calculations, we have eight weeks to get things ready, and we will just make that deadline. And guys," he said, looking around imploringly, "we have to do tours. It's perfect timing for our whiskey launch, and a great way to drum up new business for the brewery side." He turned back to Brody. "We have the money to make it happen, right? My proposal was good, wasn't it?"

"It was," Brody said slowly. Both Ed and Gabe had held up their ends of the bargain, which was to get him their proposals. It had been the matter of a few hours to see that what they proposed was going to work—with the proper precautions. "But nothing's been hashed out. I have to make a budget for the safety features and the additional insurance, and once I have those, we can talk about pricing."

"No need," Gabe said, waving his hand. "I already paid the engineers and the contractors based on my proposed estimates. I'm using Rick Johnston's crew."

"Rick always underestimates the time he'll need," Aidan growled.

"And he's always over budget," Brody added. "You should have talked to me before making any promises."

Realizing things weren't going his way, Gabe crossed his arms over his chest defensively. "I'm not going to apologize when I'm not sorry. We need this to happen. I own one-eighth of this company, same as all of you. I'll pay for the work out of my own pocket if Wolfshead doesn't want to pony up."

Brody sighed. "It's not just the money. It's the timing. I don't know if we can pull this off."

"We'll pull it off," Gabe said with steely determination.

But Emma looked worried. "I'm not so sure. Maybe if we had more time? It's bad to promise something you can't deliver."

"Just call up the Portland Eats folks and cancel the tour part," Aidan said.

"We can't cancel," Gabe said, waving at the paper in Brody's hand. "All the posters have already been printed and distributed, remember?"

"Shit," Aidan said softly.

Then everyone except Connor started talking at once. Okay, it was more like arguing, but that was par for the course with his family. Brody sighed. He'd give them a few minutes before stepping in to break things up.

As Gabe and the rest of them hashed it out in loud and colorful terms, Brody sneaked a glance at his watch. Thanks to this impromptu meeting, he was going to be late for his dinner with Juliette.

"Got somewhere you have to be?" Connor said in a low enough voice that no one else could hear.

He met Connor's gaze. "What do you think?"

"I think she's good for you. Just don't hurt her."

Of course Connor knew about Juliette. His brother might not talk much, but he was damned observant. He saw what no one else could see. What no one else was even looking for.

Hell, Brody was dressed to the nines—slacks, a button-down shirt, even a fucking blazer, and no one had asked him what he was doing or where he was going. Except Connor.

"I thought you hated the Costas," Brody said.

Connor shrugged. "I do. But I like her." He gave a ghost of a smile and shoved his carton toward the center of the table. "Anyone want the rest of my food?"

Ed, still obviously angry, snatched it up and started eating. Everyone else fell silent. As usual, Connor's quiet words had cut through the cacophony like a knife.

Brody let out a short breath. "The problem isn't going anywhere and we don't have to make any decisions tonight," he said. "So let's brainstorm independently and reconvene next week to do some damage control."

"There hasn't been any damage," Gabe said, his face flushed from the efforts of trying to convince everyone it was all going to work out.

"Yet. Look, I gotta go," Brody said. "We'll talk more later." Nodding at the group, he walked away.

The creased Portland Eats poster was still in his hand, a stubborn reminder of yet another mess he had to clean up. Crumpling it up, he threw it in the trash.

Juliette leaned back against cool leather inside the small French bistro and took a deep breath, inhaling the aromas of garlic, wine, and roasting meat. Servers wearing white aprons bustled around, one carrying a delicious-looking purple cocktail on a silver tray.

The space was long, but narrow, with maybe twelve tables and a curved bar on the far side of the room. And the decor was totally Portland, albeit upscale—red leather banquettes, a pounded tin ceiling, a mounted set of giant antlers, and within each of the small circular alcoves high up on the wall, tiny little stuffed birds, both cheerful and macabre. The clientele consisted of an eclectic mix—a couple of hipsters stuffed into the corner banquette, an elderly group sipping postprandial drinks at a four-top, and two thirtysomething women at the bar sharing a delicious-looking cheese plate.

Juliette shifted to cross her legs, making sure that her (Lucy-approved) dress didn't ride up too high on her thighs. The red jersey clung to every dip and curve, and her strappy leather peep-toes (also Lucy-approved) made her legs look super long. Lucy had done her makeup and hair, too, giving her curls an extra bit of volume. "Sex curls," Lucy had pronounced before she'd left for the evening. Juliette had been a bit self-conscious, but when she'd seen the way Brody's eyes had darkened to a deeper green, she was glad she'd let Lucy choose her outfit.

Except Brody looked tired, and a bit beat.

"Rough day?" she asked.

He gave her a rueful smile. "Yeah."

"Want to talk about it?"

"Nah. Staring at you is just as good. Maybe better." He took her hand in his across the table. "You look gorgeous tonight."

She flushed with pleasure. "So do you."

He smiled, for real this time, and pushed the drink menu her way. "Do you want something to drink?"

"Sure." She studied the menu for a moment and quickly decided on a glass of white wine.

"I like this place," she pronounced after the server had come to take their drink orders. "I'd definitely come back."

Brody laughed. "You haven't even tried the food yet."

"I like the ambiance. I like the vibe. And if the food is even half as good as you say it is, it's a no-brainer."

"You made up your mind that fast?" he asked, cocking his head at her.

"I'm usually pretty decisive about stuff like this. Something clicks in my brain and I'm done."

"Does your brain-click work with people too?"

She was saved from having to answer by the server who reappeared with their drinks—a glass of Riesling for her, a craft beer for him.

"Thanks again for helping me with my business plan," she said, holding up her glass for a clink.

"Pleasure," he said, following suit and taking a sip.

God, she loved the way he looked—effortlessly amazing in a blazer stretched over his broad shoulders and button-down shirt opened at his throat. She liked him like this—a little bit corporate, a little bit rough.

Because the beard and the longish hair were kind of rough. As was his tattoo. She'd seen a glimpse of it once on a rare sunny day when he and his brothers had come out to the parking lot to play a game of pickup basketball against the guys who owned the charcuterie place down the street. The Phelans had been skins, and she'd caught a flash of ink…before Sal had found her spying and threatened to rat her out to their dad if she didn't help him.

Now that she'd dispelled his obvious fears about being trapped in a relationship with her, he was back to the old Brody—relaxed and flirtatious.

"So you never answered my question. Does your brain-click

work on people?”

"Why don't you ask the question you really want to ask?”

He grinned. “Fine. I'll rephrase. Did your brain-click work with me?”

Deliberately, she took a sip of wine, drawing out the silence. “I don't remember.”

"Sure you do.”

"Nope. I don't even remember the first time we met, as adults, at least,” she lied.

At that he actually looked affronted. “You don't? *I* do.”

"Really?”

"Sure. It was summer. Early June, I think, because it wasn't raining as much. I'd just gotten back from Asia. Things were…not good. Paddy was running roughshod over everyone, he and Aidan were at loggerheads over every little thing, and the rest of my family was tired and on edge. And on top of everything, your brothers were doing everything they could to make our lives a living hell. There was a fight. I forget what it was about. Something stupid, I'm sure.

"I do remember that it was Gio who started it. Came right onto our lot and started up with Finn, who happened to be outside at that moment. Well, Finn gave it back to him, and soon the two of them were yelling loud enough to wake the dead. We all came piling out of the building, and your other brothers and your dad and maybe even one of your cousins came piling out of yours—it was just like when the dugout clears at a baseball game. Things got ugly, and there was some scuffling, and I remember panicking, thinking there was no way for me to rein everyone in before all hell broke loose and everyone started pounding the crap out of each other, and also I remember thinking that this was the worst fucking welcome home ever. And then, in the middle of all the hollering and posturing, you came out.

"I hadn't seen you in years, but there you were, all grown up, strutting your way across the lot and looking hotter than hell in whatever it was you were wearing—knowing now, probably something your cousin picked out, yeah?”

She didn't know what to say, so she nodded.

"Anyway, you squeezed your way right in the middle of everyone and held out your hands, and said in that sexy voice of yours, 'Settle down, boys, or you're going to have to deal with me.'

"I don't know who was more surprised, your family or mine, but everyone stopped what they were doing and just stared when they realized you meant business. Sure enough, everyone settled down and went back to what they were doing. You gave me a nod and tilted your chin up and strutted right back across that parking lot, and all I remember thinking to myself is that you were the most amazing woman I'd ever laid eyes on."

She sat there, looking at him as he looked at her.

"Amaretto cookies," she finally whispered.

Brody blinked once. "I'm sorry, what?"

"Cookies. That's what the fight was about. Some ridiculous delivery mix-up, as usual." They'd never found the damn things. Three whole crates of them, disappeared into thin air.

His eyes warmed. "So you *do* remember."

She nodded. "You didn't have your beard then." She'd thought him handsome without it—square-jawed, with small brackets around his mouth, as if he laughed a lot. Or used to.

"That's right," he said, smiling slyly. "Do you like me better with or without it?"

"It suits you."

His smile grew wider. "You love it."

"Kind of, yeah." She squinted at him. "It makes you look like an urban lumberjack."

"Better than looking like an investment banker, I guess."

"What's wrong with looking like an investment banker?"

"Nothing. It's being an investment banker that's the problem."

"What's wrong with being an investment banker?"

"Again, nothing, if you don't want a life outside of work."

Interesting. "Do you think you have a life outside of work now?"

"In some respects, yes," he said. "In other respects, no."

She nodded. "Same. I guess my question for you is this—do you want things to be different?"

He hesitated a long time before answering. "For a long time, I didn't think so. Now I'm beginning to change my mind."

"Anything I can do to help?" The words slipped out before she could stop them, and by the way he was assessing her, she guessed he was mulling over her offer.

"Maybe," he finally said. "I'll let you know."

She'd probed enough, and it seemed safer to let things lie, so she took a sip of wine and he drank some beer and they ordered their food and talked about their families and their work.

Being with Brody was easy. So easy.

But she never for a moment could forget what their relationship was—and what it wasn't. As she'd said, he came with an expiration date, but here, in the moment, she could enjoy herself with him.

And when this ended—and she was sure it would end—it wouldn't matter. Given Brody's track record, she doubted he'd miss her.

So she would take what he was offering, and when the time came to say goodbye, she could leave, knowing she never expected more. It would have to be enough.

And it was the most natural thing in the world to sit there, drinking wine, listening to Brody regale her with tales of what it was like to grow up with six brothers and cousins. She loved hearing the stories of their fights, their laughter, and their injuries, and their exasperated mothers.

Brody had coaxed her to talk about her family, too. He genuinely seemed to want to know about her life, what she was like as a girl, and how she fit into her large Italian clan. She told him of Lucy and of her wild, enormous family.

They closed the place down at 1:00 a.m., when all the waitstaff was ready to call it a night. Over her protests to split the check, Brody paid the bill and held her hand as they walked out. As if they were a real couple.

She was pleasantly warm from the wine and from Brody's hand in hers. She liked the feeling. He helped her into Connor's truck, then slid into the driver's side and shut the door.

For a long moment, they looked at each other.

Brody broke the silence first. "I have a confession."

"What is it?"

"There wasn't actually a delivery mix-up."

"I'm sorry?"

"The first time we met? There wasn't a delivery mix-up. Dylan stole those fucking cookies."

Her mouth dropped open. "What happened to them?"

He leaned closer and lowered his voice. "We ate them."

"You…ate them?"

He nodded solemnly. "Every last one. And you know what?"

"What?"

"To this day, every time I taste almond, I think of you."

His eyes were serious, his gaze searching. Brody had just admitted that his family had stolen Costa property. She should be angry, or at the very least, annoyed. Instead, all she wanted to do was to kiss him. So she did.

She started by hooking her arm around the back of his neck and pulling him close. He came willingly. And then she pressed her mouth to his. His lips were firm and urgent, and he tasted utterly delicious.

His hands were in her hair, messing up her sex curls, or maybe making them even sexier. All she knew was that his hands and his mouth felt so freaking good and she wanted more.

He kissed her fully and deeply, and then, unfortunately, pulled away.

"I want more time with you. And as much as I love feeling young, making out in the front of my truck just isn't going to cut it."

"Connor's truck," she corrected.

He smiled. "Connor's truck."

"I want more time with you, too. I would invite you back to my place," she said, "but I don't think that's such a good idea tonight. My family is having yet another party. But I wouldn't mind going someplace else."

"A detour?" he said, his eyes gleaming.

"Yes. A detour."

"I know just the place."

CHAPTER 12

This time, Brody's detour wasn't to the Pittock Mansion but to his house. It was a surprise—not that he'd take her to his place, but how beautiful it was. She'd expected a bachelor pad, one of those bare-bones places with minimal furniture and unframed posters on the walls.

Instead, he'd taken her hand and shown her a well-furnished, tastefully decorated home. It was masculine, but not overblown. There was even a full set of gently worn pots and pans hanging from a rack in the kitchen. She liked that a lot. Brody lived here. Not just crashed or used it as a glorified closet, but actually lived here.

When he'd finished giving her the mini tour, he tugged her down a hallway. "Let me show you my favorite room."

He opened a door and clicked on a light and immediately, she understood why it was his favorite.

It was his garage. He'd clearly added on to the space, since most of the others in this neighborhood seemed to be one- or two-car garages. This could easily house three cars, despite the huge amount of equipment that he undoubtedly used for his restorations.

She could tell that the space was functional and not just for show because not only did the place have a machine-shop feel to it, but it smelled of metal and fresh motor grease, and the tools looked as though they'd seen a lot of use. The wrench handles were shiny and worn, and there was a pile of old but clean rags on one of the workbenches.

There were two cars in the garage at the moment. One of

them—an old-fashioned-looking hot rod—was complete. But the other, a vintage station wagon, had the hood open, with engine parts strewn on the floor and counter around it.

This was Brody's refuge. His sanctuary. And he was sharing it with her.

"Wow," she said, stepping inside.

Brody turned to her, watching her carefully, undoubtedly to see her reaction.

"Would you tell me about them?" she asked, indicating the vehicles.

He went over to the hot rod first. "This is Casey," Brody said, running a hand lovingly over the gleaming hood, "my regular ride. She's a 1971 Camaro." He smiled broadly. "Casey is a second-generation Camaro with a unibody structure, front subframe, A-arm front suspension and leaf springs. The engine is a seven hundred horsepower built LS7 V8, headers with dual exhaust, and a turbo 350 automatic transmission. Exterior, it has a split front bumper, performance SR1000 GT 255/60R15 tires, Forgeline Concave wheels, and a factory spoiler. Interior, it has bucket seats and a custom stereo because I like my music good and loud." He stopped and looked at her expectantly.

Whoa. "It's amazing, Brody."

"Thanks," he said, and was it her imagination or did his chest puff out a fraction?

"What's that one?" Juliette said, indicating the station wagon on the end.

Brody nodded. "That's something I'm working on for Ed. He loves to fish, so he needs something long enough to hold his poles and his gear, but he's obsessed with safety. I figured I'd kill two birds with one stone by hooking him up with an old-school Volvo wagon."

"A Volvo? Really?" She couldn't imagine one of the Phelan men driving it, especially not handsome, tall, long-limbed Ed, with his dark eyes, auburn hair, and neatly trimmed beard.

But Brody shrugged. "Yeah, I know. It's kind of a family car but Ed…well, he's Ed. He has that mentality even though he doesn't have kids. It was actually his choice."

That made sense. Volvos were serious and safe, and Ed was kind of intense. At least that's how she was able to tell him apart from his twin, who didn't have that kind of energy about him. Plus, every time she saw him he was usually scowling.

"When do you think she'll be done?"

Brody scratched his beard. "I don't know. A month or two, maybe? I don't have a ton of time to work on my cars these days."

"I thought you said it was Ed's car."

"They're all mine, even when I let them go. You work on them long enough, they become a part of you." He stopped. Looked around the garage. "I've never shown this to anyone outside my family." He met her gaze. "Just you."

"I'm honored."

A smile ghosted his lips. "You should be. Maybe I'll take you up to my work shed at the cabin. Show you my Torino. The one I just restored."

That felt big, and a bit scary, but she nodded anyway. "Sure. I'd like that."

"Seen enough?"

She nodded and opened the door to the main house, waiting until he'd turned off the lights before stepping through all the way.

He'd given her a piece of himself tonight, and she wanted to give him something in return. Something private she had never shared with anyone. As he passed her in the hallway, she caught his arm. He stopped and looked down at her.

"I have a confession too. About the day our families fought about the amaretto cookies."

"Yeah?"

"I just wanted to tell you that I noticed you that day, too. Out of everyone, you were—" She stopped. Licked her lips, because this was so much harder than she thought it would be.

"Tell me," he coaxed.

"Everyone was so angry. There was so much hate in the air, like they were all so excited that they'd get to beat the crap out of each other. Except you. You were big and scary and had this intensity about you, but I knew you didn't want to fight. I'd never seen anyone so focused, and it was powerful. More powerful than the violence around it."

"Why'd you step in?"

"I don't know. I was just kind of going on instinct. Maybe it was because I didn't want your face to get mangled."

He gave her a crooked sort of smile. "And here I thought it

might have been because you wanted to save me."

She reached up and patted his chest. "I'm pretty sure you can save yourself. And anyone else who comes along." He visibly startled and captured her hand against his body.

"Are you telling me you want to be saved?"

His heart beat rapidly against her palm. There was so much Brody didn't reveal, only showing what he wanted others to see—the cool, composed deal-maker, the cocky ladies' man.

"I don't need saving. I just need you."

He tensed, her only warning before he bent his head and kissed her.

If she'd thought Brody's kisses were seductive before, this was on a different level entirely. It was deep and a hair desperate, his beard rasping against her chin as he kissed her, first with his lips, coaxing her mouth open, and then with his tongue, sweeping over hers in a possessive gesture.

He wasn't the only one who was desperate for it, and she wasn't in the habit of passively accepting things, so she gave back as good as she got. *Tonight, I'm all in.*

His kisses were powerful, drugging. Needing an anchor, she grabbed on to his shirt, gripping it in her fist as he backed her up, pinning her between the wall and his hard chest.

Then he ravished her mouth until her head was spinning and her insides were molten.

She turned her head to the side, breathing heavily. "Brody—"

"I want to touch you, Juliette," he murmured. "Everywhere. With my hands…" He slid one finger up her thigh, pushing the hem of her dress up with it, leaving tingling sparks in its wake. "With my mouth…" He tilted her head to kiss a spot behind her ear, and she shivered. "With my tongue…." He licked the hollow of her throat, and her already-hard nipples turned to stone. "Tell me you want it as much as I do."

His words. His body. His cock, pressing insistently into her hip bone.

"I want it," she whispered. Her voice barely sounded like her own—throaty and sexy and so very needy. *I want you.*

He skimmed a hand up her ribs, letting it come to a rest with his thumb directly under her breast. "This isn't going to be fast," he said. "I've wanted you too long for that."

In response, she speared a hand through his hair and pulled him down for another searing kiss.

His lips were hard on hers, his fingers even harder, and then he pulled away, but only for an instant, because a second later she was in his arms, being carried down the hallway.

It didn't take a minute before he'd kicked open the door to a room she hadn't been inside. His bedroom, dimly lit. He tipped her back on the bed and he followed her down, his mouth still moving against hers.

He was half on top of her, giving her some of his weight and Jesus, he was massive. One huge hand was up her dress and on her thigh, the other buried in her hair. He kissed her and she kissed him back, demanding and deep.

Hell, yes, she wanted this. Since she'd seen him in that parking lot, breaking up that stupid fight.

Something in his eyes flared hot, and then he was urging her up, pulling her dress over her head and tossing it on the ground. Her bra and panties followed until she was kneeling on the bed, bared to his gaze.

Any embarrassment she might have felt about her imperfect body was dispelled when she saw the look on his face—pure, unadulterated hunger.

Guess he liked women who had a bit more…of everything.

"Jesus, Juliette." He wiped the back of his hand across his mouth. "You're so gorgeous, I don't know where to start."

"I do."

She reached for his shirt and slowly pulled it up over his head, revealing inch after sexy inch of flesh and muscle. She'd seen it before, just not this close or in this intimate a setting. Which was probably for the best, because imagining Brody like this, on display for her perusal, would have been way too tempting.

He was broad and toned, his skin lightly freckled, especially on his shoulders and upper chest. He had a puckered scar right below his collarbone, white around the edges, the center a faint pink, and another thin line of white across his rib cage. A light smattering of hair adorned his upper chest.

He was magnificent.

He stood there waiting, not rushing, not pushing. Just waiting, knowing that she liked what she saw, which would probably make him even more cocky in the long run, but right now she couldn't find it in herself to care.

Itching to touch, she reached out, smoothing her hands over his shoulders and arms, then back up again. Slowly, she traced his collarbone, edge to edge, then skimmed the line of first one pectoral, then the other. Were his nipples sensitive? She wanted desperately to find out. She circled one with the tip of her finger, rewarded when it hardened into a bud. Nice. She scraped her nail over it, and he let out a hiss.

Taking note of that for the future, she moved down, enjoying the feeling of the ridged muscles of his abdomen under her fingertips.

She trailed the light line of hair to his jeans, but when she reached for his belt buckle, he caught her wrist in his hand. "My turn."

In an instant, he'd flipped her back, so that he was on top of her again, kissing her, bare skin on bare skin.

"You always stop me before I get to the good bits," she complained.

"Trust me," he said, grinning. "You don't want me to skip this."

He was dizzying in his thoroughness, and by the time he cupped a breast, she was warm and pliant. His hand felt way too good, but it was even better when he brought his fingers into play on her nipple, flicking and pinching until she was moaning. And when his mouth closed around one of the sensitive tips and sucked, her eyes nearly rolled back in her head.

Holy mother, the man knew how to use his tongue.

He played with both breasts, pinching and licking and sucking until she was almost desperate.

"Brody," she moaned, shifting beneath him.

But still he didn't touch her where she needed it the most. He splayed his fingers over her soft belly, wrapped his hand around her waist, traced the curve of her hip, taking his time exploring the same way she had him. He kissed her wrists, her belly button, her nipples, still unbelievably sensitive, making her crave something, more, anything.

By the time he eased his hand between her thighs, she was ready to beg.

He spread her folds and slipped a finger inside, groaning with appreciation. "You're wet. Is that all for me?"

Another finger joined the first, stroking in and out, then curling up, and holy crap, whatever he was doing was incredibly intense. "Brody," she gasped, grabbing on to his wrist.

"Found it," he said with some satisfaction. And then he began to rub that special spot with a firm pressure that had her seeing stars.

It was too much—too much and yet not enough. She squirmed and pulled on his wrist, trying to get him to ease up, but he simply plucked her hand away and rubbed harder, then brought his thumb into play on her clit.

And then her back was arching as she was flying, soaring, falling, the pleasure so acute it took her breath away.

When she was finally able to pry her eyes open, nothing could have prepared her for the sight of Brody looking down at her, fire in his eyes.

"You're beautiful," he said. "And you're even more beautiful when you let go."

Who *was* this man? She barely recognized this Brody, the one who had taken control of both her body and her brain.

This time, when she reached for his belt buckle, he didn't stop her. Still high from her orgasm, she got his pants off. And oh, Lord.

Brody Phelan was huge everywhere.

She hadn't had a ton of experience, and was definitely not prepared for a man of Brody's size. She pushed her hair back from her face and stared. "Um—"

"Shh," he said, covering her with his body once again.

He kissed and stroked her into a stupor, which, given her state of arousal, did not take long at all. She was panting again by the time he leaned over and riffled around in his bedside table drawer.

She rolled away and watched with no small amount of concern as he smoothed on the condom, then positioned himself on the bed, half reclining on the nest of pillows.

He crooked a finger at her. "Come here."

Slowly, she moved toward him. When she got close enough, he gripped her around the waist and hauled her up and over him so she was straddling his torso.

Brody met her gaze. "You're in control," he said. "Always."

Control. Right. Something that seemed to have slipped through her fingers the moment Brody touched her.

Carefully, she positioned herself, then dropped her hips.

He was huge, his blunt flesh forging inside inch by torturous inch. Despite her earlier orgasm, it was a tight fit, her body working hard to accommodate him.

And the whole time he watched with half-closed eyes, holding stock-still so she could set the pace, grow accustomed to his size, take that control that he had given unreservedly to her.

It took a while, but she finally worked her way onto him. Once she was fully seated, she raised her gaze. He was still watching, and something about seeing this ridiculously large and handsome man, laid out just for her made her feel unbelievably sexy and strong.

She squeezed her internal muscles around him, and he groaned. So she leaned forward and kissed him. Just once, feeling him shudder with pleasure.

"Ride me," he rasped.

She did, slowly at first, his hands gripping her hips, guiding her, but not controlling her, until she found a smooth rhythm.

Oh, she loved this. The glide of him, the feel of him, touching seemingly every part of her. She rested her hands on his chest and moved, reveling in the sensation of wielding so much power.

He'd given her this—this command, this control. Letting her set the pace, take what she wanted from his body. And all the while he watched, his eyes dark with pleasure. She went faster now, more confident in the way she slid up and down, snapping her hips to make him groan. He reached for her breasts and pushed her up to sitting, which forced her to take him even deeper.

"God, Brody."

"Too much?"

"No," she breathed. "I'm just full." So full.

She had less room for movement in this position, but that just made the sensations more intense. He flicked her nipples, then went for her clit, worrying that sensitive flesh with the pad of his thumb. When her thighs started to shake, she knew it was coming. Involuntarily, her lids slipped shut.

"Open your eyes," he whispered.

The pleasure was almost too much, but she forced herself to obey just as her body lit up in a rush so strong that she cried out. And as she came, Brody watched her with a look of supreme satisfaction as her orgasm went on and on.

"Gorgeous," he said, pulling her down for a heart-stopping kiss before rolling her onto her back and thrusting hard enough to leave her breathless.

Clearly he'd been holding back, because this? This was sheer power, one arm under her back, one hand clamped on her hip.

He thrust into her body over and over again, hitting that same special spot inside that made her crazy, dragging over her clit as an added bonus. He knew just what he was doing, too, pinning her in place while he worked her into oblivion so she had no choice but to take every bit of pleasure he was giving her.

"You feel that?" he said. "Feel us together?"

"Yes," she gasped, because he had just hit her clit again, sending shivery sparks through her.

"So…fucking…good," he breathed, punctuated by three separate upstrokes. "Tell me."

But words were impossible, especially because he was now powering into her with such force that her head would have jammed up against the headboard if he hadn't cupped his hand protectively over her crown. He stared directly into her eyes as he simply wrecked her.

She got it now. Why Brody had women hanging on him, lining up to date him, willing to do anything for him. It didn't matter that he was allergic to commitment. The chance to have this, Brody Phelan's singular focus on giving pleasure, if only for a week, a night, an hour, was the ultimate temptation.

In point of fact, she would sell her soul for it.

Still driving into her, he kissed her roughly, his tongue deep in her mouth. It was too much—Brody on her, over her, in her.

Sensation overloaded her, and she came a third time, a shockingly sharp burst that hit without warning, almost painful in its intensity.

She might have screamed his name. He definitely swore, loudly and colorfully, as he thrust one final time, then shuddered and stilled.

He withdrew and rolled off her almost immediately so he

wouldn't crush her, then gathered her close and kissed the top of her head.

"Jesus Christ, that was fantastic. I just changed my mind."

Her brain was numb and she could barely feel her limbs. "About what?"

He nestled her even closer. "Forget the garage. This is now, officially, my favorite room in the house."

CHAPTER 13

On Saturday morning, Brody woke up with a woman in his bed. This was typical. What was not typical was how he felt about that.

Depending on where he was in the life cycle of any given relationship, he would have one of three reactions. Wake her up so she could leave. Wake her up so they could fuck again and she could leave. Or wake her up so they could fuck again, get some coffee, maybe have brunch, and then she could leave.

But the woman in his bed was Juliette Costa, and he had a completely different reaction altogether.

What he wanted was for her to wake up, not so they could fuck again, though he really wanted that. Not so they could have coffee and brunch, though that would be nice, too. And definitely not so she could leave. No, he wanted her to wake up so he could talk to her. See what was going on in that big brain of hers, then see if he could make her come again while screaming his name—absolutely the sexiest thing he'd ever heard in his life—then feed her, talk to her some more, then go for another round.

He definitely didn't want her to leave, which was weird.

Even weirder? He wasn't freaked out about it. All he wanted was more of her.

She lay in his arms facing him, one thigh thrown over his leg, hair everywhere, sexy as hell, eyes closed, breathing deep, so beautiful it actually made him ache a little inside.

He'd never ached over a woman before. That was weird, too.

She stirred and moaned, then nestled into him, rubbing her

face into his side. Her body was warm and soft, and she smelled delicious. Like cinnamon and flowers.

He kissed the top of her head. Slowly, she opened her eyes.

He knew the moment she realized what they'd done last night because she stiffened in his arms.

"Hey," he said.

"Hey," she said, her voice wary, and blinked, her eyes still hazy from sleep.

"You okay?"

She nodded. "Are you?"

"Yeah, Juliette," he said, amused. "I'm okay." He brushed his lips over hers. "Last night was good."

She was still stiff. "I need coffee," she said.

"Are you sure that's all you need?"

"Yes, I—"

He didn't give her a chance to finish her sentence. Just kissed her, deeper this time. She melted.

And just when he thought things were about to get really good, she pulled out of his arms and swung off the other side of the bed.

"I have to go." He got a prime view of her luscious bare ass, then a slightly more blurry view of her sexy curves because she was moving so damn fast, flicking through the clothes they'd tossed to the floor last night.

He watched her, bemused, as she found her dress and held it up with an expression of dismay. "Lucy's gonna kill me."

"Lucy's gonna love that the dress served its purpose. Tell her it worked."

She shot him a look and wiggled the dress on over her naked body. "I am not doing this."

Distracted by her going commando and everything he could do with that information, it took him a moment to answer. "Doing what?"

"This." She gestured between them, and her unfettered breasts gave a delightful jiggle. "You, me, the morning after, the walk of shame? This isn't happening."

He jerked his attention away from her breasts and focused on her face. "It is so happening. And you know what?"

"What?"

"It's going to happen again." Even as he said the words, he heard their truth. He liked her, and he wanted her. Wanted to see where this could go.

"Nope." She'd found her bra and panties and was jamming them into her handbag, which she then placed on his night side table. "We've already established you don't do commitment."

The blithe way she was dismissing him pissed him off. Or maybe it was because there was truth behind her words. "I'm not kicking you out here."

"That's right." She bent down to slip on her shoes, then straightened. "I'm kicking myself out. And besides, I have to get home, and what time is it anyway?" She peered at his alarm clock. "Ohmigod, it's ten thirty already? Crap! I have an important interview scheduled for eleven. I'm never going to make it." She reached for her handbag but missed, tipping it over and spilling everything inside onto the floor. "Crap!"

She scrambled to her knees and began tossing things in as fast as she could.

He swung his legs to the side of the bed and stood up. "You'll make it," he said, reaching for his jeans.

"How? In case you didn't remember, you drove! My car's at the house and"—she picked up her cell phone and glowered—"my cell phone's out of juice. Stupid phone. I'm trapped here." She was really panicking now. "I can call Lucy. Maybe she'll be able to leave work to come get me. Can I borrow your cell or your home phone? Do you even have a landline?"

It was cute, seeing her all flustered like this, her hair wild, her eyes bright. Still, he wasn't in the habit of letting people suffer unnecessarily. "I don't have a landline, and you don't need to call Lucy."

"Seriously, Brody? Come on! I scheduled this interview months ago. I spent three full evenings prepping. I need to make it."

"You will because I'm driving you home."

"You…will?" She narrowed her eyes and crossed her arms over her chest. "What's it going to cost me?"

"Nothing." He tugged on his jeans and zipped them up.

"Nothing." Her tone was one of complete disbelief. "That's not how you operate, Phelan."

"So suspicious."

"For good reason."

"Can't I just do something nice for you?"

"Without payment in return? As a rule, no."

"That's going to change," he informed her. "Starting now."

"Really," she drawled. "Sorry if I don't believe you."

He shrugged. "That's on you. Right now, what I need you to do is to get your stuff together so we can get out of here."

"It's not like I'm in a position to argue." Eyeing him warily, she tossed her dead cell into her handbag and did a sweep of the floor while he went to put on some fresh deodorant and pull on a clean T-shirt.

When he returned, she was standing stiffly by the bedroom door. "Got everything?" She nodded. "Good. Then let's roll."

Brody drove like the wind and there wasn't much traffic, so they made it to Juliette's place in less time than he thought they would.

Within minutes of arriving at her place, she'd gotten all her recording equipment set up and her notes pulled up. She even had a few moments to spare before she phoned her interviewee to review everything and take a deep breath.

Once the interview began, he realized why she was so insistent about getting back to her place in time. The person she was interviewing, Kara Killian, was a founding member of one of the most influential rock bands to come out of Portland—a woman who'd gone on to star in tons of indie films and an award-winning sketch comedy show based on life in Portland.

Juliette had been nervous beforehand, but as soon as that call started, she was completely on point, nailing her questions, speaking knowledgeably, and shaping the interview into something magical. Brody had intended to work while she was recording, but he found he couldn't take his eyes off her. She was on fire, and it was a beautiful thing to watch.

When the final question was asked and answered and goodbyes were said, Juliette clicked off her recording device, pulled off her headphones, and leaned back in her chair with a satisfied sigh.

"You're amazing."

She turned only her head to look at him. "No, Kara is."

"She is," he conceded, "but I've heard her speak before. She can be stiff and dismissive if you don't hit the right notes. You did."

"Thanks. She gave me a lot of good stuff."

"If she did, you got it out of her."

"It's definitely an art, giving good interview. But a lot of what comes out has to do with the subject, too." Juliette smiled. "I like that she drinks rosé. For anyone else it'd be a cliché, but for her it's just kind of badass. Like she doesn't give a crap what anyone else thinks and she's going to drink what she's going to drink."

"You still want your wine bar?"

She looked over at him. "More than anything."

"You've been working on your business plan?"

"Every day."

"How's it reading?"

"Okay. I'm almost ready to show it to you."

"Soon, yeah?"

She nodded. "Soon."

Now that she wasn't panicking, she was back to being sweet-tart Juliette. He liked that.

"You done with your work?"

"For now." She sat up in the seat and clicked a few buttons. "Now all I have to do is upload this to my backup server and I'll be set. Excellent." She looked over at him. "What time is it?"

"Twelve thirty."

"I'm hungry."

"I'll bet. You didn't eat any breakfast."

She rose and stalked over to him, all sultry curves and sly smile, and hooked her fingers in the waistband of his jeans. "Food's not really what I'm thinking about right now."

His libido went from zero to sixty in zero-point-one seconds. "You're jazzed up?"

She nodded solemnly and looked up at him. "Totally jazzed up."

"And what would you like me to do about that?" he said, playing along.

"I have a few ideas," she said, right before she pulled his head down and kissed him with lots of tongue. He let her have control for a while with them standing up, then finally walked her backward to the bedroom and onto the bed, laying her flat with him half on top. He gave her some, but not all of his weight because it would probably crush her—just enough so she would feel pinned, but not enough to make her feel trapped.

God, she was luscious, all smooth, curved flesh. Last night he'd finally laid claim to her, to that thing that had been simmering between them for so many years. He thought once he'd done it that he could let her go, but just like every other time they'd been together, he wanted more. And not just more sex. More her. More everything.

She was as into this as he was, one hand speared through his hair, the other gripping his shoulder as if her life depended on it.

This was going to go hard and fast unless he reined himself in, so to bide some time, he went for her neck, especially that spot right by her collarbone that seemed to give her the shivers every time he passed over it.

She was shivering a hell of a lot by the time he was through, and she still wasn't wearing a bra, so every time she did, her hard little nipples poked through her dress and rubbed against his chest. Fucking fantastic.

It was then he felt it. Her little hand between them on his cock, stroking him through the denim. Already at half mast, he got hard fast, and she hissed through her teeth. "I still can't believe this is real."

"You took all of it last night," he reminded her.

"Is this a ploy to get me to tell you how big your cock is?"

He grinned. "You think my cock is big?"

She unbuttoned his jeans and shoved them down his ass, then stroked him through his boxer-briefs. That felt even better.

"Mmm, you'd better cool it with the attitude. You know where my hand is. One wrong move and…" She squeezed her fingers around him.

"You play dirty," he said, then groaned as she resumed her easy slide.

"Your mouth is dirty."

"You like it." He brushed a thumb over her already-hard nipple, then rolled it between his thumb and forefinger. "You get off on it."

"Yeah," she said on a sigh. Sexy as hell.

"I'd bet if I touched you, I'd find that you were wet and ready for me," he said, still working her breasts.

"You think?" she said. Challenge.

"I know. Let's find out." He placed the flat of his palm on her leg, and slowly started moving it up her thigh, pushing her dress along with it. "Did I tell you that you have fantastic legs?"

"No," she breathed, maybe because of his words, maybe because he was pinching one of her nipples just a tiny bit harder.

"You do. They're long and silky and built and feel fucking amazing around my back." He pulled the top of her dress down to bare one perfect breast, then plumped it in his hand. "But these are amazing, too." Then he bent his head to taste, sucking and nibbling until she let out a soft moan. He used his mouth on the other until her breaths were coming in short pants.

She did love his dirty mouth—whether it was his words or the way he used it on her body, he didn't rightly care—but he intended to use that knowledge to his full advantage. He continued to slide his hand up over that long expanse of silky skin until he reached the crease of her thigh.

He looked up at her flushed face, and his cock throbbed. "I've been thinking about your lack of underwear for hours."

"Yeah?" she said, sounding breathless.

"Yeah. You do this often?"

"No," she admitted. "Just with you."

Like last night, she wasn't holding anything back. He could see everything reflected in her gaze—her doubts, her fears.

And lust, clouding over everything, making him feel like a god. He could give her this, at least.

He sank a finger into her warmth, and she gasped. He was right. Wet and ready and so tight. Ramping her up didn't take long at all. Just a few strategic slides and curls, and her thighs were already starting to shake.

"Do you want me?" he asked.

Her only answer was to stroke him faster. Then she moaned. Maybe because he'd now brought his thumb into play over her clit.

"I want to hear you say it," he said, stroking her clit, then backing off before she got too close.

"Brody…" she said, her voice inching into warning territory.

"What?" He flicked her clit again and she shuddered, then went back to using just his finger.

Her hand had stilled on his cock. "I don't…I can't."

"Say it," he crooned. "Say, 'Brody, I want you.'" He kept on doing the same thing, alternating his finger with strumming her clit, until she was quivering and needy. Her face was flushed, her hair messy, her body shaking. Fire. He wanted it. He wanted it all.

"You…are…so…mean," she gasped out.

"Awful," he agreed, and gently bit one of her nipples.

"It's too much. Too much," she moaned.

"All you have to do is tell me."

She finally snapped out of her stupor and glared at him. "Fine, Brody, okay. I want you. I want you so badly I ache. Is that what you want to hear?" And there it was. All that sass and attitude he loved so much.

"For a start," he said. He kicked off his jeans, slipped on a condom, pulled her knees up, and slid into her in one smooth thrust.

She gasped his name.

She was so warm and wet and tight, it was almost unreal, but she took all of him, and it was made all the sweeter by him knowing that he'd earned his spot in her bed.

He stroked faster, then slower, denying her the chance to peak, knowing it'd be even better when she finally did. She cursed and pleaded and actually tried to physically get him to go faster, but all that did was strengthen his resolve to make her wait.

Soon enough, she was literally begging, so he switched it up a final time, angling himself just right.

And then she detonated, shouting his name, crying out in satisfaction.

He followed immediately after, gripping her tightly as he came.

There was no way to top what they'd just shared by speaking, so he didn't. Just quietly withdrew and held her in the aftermath while she came down from her high.

He finally glanced over at the bedside table at her clock and caught a glimpse of the time. It was pushing two, and he had places to be.

"Shower," he said.

She was lying on the bed, one arm crooked over her eyes, shielding them from his gaze. "I don't think I can move," she moaned.

He swung out of bed, went to the bathroom, flicked the

water on, and adjusted it. Then he went back into the bedroom. She was still lying on her back in the exact same position.

"Still can't move?"

"Nope."

He picked her up, and she tried to protest that she was too heavy, but he quelled that with a completely consuming kiss. After confirming she could stand, if not move, he put her in the warm shower and slowly washed her hair and body. She returned the favor, which continued on to him making her come with his fingers and her making him come with her mouth.

It was a fucking amazing shower.

They'd just dried off when there was a knock at the door. Juliette went very, very still, until a female voice rang out.

"Juliette? Are you home?"

"Thank God, it's my cousin Lucy. She'll be cool with you. I think." She bit her lip, then yelled loudly. "Hey, Luce. Give me a minute."

"Okay," the woman called back.

Juliette dressed in record time, then went to answer the door. Brody took his time, toweling off his hair, swiping some of Juliette's deodorant, and pulling on his clothes.

When he came out into the living room, he found Juliette in a heated discussion with a tall blonde woman dressed in workout clothes. She was beautiful in a classic sort of way, with willowy limbs and delicate features. She looked nothing at all like Juliette, and yet you could tell by the way they were standing together that they knew each other, intimately.

The woman saw him, and her eyes went big. "Is that him?" she hissed.

Juliette flickered her gaze over to him. "Yes."

"He's way hotter in person than he is on the Wolfshead website." Juliette shot the blonde a dirty look. "What? Of course I cyber-stalked him when you told me you were going on a coffee date with *the* Brody Phelan. Looks like you went way beyond coffee and just skipped to dessert. Which is awesome. I mean, everyone loves dessert, right? Except me. I don't love dessert so much. I'm more of a salty-snack-food gal, myself."

"My cousin, Lucia Palladino," Juliette said, her voice weary. "She was just leaving."

"Not leaving," she chirped, coming toward him with her hand outstretched and a huge grin on her face. "I'm Lucy. And I'm really excited to finally meet you."

"Are you?" he said.

Lucy's eyes almost bugged out of her head. "He even has a hot voice," she faux-whispered to Juliette.

"He can hear you, Lucy," she said.

"Oh, yeah, right." She turned back to him. "You have a hot voice."

"Thanks," he said, with very real amusement.

She turned back to Juliette. "So I just came over to tell you that my mom's coming back with your mom and they're already plotting your hookup for tonight."

"What?" Brody growled.

Lucy looked freaked out at his probably murderous expression, but Juliette waved her hand at him as if she'd seen it all before.

"It's not a hookup, like sleeping with someone. It's just a hookup."

"It could lead to sleeping with someone," Lucy said.

"No, it could not," Juliette said firmly.

"Absolutely it could. If done right. Which unfortunately for our moms, Juliette does not. Do it right, that is."

"You are not helping me here, Luce," Juliette hissed.

Brody crossed his arms over his chest. "Explain."

Juliette sighed. "A hookup is when my meddling relatives try to get me to go out with some guy they want me to marry."

"And have babies," Lucy chimed in. "They really want babies. Lots and lots of babies. They've been jonesing for a whole passel of grandkids to grow up and run the family business."

For some reason, that thought made him feel even more murderous.

Juliette must have caught on to the fact that he was none too pleased to hear this, because she cleared her throat. "Come *on*, Lucy."

Lucy's eyes went wide again, and she looked back and forth between the two of them. "Sorry."

"Forget the hookup," Brody said, his voice as smooth as

butter. "You can be busy for the rest of the day, can't you?"

"I have work to do."

"But it's such a gorgeous day. Why don't you do it later?"

She made a hand gesture in his direction, pure Italian. "This, from a man who sleeps in his office. Work later, he says. Guess what, Brody? My office doesn't have a couch like yours. It doesn't even have a door!"

"So work in my office."

Juliette simply goggled at him. "Are you insane? What would my parents say if they found out I was working with the enemy?"

"Um, Juliette?" Lucy interjected. "You're kind of already sleeping with the enemy." She turned to him and smiled. "No offense."

"Again, not really helping," Juliette said through clenched teeth.

"Honestly, you're being ridiculous. If I had the choice between hanging out with our moms and getting set up with some dude just because they think you're on the shelf and can't take care of yourself, or hanging out with this—" Lucy paused to gesture at him, as if she were giving a lecture and he was exhibit A. "I would choose this"—she did the gesture again—"any day of the week."

He liked Lucy.

Clearly, at that moment, Juliette did not. She was standing there with a horrified look on her face. "This is not happening," she moaned.

"Maybe I should go," Lucy said.

"Maybe," he said.

"Seriously hot voice," she muttered. Then she crossed over and held out her pinkie to Juliette. With obvious begrudging, Juliette hooked her pinkie in Lucy's, and her expression softened. This seemed to pacify Lucy some, because she smiled.

"Love you."

"Love you, too."

She turned back to him and gave a little wave. "Goodbye! It was nice meeting you."

"Ditto."

The door clicked shut.

"Nice," Juliette said. "You two conspiring against me."

"There was no conspiracy," he told her. "Your cousin

obviously has good taste in men."

"Why don't you go out with her then?" she snapped.

"Don't want her," Brody said, crossing the room. "Want you."

Then, before she had a chance to protest, he kissed her. He did it hard and he did it deep and he was thorough. By the time he raised his head, she looked practically drunk. Excellent.

"Got your keys?" he murmured.

"What?"

"House keys. You got 'em?"

"Yes."

"Great."

And with that, he shoved Juliette out the door and into the courtyard. The sun was a muted yellow in the cloudy sky.

"What? Where are we going?"

"I know you're hungry, so first I'm gonna feed you."

She kept walking. "Food's okay. Then we come back?"

"Nope. Going on a detour."

"No," she said, digging in her heels. "I have stuff to do. I can't just hang out with you all day. I have to work."

"Later."

"Brody—"

"Food," he said firmly, steering her down the path toward the sidewalk.

"Food is okay, a detour is not okay."

"You'll change your mind after the food."

"I will not," she said.

"You're forgetting something."

"What's that?"

He leaned in, his lips brushing her ear. "How persuasive I can be."

Her delightful shiver was all the answer he needed.

CHAPTER 14

Juliette stared down a row of vintage candy-colored cars angled facing out from the curb for maximum visibility. Hundreds of people milled around, peering under the hoods of vehicles, scoping out whitewall tires, and checking out paint jobs.

"Nice detour." She met his gaze. "But you promised me coffee."

He just grinned at her attitude. "Sure did. Come on. Let's get you caffeinated."

Clasping her hand firmly in his, he pulled her into the crowd, and *damn it* the warmth was back, spreading through her body. He'd fed her at Laurelhurst Market, one of her absolute favorite places, where she'd eaten an insanely delicious smoked turkey sandwich with bacon and cheddar cheese made fresh at the butcher counter. They'd sat outside on a bench, and he hadn't even minded that she'd picked off all of the pickled zucchini on her sandwich. Or asked for a bite of his.

Then, just as he'd promised, he sweet-talked her into joining him on this "detour" by pledging to buy her unlimited amounts of coffee to fuel her through her afternoon and evening.

She could never say no to coffee.

Or maybe it was that she was finding it harder and harder to say no to him.

"Seriously, Brody, what *is* this place?" she asked as he steered her through the crowd.

"It's a cruise-in."

"A what?"

"It's a Portland tradition. Actually, it's pretty common around the country. Anywhere you have car collectors or admirers, you get a cruise-in. It's like a meet-up, but for cars. You have a vehicle you want to show off, you drive it up and park, and let other people check it out. There are a couple of bigger annual meetings, usually sponsored by classic car groups in the area, but this time of year, there's at least one smaller cruise-in each weekend, run by different groups. Sometimes they do them for charity."

"I noticed you dropped off some canned food when we came in."

"Yep. That was our entry fee. I've also been to cruise-ins where the entry fee is a new toy for a shelter around Christmastime or cash to support a high school sports team. It just depends on who's running the show. The one we're at today is sponsored by Second Harvest, so the entry's a couple of cans of food."

She looked around at the gathering. There must have been a couple hundred people there, and while there were a few folks just hanging out by their cars or milling around in silence, most were chatting. "Is it just me, or does everyone know each other?"

"We're a pretty tight-knit group. Makes sense, given that we're all obsessed with the same thing. Probably like you with your podcast, right? Do you hang out with other people who have their own shows?"

"Never," she told him honestly.

"You should. You're a huge deal."

"How do you know that?"

"I was curious and I had some downtime when you were doing your interview to do some research. Most of what I found was on chat boards and articles from indie mags. People love you. And I also have to admit, I downloaded a couple of episodes and listened to them. They were fun. And your voice is sexy."

She blushed hot. "Seriously, Brody."

"I loved hearing you do your interview in person today. You were so natural. And even though you were nervous, you never let it show. You have a gift."

"Thanks. It's still a bit surreal. I mean, I started doing it for me. It just kind of...grew."

"I can't believe your family doesn't like what you're doing.

Seems like they should be proud of your efforts and your following."

"I don't think they really get what it could do for them." She shook her head, then shrugged. "It's okay. I can't please them, and honestly, I've stopped trying. I just do what makes me happy. Keep looking forward. It's the only thing I can do, right? Besides, you of all people should know that families are tough."

"Yeah," he said. He gave her a strange expression again, just for a moment, and then it was gone. But she noticed the difference in his before-and-after moods. Before he was relaxed, even happy. After she'd brought up his family, he…wasn't.

Which was weird, because she thought he lived and died by his family. All the Phelans were super tight. You could just see it in the way they interacted. Sure, they fought. All families fought, but the Phelans did it with love. But that look said there was something more. Something he hadn't told her and probably never would.

She'd just have to be okay with that. After all, that was the deal.

He bought her some cold-brewed iced coffee at a nearby stand, and the two of them strolled around for a while, looking at all the tricked-out vehicles and talking with a few of their proud owners.

As they walked through the show, many people said hi to Brody or came up to chat. He was friendly to everyone—friends, friends of friends, whoever. And it was obvious that the people who didn't know him had heard of him and were excited to meet him.

"I love that you know so many people," Juliette said.

"I've been around the industry for a while and I enjoy coming to events, seeing what the latest trends are, and checking out other people's work for inspiration." He'd tucked his hand in hers and was leading her down a row filled entirely with Dodges. "I also belong to a car club. We sponsor an event every year, and I meet a lot of folks that way. Plus, people know me from Wolfshead."

That made sense, given that Wolfshead was pretty famous around Portland. But Brody was being modest. People didn't just know him—they liked him. A lot. And it wasn't an act. This was him. He'd found his people, built yet another family for himself.

Which made her rethink everything she was supposed to think about him.

According to her family, Brody Phelan was the enemy. A beautiful, bearded enemy, someone to hate, to dehumanize.

Except now that she knew him, she realized that just wasn't true. He was generous with his time, with his family, with his friends, with *her*. Deal or no deal, underneath it all, he was a decent person.

He stayed silent, so she braved a look up at his face. He was looking at her, his head cocked to the side, his eyes soft.

"Don't deny it, Brody Phelan. You really are a nice guy."

"Not really," he said.

And then, before she quite realized what he intended, he speared his hands through her hair and kissed her.

This wasn't a gentle brush across the cheek, either. This was a full-on, openmouthed kiss that was hard and hot and wet and very public.

Not that she cared about the public part at that particular moment, because *damn* the man could kiss. His mouth opened hers and when his tongue stroked inside, she felt it *everywhere*.

So, so good.

Despite the fact that she'd had him three times in the past twenty-four hours, she needed more of him. Right now. She grabbed on to his shirt and hung on while his mouth ravished hers. Beneath her fingertips, the muscles of his abdomen were hard and solid. She moaned into his mouth, and he tightened his grip.

And just when things were getting good, he pulled away, tucked her hand back in his, and continued on.

"Later," he promised.

They wove their way through the crowd and ended up on a patch of grass where there were maybe a dozen old-fashioned cars lined up in a row.

"Hey! Brody!" a man called out.

"Come on," he said. "Let me introduce you to my friends."

Brody ushered them in the direction of a group of men standing near a cool old-fashioned truck painted a deep, dark blue.

One of the men she knew by sight—Finn, Brody's brother. Like Brody, he had reddish hair that was a bit too long and curled around the nape of his neck. Unlike Brody, he didn't have a full beard, but more like a couple days' worth of stubble that outlined his sharp jaw and defined cheekbones. He was tall, maybe six three, but leanly muscled, which made sense, because he played bass guitar in a local indie rock band that had achieved some success, and was as close as they came in Portland to local celebrity. Effortlessly cool, he had on a T-shirt and low-slung jeans held on narrow hips by a grommet belt. The look definitely worked for him, because the man was gorgeous.

He'd been laughing, but when she approached with Brody, his eyes got cool.

There were two other men standing in the group, and when they spied her, their eyes got warm.

The first one was tall and built, and probably in his mid-thirties. He had cropped black hair and striking deep-set blue eyes. His features were so perfectly chiseled, he could have been a model. His collared shirt was tucked into a pair of blue jeans worn in all the right places, and his cowboy boots looked authentic—as if they'd actually been worn on a ranch. She hadn't seen anyone in Portland wear cowboy boots, at least not in recent memory, but this guy pulled it off just fine.

The other man was a bit older, probably in his late fifties, with salt-and-pepper hair that was still more pepper than salt. He had warm brown eyes, a square jaw, and a deeply cleft chin. He had on a plain black T-shirt that was tight enough to show off all the definition in his chest. His jeans were darker and not worn at all.

Brody stepped up and gave his brother a fist bump, then proceeded to give the other two those half-handshake, half-hugs that men who are confident in their own masculinity do. Then he stepped back to make introductions.

"Guys, this is Juliette. You already know Finn," he said, and Finn, still with cool eyes, gave her a head nod. "And these are Tex and Marino."

Juliette smiled at them. "It's nice to meet you."

Tex gave her a huge smile. "Howdy."

Marino didn't smile the way Tex had, but it was still a nice one. "Hey."

Before Brody could say anything else, someone tapped him on the shoulder and he was quickly pulled into another conversation. She noticed that Finn left the circle and went to join him.

When she turned back, she found Tex and Marino watching her carefully.

"So," Marino said, eyes alight. "Brody finally has a woman."

"I'm not his woman," she said quickly, hoping that both Brody and Finn were out of earshot. "We're just"—she didn't know what they were, exactly, so she settled for the truth—"business associates."

Marino kept his face neutral. "Is that right? That might explain why we haven't seen you around until now."

"This is gettin' more and more interestin' by the minute," Tex said, eying her intently.

"How'd you two meet?" Marino asked.

"My family's business is on the same block as Wolfshead, so I guess we've known each other…well, forever. Except we didn't really get reacquainted until he came back from Asia a few years ago."

"What kind of business is your family in that you're associated with Wolfshead?" Tex asked.

"Italian imports. Food mostly, but we do wine and some dry goods."

Tex raised an eyebrow. "I'm not seein' the connection."

"Oh, there isn't one. Our families hate each other." They stared at her, so she went on. "There's this feud, one that's been going on for ages, and it seems like our brothers just can't give it a rest. They all fight like cats and dogs, and Brody and I try to keep the peace. We're usually pretty successful, but I have to say that he's kind of into it and I'm kind of not. But we work well together, which makes the whole process a lot easier. Which is why I call him my business associate."

The men were still looking at her extremely intently. "So, um, how about you? How long have you all known him?"

"I've known Brody since he was a kid," Marino said. "I served in the army with Brody's father. We were in the same unit."

"Is Brody like his dad?"

"Not in the slightest," Marino said, rather tightly.

She wanted to ask him more, but Tex spoke up.

"Brody and I had a mutual friend who knew we'd be in Thailand at the same time and hooked us up. The first time I met Brody, we met up after work, went out for a night on the town. There was this amazin' little club…" His smile got downright dirty. "You should ask him to tell you about it sometime."

Marino shook his head in the negative. "Juliette doesn't want to hear about stuff like that."

"What would she like to hear about?"

"More pleasant things, such how talented Brody is at

restoring cars. Self-taught in everything, but his skills are legendary. Even taught me a thing or two. And he helped me out with this baby." He reached behind him and patted the side of the truck.

She looked at his truck with interest. "You restored it?"

"I'm proud to say I'm the original owner, but I did a full rebuild seven years ago. Brody helped with the engine, and he got me these custom rims. Didn't know how amazing they'd look until they were on, but Brody's got a good eye. Despite not doing exteriors, I trusted him. Glad I did because like I said, the man's got talent."

"Yes," she murmured.

"He's sharp, too. Like a tack. Got a real head for numbers. And he makes a damned good beer. Yes, I'd say Brody's the full package."

"Why are you talkin' him up to her?" Tex demanded.

"Why do you think?" Marino said with a grin. "He's kept her away from us. That should tell you everything you need to know."

"You know, Brody and I, we…" Juliette began, but before she could say anything else, she felt a warm hand on her shoulder.

"Sorry I left you alone for so long. What lies have these guys been telling you?"

"Nothing," she said quickly.

"Just tryin' to figure out this business associates thing you two have goin' on," Tex said, eyes keen.

Next to her, she felt Brody's whole body tighten, and then his hand was at her waist, tugging her in to his side. "Business associates?"

"That's what she said."

Brody squeezed her tighter. "There's a little bit more to it than that."

Tex didn't blink an eye. "You ever get tired of Red, darlin', you look me up. Last name's Yearling, but there's only one Tex in this town."

"She won't be looking you up," Brody said in a dark voice she'd never heard before.

"Brody," she said, her voice a warning.

"Sounds like the woman has a mind of her own," Tex said with a smirk, which actually made him look even more handsome. Brody was still scowling at him, but he didn't even blink. "See you two later. Right now I got a hankerin' for a beer. Nice to meet you,

Juliette."

"Cut Tex some slack," Marino suggested quietly when Tex was out of earshot. "He's still raw that you got president."

Juliette looked up at him. "You're the president?"

"Of our club," he said. "But only for one year."

"Except what he's not telling you is that he's been president three years in a row."

That did not surprise her at all. Brody seemed born to lead.

"It's not a big deal," Brody said.

Juliette smiled. "I think that it's cool."

"Hear that, Brody?" Marino said. "She thinks it's cool."

Then Marino winked at her and smiled, showing off white teeth and a dimple. Holy cow. For an older gentleman, Marino was *hot*.

She dragged her gaze away from that gorgeous dimple and looked up at Brody. "He told me how you helped him rebuild his truck. He says he couldn't have done it without you."

Brody gave a short laugh. "He was doing just fine on his own. This guy's restored more vehicles than I can count. Well into the double digits, right, Marino?"

Marino cleared his throat, obviously embarrassed. "I almost forgot to ask. How's your mom?"

"She's good. Keeping busy at Wolfshead. A little too busy, if you ask me, but she says she likes it."

"Give her my best, will you?"

"Always," Brody said.

There was something more there. Something Juliette couldn't quite put her finger on, but before she had the chance to figure it out, Brody had his hand on her waist again. "It was great to catch up, but I want to take Juliette to see the rest of the show before they shut it down."

Marino nodded. "Make sure you don't miss Keller's Ferrari 250 GTE. He just gave it a fresh paint job and it looks incredible."

"Will do. Good to see you, man," Brody said, briefly clasping hands.

"Catch you at our next meeting."

"It was nice to meet you," Juliette said.

Marino gave her a warm smile. "Same. I hope to see you again soon, Juliette."

"See you, Marino," Brody said.

As they turned, Tex came sauntering up, a sexy smile on his handsome face.

"Juliette," he drawled. "We meet again."

"We were just leaving," Brody said.

"But we didn't get to see the Ferrari yet," she complained.

"Another time," Brody said tightly.

Tex's eyes gleamed in challenge. "I'll take you to see it," he offered.

"Back off, Tex," Brody said, ice in his tone.

"What's the problem, Phelan? Afraid Juliette's gonna leave you high and dry?"

Brody glowered at him. "Don't push me."

Same story, different guys. It seemed that everywhere she went she was faced with alpha males throwing down.

"Gentlemen," Juliette said, keeping her voice deliberately light, "I've had a little too much excitement today. Let's take the testosterone down a notch. Tex, I appreciate your generous proposal, but I'm feeling a bit tired. Brody, why don't you take me home?"

"Goodbye, Juliette." Tex reached for her hand, but Brody gripped her arm and tugged her out of reach. And before she could even return the sentiment, Brody started towing her in the opposite direction.

At that moment, rain started coming down, one of those out-of-nowhere storms that always took her by surprise. They walked quickly to his truck, he opened the door for her, and she got in, immediately snapping on her seat belt.

In silence, Brody started the truck and slowly pulled out of the lot and onto the road. Fat water droplets hit the front window. After they'd been driving for a few minutes, she finally spoke.

"Are you angry with me?" She couldn't understand why, given that she thought she'd handled Tex pretty well.

Brody didn't answer.

"Come on, Brody. Speak to me."

"Why did you tell Tex that we were business associates?"

She blinked. "I thought Tex was your friend."

"He is," he said, his voice dark and low. "And you told him we were business associates."

She gave him a side-eye. "Um, we are."

"No, Juliette. We are not." His grip was tight on the wheel, his jaw stubbornly set.

"How would you characterize our relationship, then?"

He stopped the truck, and dimly, she realized that they were nowhere near her house, but instead were at his, parked in his driveway.

"I thought you were taking me home."

He shook his head and got out of the truck. She got out, too, uncaring that she was getting wet.

"Fine," she said, pulling out her cell phone. Immediately, rain pelted it, but she didn't care. "I don't need you to drive. I'll call someone else." But before she could press a single button, he'd snatched her phone from her hands and pocketed it. "Have you gone crazy?"

He finally turned his gaze on her. "Maybe," he clipped out. "But last night felt like a hell of a lot more than business associates."

"Agreed, but we've had two dates." She waved two fingers in his face. "Two! And you're the guy with a three-strikes-and-she's-out policy."

"I'm not that guy."

"Yes, you are!"

"No." He ran a hand through his wet hair.

"You're exactly that guy—the kind who's out the door the minute he gets bored."

"You don't understand."

"What's to understand? We have a deal. A deal where we have sex and it doesn't go further than that, and I'm good with that because God knows why, but I'm incredibly attracted to you. But you trying to make this more than it is isn't going to be good in the long run. I'm not saying what we have isn't good. It's just temporary. So it's easier if we don't make a big deal about it."

"It is a big deal. A fucking big deal." He was staring at her, with such wildness and intensity he looked half-feral. "Because business associates don't do this."

And then before she knew what he intended to do, he stepped forward, grabbed her by the shoulders, and slammed his lips down on hers.

CHAPTER 15

Juliette froze under the onslaught of sensation and made a shocked sound in her throat.

What. The. Hell?

This wasn't the Brody Phelan she knew, the in-control man who seduced in the bedroom and the boardroom, the one who had everything all laid out, who planned for every occasion, and who never got rattled. This Brody was rough and vaguely harsh, taking what he wanted and teetering dangerously on the edge.

She should put a stop to this. Demand he let her go so they could cool off and talk things out, or at the very least, get dry.

But all she tasted was rainwater and him and then every single brain cell short-circuited.

Want. Need. Now.

"Brody," she moaned, and he capitalized on her open mouth to slip in his tongue.

Talking was overrated. Ditto arguing and analyzing. All she wanted was to feel, the weight of his hands, the heat of his body, the glide of his lips against her lips.

And the hard, hot proof of his arousal, pressing into her stomach.

Brody gripped her tighter, as if at any moment she might flee. His mouth was hard, almost punishingly so, his lips bruising hers.

She fisted the front of his shirt and dragged him closer, showing him just how much she wanted him.

"Brody," she said, and this time it was a plea. To keep going.

To finish what he started. To send them both soaring.

He must have sensed the moment her mind-set shifted, because his hands slipped from her shoulders down her arms and around her back, tucking her against him.

She wasn't going anywhere.

This was beyond anything she'd experienced, this unrelenting want that would never be slaked. This wasn't normal. This probably wasn't even healthy.

And she didn't care. Especially when he slid a hand up her shirt. She'd never known that a hand on her bare back could feel so erotic, but that's exactly what it was, stroking up and down, as if he were trying to memorize the gentle slope. But her bra strap was in the way, and it was still raining, and they were on his freaking driveway, and there was no way she could possibly get him naked and horizontal where they stood.

To get him to pick up the pace, she bit down on his lip. His fingers tightened again, and a muttered curse slipped from his mouth.

Then he was backing her up to the door and fumbling for his house key and dragging her inside. He shoved her up against a wall, but she was on him first, sliding his T-shirt up and over his head and scoring her nails down his chest.

He hissed at that and captured both her wrists in one hand, holding them high above her head as he plucked at her already-stiff nipples through her wet shirt.

She moaned and pulled free, then attacked his jeans, working the top button free.

"Now, Brody," she demanded.

He tugged her hands away. "Not yet."

She shook her head and went right back to his fly. "Now."

He captured her mouth with his, then pinned her arms to her sides once again. "You do realize that challenging me is just making me hotter?"

Her lips curled up. "Yes." Challenges were always foreplay to guys like Brody.

"And it's going to make me go slower."

"Nooo," she moaned, as he went back to her breasts to tease and stroke without mercy. She did everything she could to get him to go faster. Kissed and sucked. Stroked and sighed. Even took his hands and placed them where she wanted.

All he did was laugh and go slower, tormenting her with touch. Every inch of her was sensitized, every nerve ending firing with sensation. It was too much and yet not enough.

"Brody," she said surrendering. "Please."

His eyes gleamed, his hands went to her shirt, and then, in one jerk, he ripped it right down the center, buttons pinging on his hardwood floor.

She gasped, eyes going wide.

"Fuck, that's hot," he said, covering her body with his once again as he kissed her so hard it took her breath away.

Clearly, he was making up for going super slow, because the next few minutes happened in a blur. They made their way down the hallway, leaving a trail of damp clothes in their wake.

Juliette finally got his jeans off and took him in hand, glorying in the long, hot length of him. She got all of half a minute to play before she was in his arms, being carried into his bedroom. And then she was flying through the air, landing on her back on his bed.

Before she could even blink he had rolled on a condom and was between her thighs, urging her legs up, and slamming inside her in one impossibly deep thrust.

"Oh, God, yes." The size of him, the feel of him. So, so good.

It was even better when he started moving.

He powered into her fast, then faster, giving her no time to catch her breath.

"More," she breathed.

He gave her more, pounding into her with an intensity that had her seeing stars as she writhed beneath him in pleasure.

She wrapped her legs around his back and dug her heels into his ass, snapping her hips up to meet his. She wanted more. She wanted everything.

And he gave it to her. Over and over again.

"Brody," she gasped, as his mouth found that sensitive spot on her neck. Pressure built unbelievably fast and she simply detonated, screaming his name and clawing at his back.

But he wasn't done. Not even close.

He'd given her what she wanted, and now it was his turn. Before she even had a chance to recover, he pulled out, flipped her over onto her stomach, pulled her hips back, and thrust into her from behind.

Oh God, she was so full like this, and before she came down from her high, he simply built her up again, one hand on her hip, a finger stroking over her clit in just the right way to make her shudder and cry out.

She came even harder the second time, burying her face in the comforter to scream out her pleasure.

Head fuzzy and body tingling from her second orgasm, she didn't question when, still deeply planted within her, he lifted her upright until her back was against his chest and she straddled his spread thighs. She barely had time to take a breath before he gripped her in place, then thrust.

Oh. My. God. His power. His strength.

She thought he'd been giving her everything. She was wrong.

He slammed into her so hard and so deep, she felt it in her throat. She was quivering, but he had strength enough for the both of them.

With a final mighty thrust, he squeezed tight, drove deep, and groaned.

She was flushed and sated and boneless. The only thing keeping her together was Brody's arms locked around her body, his cock still inside her.

"Juliette." Her name sounded like a prayer on his lips. He buried his face in the crook of her neck. "I'm really falling for you."

Brody loved his house. He loved the garage he'd built out specifically to hold his cars. He loved the size of the space, much more spacious than the tiny shoebox of an apartment he'd had in Hong Kong. But most of all, he loved the backyard—a small sliver of grass beyond which was three-quarters of an acre of forest.

Technically, they were still in the city, but because the house was high in the hills and close to Macleay Park, a nature preserve with tons of hiking trails, it seemed as if they were far from civilization.

He'd had a giant old-fashioned swing installed on the covered back porch, mostly because it reminded him of their cabin up near Mount Hood. He could sit for hours, gently swaying in the breeze, listening to the wind rustle through the trees.

Or, like now, watching the rain fall in shimmering sheets,

pattering softly as it hit the leaves and dripped to the ground.

Juliette was lying on him against his chest, her back to his front. His long arms were wrapped around her body, holding his woman close. His woman. He'd had women before. Plenty, but not one of them had been like this, by turns infuriating and generous, challenging and giving.

Brody smoothed her hair back from her face and kissed her temple. "You okay?"

It was the first thing either of them had said since Brody's confession back in the bedroom.

She nodded once. "Yep."

"You sure? You seemed kind of freaked out back there."

She stiffened a bit. "I wasn't. I was just…surprised, is all."

"Do you want to talk about it?"

"Do you?"

He did. He really did. But then he had the thought that she might not want to. "It's not part of the deal," he said softly.

"Neither was me spilling my guts to you about my family," she reminded him.

"Right. It's just…I've never said anything like that to anybody before."

She shifted in his lap so that she was more squarely facing him. "Then you don't need to ask me if I want to talk about it," she said gently. "Because *you* do." When he hesitated, she took his face between her hands and kissed him once, very softly. "Tell me, Brody. I'm listening."

His gaze slid to the corner of the porch, where a steady stream of water was dripping from the roof down to a small shrub below.

"It all starts with my dad," he said, his voice quiet.

She settled into him, resting her cheek on his shoulder. "What was his name?"

"John. John Phelan." He couldn't remember the last time he'd said it.

"It's a nice name."

"Yeah, well, he wasn't a nice man."

One of her hands was wrapped around his side, just under his rib cage. "Why not?" She squeezed him, letting him know it was okay to go on.

"Because he was selfish."

"How was he selfish?"

"He always had to come first. Even though he was born second, three minutes after Patrick, he always came first. Uncle Patrick didn't have anything to prove. He'd walk into a room and people knew who he was and what he was. It could have been the same for my dad, but it wasn't. I don't know why, but he had a chip on his shoulder from the time he could walk. Everything—and I mean *everything*—was a competition with him. School, sports, life, women. Everything. But Patrick loved him. Put up with his shit. But he was charismatic as hell. That's how he managed to land my mom."

"I've met your mom. She seems really nice."

"Mom's a good woman. Quiet, pretty, loyal, and smart. Crazy smart. Except when it came to my dad. See, she loved him, too. And he crapped all over that love every fucking day by cheating on her. And not just once. Dozens of times. There were so many women. So many times that he didn't come clean. He kept secrets. Too many secrets. And they destroyed my mom. I begged her to leave him—we all did—but she stayed. At first I think it was because of us. And then, I think it was because she didn't know what the hell else she was going to do."

"I'm so sorry, Brody. That must have been awful."

"It wasn't so bad when I was little. I mean, I knew something was wrong. I just didn't know what. It was when I got older and started to really understand what was going on that things got worse. I remember thinking that my mom was this tragic figure, having to watch Christine married to Patrick, living the life she wished she had.

"Patrick was great with his boys—loving, and caring, and just there for them, you know? My dad wasn't like that. He lied and hid. Hurt and bullied. And once he knew that I knew what kind of man he was, I became his main target."

"Did he hit you?" Her voice was a whisper.

"Sometimes. But the abuse was mostly emotional, and he usually targeted us, not our mom. It's why I locked myself in my shed, buried myself in cars and numbers so I wouldn't have to deal with him. And I left the first chance I got. Dad was furious, but there wasn't much he could do. Connor split fast, too. Signed up for military service instead of going to college so he could get out of there, make his own way. Finn took off first chance he got to play gigs. Swear that was why he learned how to play the guitar to begin with. Even after all of us had left the house, my mom still didn't leave him." He laughed, and it came out sounding sorry and bitter. "My dad was the one driving when the Jeep flipped. When I heard he was dead, I didn't cry. I didn't feel anything. I always knew that I didn't want to grow up to be like him. I never wanted to make promises I didn't keep. I never wanted to have secrets. And I never wanted to get involved with someone seriously, because I saw how fucked up things got when people fell in love. How they cheated on each other, hurt each other. And now I find myself falling for you, and that scares the hell out of me."

He fell silent.

The dripping from the roof had slowed a little, the patter morphing into a softer sound.

A summer shower, fading fast.

Juliette spoke into the damp air. "I'm so sorry you had to go through that."

Brody shrugged, wishing he could say it was over for him, wishing he'd moved beyond it.

"Your mom didn't leave your dad because she loved him," she said quietly.

"I know."

"You loved him, too."

"Yes." No matter how many shitty things the bastard had done. "Which makes no sense."

"Love doesn't have to make sense. Love makes you do stupid things."

He only had to look at Emma and Aidan to know that was right. Aidan had fucked up his relationship with Emma, but she'd held out for him for years, waiting for him to get his head out of his ass and come to his senses because she loved him. Luckily, he finally had, but if that wasn't the height of stupidity, he didn't know what was.

"You ever done anything stupid for love?" he asked. "Anything really brave?"

"No," she whispered.

"Me neither," he said.

Except this.

This was what love was. No secrets. Laying yourself bare. It was scary and real, exhilarating and exhausting. Most of all, it was truth.

And he hadn't felt truth in a long time.

He was falling for Juliette, and it scared him. But he was honest enough to embrace it, to lean into it instead of pulling away as he always did. Because the woman in his arms—and yeah, at this point she was his woman—was worth it. She was as scared as he was. He could see it in her eyes, but he wasn't going to let that stop him from going all in.

He wasn't his father. Maybe that was why the old man had been such a bastard—because he knew that Brody knew and had judged him for his failings.

Not Juliette. She was still right there, the warmth from her body seeping into him, making him whole again. There was only one thing to do. He pulled her closer to him, kissed her temple, and slowly rocked them to the sounds of the dying storm.

CHAPTER 16

Brody was on the phone in his office bright and early on Monday morning when a movement by the door caught his eye. It was Gabe, poking his head inside. He motioned for his cousin to come in and raised his pointer finger, the universal symbol for *I'll be with you in a minute*, while he finished up the call. Gabe nodded and crossed the room, where he sprawled on his couch right next to Ulysses, who had found a rare patch of sunshine. Lazily, he stroked Ulysses's fur while the dog rumbled in pleasure.

The call was an unpleasant piece of business—one of their distributors was three months in arrears on their payments—so Brody finished it up fast and tossed the phone onto his desk in disgust when he was through. Stuff like that was necessary, but it always made him feel like a coldhearted machine afterward.

Clearly Gabe didn't see it that way, as he was grinning at him like a maniac.

"What?'" Brody asked, taking a swig of coffee from his travel mug.

"You're good at ballbusting."

"I wasn't ballbusting."

"Dude. I know ballbusting and that was it. You went after them like a boss, using phrases like *breach of contract* and *you'll be hearing from our lawyer if the situation is not resolved immediately*." Gabe grinned. "I especially liked the part where you told them if they didn't pay by the end of the week they could go fuck themselves."

Brody gave him a repressive look. "What I said was that if

147

they didn't pay by the end of the week, we would cancel our distribution contract, find a replacement distributor within the month, and ban them from future distribution of any Wolfshead brand products. And when word got out that they'd failed to pay us for product, they would be blackballed from the rest of the West Coast craft beer industry, as well."

"Same thing."

Brody sighed and folded himself in his desk chair. "So what brings you to my office at"—he looked at his watch—"eight-oh-six in the morning? Kind of early for you, no?"

Hurt flashed in Gabe's eyes, but just for a moment, replaced by a sharp look Brody hadn't seen from his cousin in recent memory. "I just stopped by to give you a report. I'm on top of the construction situation. The contractors are starting work tomorrow, and they say they should be finished in two weeks, which should leave us a week to get things cleaned up and ready for Portland Eats. They're under strict orders not to disturb production, and I'll be doing the supervising to ensure work is done on time. Our margin of error is pretty small, so we have to stick to a schedule, and I will make sure we do by checking in with them every day. I've actually curtailed my travel schedule for the next couple of weeks and canceled any noncritical meetings to make sure it gets done."

Brody blinked, not sure what to make of this coolly calculated Gabe. "Anything else?"

"Yes. I need to know what to code the tours. We'll be doing the ones at Portland Eats for free—first come, first served that day—but after that we'll be charging, and I want to make sure my entries jibe with your system."

"I'll get Fiona on that."

"Great. And don't be worried about what I'm going to say on the tours. I know the history of this place like the back of my hand."

"I'm not."

"Good. One final thing. As soon as I know the construction work will be completed on schedule, I'll have Emma update the website. I already prepared all the content, and she's going to deal with the editing, uploading, and formatting. I already talked to her, though, and she'll be able to get on it right away."

Brody eyed his cousin critically. "You are really on top of things, aren't you?"

"Of course I am," Gabe said. "I'm not totally helpless, you know."

"Just easily sidetracked."

"Not this time," he said, determination in his voice.

"No," Brody agreed. "But I take it not everyone sees it that way?"

"You know how everyone is. Always busting my chops for stuff I do…or stuff they think I do."

"Or don't do."

"Don't start," Gabe said.

"I'm not. I came down on you hard before because I was worried about the timing, and I'm sorry I did that. But you have to know that I believed in this project from the beginning. Why do you think I approved the outlay in construction costs?"

"Because you wanted to give Ed a hard time?"

Brody shook his head. "Not at the expense of our bottom line. I did it because I thought you could really make a run at this, improve our profile, and make Wolfshead a destination, not simply a product. If we make some money doing it, great. But I also saw the merits of community outreach, and I think with you spearheading this effort, it's really going to succeed."

"Seriously?"

"Seriously. And again, I'm sorry I doubted you, even for a minute."

Gabe puffed up a bit at the praise. "Thanks. Maybe you could let Ed know. Aidan, too. Both of them have been giving me a hard time lately about, well, everything."

Ed was pretty set in his ways, and Aidan was Aidan. "I could. But don't you think it'd be better to show them? The construction will be done in a matter of weeks. Think of how impressed they'll be if you can pull this off for Portland Eats."

"Yeah," Gabe said thoughtfully.

"From what you just told me, I think you can."

"Thanks, Brody. I can always count on you to have my back." Gabe gave Ulysses another stroke on the head, then rose and stretched. "All right. Gotta get back to work."

"What's on tap for today?"

"I've been making the rounds at local watering holes, getting the word out about our new whiskey. It's my goal to make sure that when that launches, we have buzz, and lots of it."

Since they'd lost so much whiskey, their commercial distribution deal had fallen through—after they'd all had a crisis of faith about the direction the brand was going to go. Emma had convinced Aidan that their whiskey was gold, and they should hold out for smaller distribution deals at higher price points. She and Gabe had been working together since then to make that happen.

"How's it going?"

Gabe flashed a huge smile. "Really well. The whiskey speaks for itself. I haven't even had to pull out my, erm, charms."

Read: sleep with anyone.

"Good. Keep up the great work."

Gabe smiled. "Thanks," he said. With a nod, he left.

Brody smiled with satisfaction. The way Gabe had handled the tour thing hadn't been that diplomatic, but at least he'd taken ownership. Brody liked that a lot. Anything his brothers and cousins handled that he didn't have to was a win in his book. And Gabe was finally growing up. That was an even bigger win.

He turned back to his desk. Strange, there was still the same pile as there was when he'd left the office for the weekend, but it didn't seem as daunting to deal with today. It would take some time, but he'd get to everything. And when he finished, Juliette would be waiting for him to come out to play.

It took Juliette four more days to finish up her business plan. When she wasn't at work or with Brody, she focused on it nonstop, and she'd stuffed as much information as she could into the document, which now topped out at a whopping forty-two pages.

She figured it would be easier to cut than to add. In a moment of bravery, she'd emailed Brody a copy. And now he was coming over to give her comments so she could finalize it and start talking to prospective lenders and partners.

There was a sharp rap on her cottage door—Brody's knock, always one long rap followed by two short ones. Juliette went to the door with anticipation.

Brody was standing there, one hand in his pocket, his eyes glowing in the muted porch light. He wore jeans, a collared shirt, and a half smile.

"Hey," he said.

"Come in," she said, ushering him in fast and then doing a visual sweep of the yard to ensure he hadn't been seen. Granted, it was after dark and there was no party going on tonight, but her Aunt Violetta had eyes like a hawk.

No one seemed to be about, so she swiftly locked the door and once it was sealed shut, flung her back on it, breathing a little bit faster with all the adrenaline rushing through her system.

"What?" she said to Brody, who was watching her with a bemused expression.

"Nothing," he said with a smile. "Do you want to get down to business or should we eat first?" From behind his back, he pulled out a bag. "I brought sustenance."

"Great, I'm starving."

She practically pounced on the takeaway bag and dragged it—and by extension Brody, who actually hadn't let go because it was pretty heavy—into her small eating nook just off the kitchen.

"Where'd you take out from?"

"Pok Pok."

"Thai? Really?"

"I can't tell from your voice if that's excitement or dismay."

"Excitement. I love Thai." Even if she didn't, right now she was hungry enough to eat anything.

Placing the bag on the table, she eagerly unwrapped everything. There was a spicy green papaya salad, glass noodles, roasted eggplant, and flank steak served with fish sauce, lime, and chili, which was going to taste awesome with the accompanying container of sticky rice. The final to-go container, which also happened to be the largest, had a whole roasted chicken, Pok Pok's signature dish.

Brody laughed at her exuberance and let her take charge of setting everything out while he went to get plates and silverware and cracked open a beer. The look on his face when he took the first sip wasn't satisfaction or pleasure. It was relief. He'd had a rough day, although he was trying not to show it.

"What's that?" she said, peering at the label. "You're not drinking Wolfshead?"

"Singha always goes best with Thai food. Want some?" He offered her the bottle.

"No, I'm good with water."

"Have you ever tried this beer?"

"Nope."

"Come on. Try some."

"Okay." Tentatively, she took a sip.

"What's it taste like?" he asked expectantly.

"Beer. What's it supposed to taste like?"

He just smiled. "Beer, I guess. But to me it tastes like memories."

They tucked into the food and after eating quietly for a few moments, Brody swallowed and said, "So I took a look at your business plan."

Juliette froze, a forkful of noodles halfway to her mouth. Suddenly, she wasn't very hungry anymore.

"Come on, Costa. Don't freak out on me now. You'll ruin your tough-girl image. Anyway, there's nothing to be worried about. I have some suggestions, but overall, you did a great job."

"Really?"

"Yes. Really. Not that I had any doubts. You could do anything you put your mind to, I'm convinced of that."

She felt her cheeks heating. Compliments from Brody were new, and as such, a bit unsettling. "Thanks, but we can work on it after you tell me what's going on."

His eyes flashed with surprise, and she knew she'd read him right. "I'm not complaining. Our brewery side is doing great— meeting our production and sales targets. It's just the distillery side is struggling. Oh, but earlier this week, I had a breakthrough."

"Tell me."

"So you know how Gabe's hung up on giving tours of the brewery and distillery?"

"You mentioned that, yes."

"He wants to start doing them at Portland Eats."

"But that's in three weeks."

"Yep. Not a lot of time to get ready, but believe it or not, Gabe actually got the construction permits and is all fired up about getting the work done beforehand. They started today, putting up safety rails and cordoning off the actual production area."

"Do you think you can pull it off?" she asked, taking a bite of papaya salad.

"I don't know," he admitted. "But Gabe's determined to try, and I'm determined to let him. To be honest, it's nice to see him taking some initiative, and if he can actually get it done, it'd raise the status of his reputation."

"You don't think highly of him?"

"I do. I just think he sometimes goes about getting what he wants ass-backward. I'm a straight-up kind of guy. I'm honest. I ask for what I want directly. People know where they stand with me. With Gabe, you never know what you're getting."

"I bet that's hard for him, having all these older brothers and cousins who are big and smart and talented, always telling him what to do."

"I think you meant to say, 'giving him good advice.'"

"Nope. I mean telling him what to do. Or telling him that whatever he's doing, he's doing it wrong and he should be doing it a different way."

"Actually, I was relieved when Gabe told me he was taking charge of the tours. One less thing on my plate."

"Then you're probably the only one who treats him like an adult. I can just imagine what a hard time he gets from everyone else. Trust me. I would know, and I'm not even the youngest."

Brody looked thoughtful. "Maybe."

"I'm glad that you're giving him some autonomy, and not just because he deserves to show what he can do, but because like you said, it frees you up to do other things. Like look at my business plan."

Brody raised an eyebrow. "Eager to get to it, are we?"

Not really, but the sooner they got it over with, the better. "Don't keep me in suspense. I'm dying here."

It took forty-five minutes for Brody to walk through her plan. He was extremely thorough, and by the time they reached the final page, her head was swimming with information. Good thing she'd taken copious notes, because there was no way she'd remember everything clearly otherwise.

"Remember, these are all just suggestions. This is your plan, so I'll be good with whatever you want to do with my comments."

"Are you kidding?" she said. "Your suggestions are gold."

"You think?"

"Yeah, Brody." She covered his hand with hers. "Gold."

He grinned, showing her a flash of white teeth. "I like that."

"What? People don't tell you your suggestions are gold?"

"Not usually. No. They usually just do what I suggest and that's that. No one really compliments me for a job well done."

"Well, they should." She gathered his hand in hers and squeezed. "Can I tempt you to stay the night?"

At this, he actually looked apologetic. "I wish I could, but Finn's playing at the Doug Fir Lounge and it's going to be a late night." He glanced at his watch. "I've actually got to get going soon if I want to make the show. Finn put me on the VIP list. I would ask you to come with me, but it'll just be me and the rest of the guys, except Aidan, who's bailing to hang out with Emma. And I think maybe it's too early for you to feel comfortable with that?"

He said it like a question. As if there were some point in the future she *would* be comfortable hanging out with Brody and his family. That day, however, was not today.

"No, no. It's fine." She slid her hand away and busied herself with tidying her papers. "You do your thing."

Brody's brow crinkled a little. "Are you sure?"

"Of course I'm sure," she said, deliberately keeping her voice light. "I know how important it is for you to hang out with your family. Besides, you've given me a lot of homework, and if I'm going to get this business plan into fighting shape, I need to put in the hours." She tapped the stack of papers on the table to make sure no loose edges were poking out, placed them on the table, and laid her pen on top to keep the whole stack anchored.

Brody didn't look convinced, so she made a shooing motion with her hands. "Please. Go. I don't want you to be late."

"Okay," he said, sounding reluctant. "Text if you need anything or have any questions."

"I will," she promised. "Now go."

He rose and brushed his mouth against hers. "See you soon, Juliette. Thanks again for having dinner with me."

"Thanks for feeding me. And giving me gold."

She walked him to the door, where he kissed her once more, then disappeared into the dark garden.

After Brody left, Juliette got herself a glass of ice water, then padded into her small family room and flicked on the light. She powered up her laptop and made herself comfortable on the couch.

Slowly and systematically, she plowed through all of Brody's comments and suggestions. He texted her once to see if she was okay, but she didn't want to disturb him on his evening out, so she texted a perfunctory response and kept working. It took several hours to address all of Brody's issues, but when she was done and had given the plan another read-through, she couldn't deny that it was much stronger.

As she'd said: gold.

With bleary eyes and fuzzy head, she washed her face, brushed her teeth, and climbed into bed. She was exhausted, but that didn't stop her from thinking of what it would have been like to hang out with Brody that night, surrounded by him and his family.

The truth was, she *had* wanted to go out with him. Yes, it would have been awkward to be with the Phelans, but it would have meant she'd have gotten to spend more time with Brody.

She could no longer ignore the fact that she was falling for him, too. That scared her more than she could possibly say. Because nothing had changed. Their families still hated each other, and she wasn't convinced he was in this for the long haul. But it was too late for her. She was already gone. Ultimately, he was going to break her heart.

And there was nothing she could do about it.

CHAPTER 17

It was pushing eight when Juliette arrived at Grands on Thursday night. She would have been there sooner, but she'd gotten caught up in another round of arguing with Sal about the spreadsheet and barely extricated herself in time to make the drive across the bridge and into the downtown area where the restaurant was located.

She was obviously a few minutes early—or her watch was a few minutes fast—because Michael Sutherland hadn't yet arrived. The maître d', a stunning woman with long black hair and a gentle smile, directed her to the bar to wait for him. She didn't mind. The space was chic and polished, with an onyx floor, glittery chandeliers, and brocade mirrors on the walls. Yet it wasn't at all cold—there were plush banquettes and lavish seat cushions. Whoever had decorated this place valued both substance and style.

The bartender came over right away and handed her a wine list, which she reviewed with a swift and practiced eye. She had just placed her order when she felt a hand tap her shoulder.

She turned and looked up at a tall, handsome man with dark hair and warm brown eyes.

"Ms. Costa?" he said.

"Juliette, please," she said as she rose with a smile to take his hand. "And you must be Mr. Sutherland."

He was wearing a blazer over jeans, and there was a touch of gray at his temples that in no way diminished his attractiveness. He was a bit like the restaurant itself—a shade formal, a shade not. She liked him immediately, especially when he shook her hand with a warm, firm grip and smiled broadly. "Call me Mike. And please, sit." He settled into the seat next to her and gave an approving look around at the space. "Thanks for meeting me here. I'm glad we were able to make this work out."

"I should be the one thanking you," Juliette said. "I truly appreciate you taking the time out of your busy schedule to speak with me."

"Not a problem. I had a short window before dinner. Hiya, Charlie." The bartender had returned and was standing in front of them holding two identical glasses of wine.

"Good evening, Mr. Sutherland," he said, nodding his head as he placed the glasses on the dark wood in front of them. "Heitz Grignolino for the lady." He placed another glass of red in front of Mike. "And your usual, sir."

"Thanks, Charlie. Put both of these on my tab, would you?"

"Of course, sir."

When the bartender had gone, Mike turned to her. "Cheers," he said.

"Cheers," she responded, and clinked glasses with him.

"You chose a very unusual wine," he said.

Juliette smiled. "I couldn't resist. Not everyone carries Grignolino."

"Oh?"

She explained, "It's not a well-known varietal. Grignolino comes from a region in northwest Italy called Piemonte. It's most famous for Nebbiolo, from which Barolo is made, but another varietal that's grown there is Grignolino. It's light and easy to drink, but I also love the name. It comes from the Italian *grignole* which means 'many pips,' or seeds. There are only a couple of winemakers outside of Italy who produce it, most notably in California at Heitz from Napa, which I have in my hand, and Guglielmo Winery, in Morgan Hill." She gave him an apologetic smile. "I'm sorry. I hope I'm not boring you. I tend to get a little too enthusiastic when wine is the topic of discussion."

"I find it fascinating," he said, taking a sip of his own wine. "What else can you tell me…say, about the list?"

"Balanced, with a good representation of different varietals, regions, vintages, and price points. In particular, I like the fact that it focuses on wines from the Northwest, but also showcases some interesting wines from Europe."

"Your assessment is dead-on," he told her. "The wine list was prepared with an eye toward all the factors you just listed."

"If you know the motivation behind the wine list, I'm guessing you know the owner."

"Actually," he replied, his voice mild, "I'm the owner. One of them, anyway."

Of course he was. Juliette blushed furiously, mentally kicking herself for not doing as much due diligence as she should have. She'd done enough to know that Mike was a high-powered restaurateur with a lot of clout in the Portland community. He owned a company that invested in several high-end restaurants, but she should have checked to see which ones.

"It's okay," Mike said. "I'm more of a silent partner, anyway." He leaned his elbow on the bar. "So let's get down to business. You were referred to me by Brody Phelan, a man whose opinion I respect very much."

"Thank you," she said with a coolness she didn't really feel.

"He also tells me you want to open a wine bar."

"That's right. I've spent many years in the food and wine import business, and I'm ready to take my knowledge to the next challenge. If there's one thing I know and know well, it's wine."

"I know. Brody forwarded a copy of your business plan. It's solid. Really solid."

"Thanks," she said, trying not to scream. Michael Sutherland thought her business plan was solid! When Brody had told her last week what he'd done, at first she was furious that he'd gone behind her back to pass along her plan. That fury had dissipated a mere twenty-four hours later when Mike's secretary had called her to schedule a meeting.

Talk of the meeting had set off a chain of events that ended up with Lucy spending way too many hours finding the perfect outfit for her to wear. After the dust had settled, she'd ended up wearing an elegant silk wrap dress, stilettos, and minimal makeup designed to accentuate, but not overwhelm. She looked professional and put-together. *I'd do business with you*, Lucy had pronounced.

Mike regarded her evenly. "I also looked you up."

"Online? I'm afraid there's not much to find. I keep a fairly low profile," she said, giving him a rueful smile.

"Juliette Costa does. But JC doesn't."

She froze, the smile pasted on her face. Damn Brody, spilling all her secrets. "My podcasts are just for fun."

"That may be true, but it's a very powerful platform. Not only is that medium of the moment, but they're really well done. Your voice is amazing, and I love the interviews, love the local spin you have on everything, and I especially love how you integrate wine into everything. I thought the episode you did on Zoobomb was particularly good."

"I enjoyed that interview," she murmured. Zoobomb was one of those strange Portland traditions that seemed as though it shouldn't exist, but totally did. Cyclists would take their bikes on the MAX light rail up to the Washington Park station, right by the Oregon Zoo. Then they would speed down the west hills. Unusual bikes, particularly minibikes, and costumes were prized. Her interviewee that day had been a young man obsessed with his minibike and how he customized it specifically for the events, which took place every week. He'd built his life, his relationships, and his work around it. Since it was a fall episode, she'd featured a seriously odd pumpkin spice wine from California that tasted like pie. Much like Portland itself, the episode had turned out weird, but excellent.

"Honestly, even if I hadn't already heard your podcast, I would have figured out your deep understanding of wine in the first moment of our acquaintance based on your wine choice alone." He raised his glass. "Guess what I'm drinking?"

"The Grignolino?"

"You got it. So not only did you go for one of my personal favorites, but you clearly knew your stuff when you waxed poetic about its origins."

"Like I said, I tend to get a little carried away when I'm talking about wine."

He leaned forward and looked at her intently. "Opening a business isn't just about having the numbers and a strong financial sense. It's not even about providing a service people need or want. It's about passion, because without passion, you're going to fail. Passion for what you're doing keeps you going through the bad times and powers you further through the good times. I never invest in any place where I can't see that my partner is as excited and into the project as I know I will be. When you talked to me about that

Grignolino, I heard the excitement in your voice, saw the light in your eyes. That's what I look for—that light. And you have it."

"You hardly know me," she murmured.

"You come recommended from Brody. That alone should be enough. But I also know wine and I know people. I've listened to your podcast, heard how you connect with others. You've already put yourself out there, and your podcast shows me that you have a strong understanding of culture and marketing. Your business plan shows me you have an even stronger understanding of your product and your place in the market."

He leaned back and took another sip of wine while she blinked at him, surprised and pleased. Mike was an experienced entrepreneur who knew how to read people. Brody trusted him, and she should, too. "So if you were me, where would you suggest I go from here?"

"If I were you," he said slowly, his eyes never once leaving hers, "I would ask me how interested I was in investing."

Shock pervaded her system. "How interested are you in investing?" she managed to croak out.

"Before I answer that, I need to know something. How wedded are you to staying in Portland?"

"I—I don't know. I hadn't thought about that." Leaving her family's business was one thing. Moving to a different city was another. "What are you proposing?"

Mike took a sip of wine. "My business partner and I have been thinking about expanding our portfolio for a while—somewhere that's a natural extension of the Portland market. Somewhere bigger, a bit more cosmopolitan, but with a similar demographic."

"Seattle?" Juliette guessed.

"That's right," he said, nodding. "When I showed your proposal to my partner, he was impressed. We both were. The place would be sophisticated, yet warm and accessible. It'd be fine in Portland, but we think Seattle would be an even better fit. What are your thoughts?"

"Seattle is…nice."

"Yes. Yes, it is. And it'd be even nicer with a high-end wine bar. But I'll be honest with you—when we invest, we don't just invest in a business. We invest in people. In relationships. From the minute

I met you, I knew you were someone I'd like to do business with. I'm speaking for my partner, too."

Juliette swallowed. This was moving in a completely different direction than she thought it would. "Are you saying you're interested in investing in my business?"

He assessed her coolly. "If you're stuck on Portland, then we're going to have to pass. But if you open in Seattle, we'd be willing to offer you a term sheet. Sure, we'd be taking a risk because you've never done food service before, but it's a risk we'd be willing to take given your personality and background. We'd need to see a revamped proposal, but I'm sure you can handle that."

Mike said some other stuff about percentages and risk and upside, but she heard very little of it. Finally, she got herself together enough to tell him she'd think about it.

"Good," Mike said, nodding. "Don't rush into anything. Do you have a lawyer?"

"No."

"If we're going to move forward, you'll need one. Someone good. I can give you some recommendations if you'd like. In the meantime, you can work on that proposal."

"I'll need some time." Not just for the proposal, but to truly think about what Mike was offering.

"No problem. Whenever you're ready."

The meeting didn't last much longer. They chatted for a few more minutes about wine and restaurants and even Wolfshead, but the business portion of their meeting was clearly over. Finally, Mike looked at his watch. "I'm terribly sorry, but I've got to run. I promised a friend I'd have dinner with her tonight."

"No problem. I truly appreciate your time. It was a real pleasure meeting you."

"Same here. And I'm looking forward to continuing the conversation." Mike rose, then gripped her hand in his. "Good night."

"Good night."

He released her hand, then turned and disappeared into the crowd.

The meeting had gone well. Better than she'd ever expected. Mike Sutherland thought her plan had merit, and he was exactly the kind of person she would love to go into business with. He was smart and savvy, and appreciated wine as much as she did. Plus, he was willing to invest in her business…and in her. So why did the thought of revamping her proposal give her the hives?

Because even though she desperately wanted to do her own thing, deep down, she knew that it would be the first step to leaving Portland. Which would mean leaving her family. And Brody. Truth be told, as ready as she was to start handling her own business, she wasn't quite sure she was ready to leave her world to do it. At least, not without thinking it through.

Juliette sighed and drained the last of her wine—it was too good to waste—and left a few bills for the bartender. Then she grabbed her purse and rose.

She'd promised to go to Brody's place directly after her meeting with Mike, so that they could debrief.

Part of her was eager to get to Brody's house to share the good news because she knew he'd be thrilled, but the other part of her hesitated. She wasn't going to tell him everything. Just the good bits about her talk and Mike's interest, but definitely not about Seattle, not until she had it straight in her own head.

Which felt a lot like lying.

She should go home. Forget her promise so she could think things over, but doing that would mean that she was not only a liar, but a coward, too. So she forced herself to finish the walk to her car, slide in, and start the engine. It came to life, practically purring—all thanks to Brody and his automotive belt replacement.

Brody again. Since when did her life start revolving around the man? Since when did she want to go to sleep in his bed and wake up in his arms? Since when did she miss him when he wasn't there and think about him at random moments during the day?

Nervous energy dogged her the whole way up to Brody's place, a jittery unease she couldn't quite contain. It seemed to take forever to drive through the city and up the hill. She parked in his driveway and slowly got out of the car. With leaden feet, she dragged herself to Brody's front door.

What would she say? How would he react? She couldn't think.

She hadn't even knocked on the door before it was flung open. Brody stood there, bathed in the hall light.

"Well?" he said looking, down at her. "How'd it go?"

He'd clearly settled in for the evening, because he wasn't as put-together as he usually looked. His shirt was a little open at the throat, his jeans skimmed his long legs, and his feet were bare. Sexy man.

Juliette tipped her head to meet his gaze. "He wants to work with me."

He grabbed her waist, lifted her up, and spun her around. "Yes!" He deposited her just inside the door and kissed her, hard and fast. "I knew it! Did he make you an offer?" He shut the door behind them and started to usher her down the hallway, obviously excited about her success.

"Not yet." She halted and slipped off her shoes, then continued on. "He wants to see some revisions to the plan."

"No problem. We'll deal with it. And when he falls in love with the revamped plan and sends the term sheet over, forward it to me. I'll take a look at it."

"He told me I should get a lawyer."

"He wouldn't have said that unless he was confident he'd love it." He kissed her swiftly, then grabbed her hand and tugged her into the kitchen. "Do you have one?"

"No. Do you have any recommendations?"

"We just retained new counsel for Wolfshead. The firm's solid, and the partner we're working with does good work. I can make a referral. Get you a discounted fee."

"I'd appreciate that, thanks."

"No problem." He turned to open the fridge and pulled out a bottle of champagne and a small pastry box.

She looked up at him quizzically. "What's this?"

"I was hoping you were going to come ready for a celebration, so I prepared a little in advance. Go on." He pushed the box toward her. "Open it."

It was impossible not to smile in the face of such enthusiasm, so she did, untying the string and opening the box. When she saw what was inside, she clapped with delight.

"Oh, macarons!" She threw her arms around him and hugged him tightly. "Thank you! I love you. Let me get some plates." She let him go and turned to the cabinets, but before she even took a step, she was halted by a strong arm around her waist, which hauled her backward against his chest.

"What was that you just said?" He spoke directly into her ear, and she shivered a little at his tone.

"Let me get some plates?"

"Before that."

"Thank you?"

"No, Juliette. The other thing."

Her throat convulsed. "I...love you?"

He spun her around so that she was facing him. "Why are you saying it like a question?"

"Because I'm afraid," she whispered.

"But you do love me?" he pressed.

She bit her lip and nodded. "Yes."

A strange look crossed his face, but before she could figure out what it meant, he'd wrapped both arms around her and held her close. "I'm afraid, too. But whatever it is, whatever we're scared of, we'll figure it out together."

Now was the time. She should tell him she might be leaving Portland, but the words just wouldn't come. Panic rose in her chest. "What if there are things that we can't overcome? What if there's a problem too big to solve?"

"There isn't," he said, sounding confident.

"But what if there is?"

He lifted her chin with a finger, forcing her to meet his gaze. The look on his face was infinitely patient and wise and calm.

"We'll just have to be stupid and brave, then."

She laughed, except it came out all choked, and to her shock, she realized she was on the verge of tears. "Why?"

"Because I love you, Juliette Costa. And for the first time in forever, I can see my future."

CHAPTER 18

Brody was never going to forget this night for as long as he lived. His woman loved him.

Loved. Him.

There were no secrets between them, no fights or arguments, no families or feuds. It was just the two of them, here and now, together.

He was flying, so fucking high he was never going to touch the ground again. He wanted, no, needed to show her how much her words meant to him.

He started by leading her to the bedroom, where he undressed her slowly, peeling her silky dress from her body and letting it fall to the floor. She was left standing in only her underwear and a crimson swipe of lipstick that accentuated her kissable lips.

Delicious.

Swiping the back of his hand over his mouth, he simply stared at the deep curve of her hips, the soft flesh of her belly, the swell of her breasts. When she went to cover herself, he shook his head. "Just…just let me look at you a while longer. Please."

Her eyes darkened. "Only if I can do the same."

Without hesitation, he started to unbutton his shirt, but she halted him with a breathless word.

"Wait." She covered her hand with his. "I want to do it."

He took her hands in his. Kissed them one at a time. Then gently placed them back on his chest.

She kept her eyes trained on his as she slowly, methodically unbuttoned each button in turn. Tugging his shirt out of his waistband, she undid the last button, then slid her warm hand inside. He hissed at the touch of bare skin on bare skin, especially when she swept her palms up and over his shoulders, pushing off his shirt as she went.

She stepped forward and kissed the edge of each shoulder blade, then light as a feather, slipped her hands down his chest and undid his jeans. Before he could stop her, she knelt at his feet, tugging the fabric down his legs along with his boxer-briefs, her glossy hair tickling his thighs.

Nothing could be more erotic than this. His woman undressing him, gliding her fingers over him as she slowly, methodically stripped him bare.

The look of anticipation on her face took his breath away. He urged her up, then went for her bra, a lacy black confection that reminded him of the bow on a particularly luscious package. Slowly, he unclasped it and tossed it to the floor. Her panties, a matching pair to her bra, followed.

And then she was as naked as he was.

"Brody," she whispered as he drew her close. He kissed her cheeks, her mouth, her neck, the little beauty mark on her chin. All the while, she caressed him with those smooth hands.

When he bent a head to her breast, she inhaled sharply, then moaned as he licked and sucked on her stiff nipples. She gripped his shoulder hard, as if she would fall without some kind of anchor. She was so responsive, so beautiful. And all his.

He worked her until she was making little mewling noises and grabbing at the bunched muscles of his arms. The moment her knees buckled, he scooped her up and laid her on the bed.

She looked up at him, panting, lips red, nipples hard and wet from his mouth, hair wild, eyes needy. If he slid a hand between her legs, he'd find her wet and wanting, completely aroused and ready for him.

She propped herself up on her elbows and wrapped her hand around his cock, then squeezed gently. "I want to taste you. Put my mouth on you."

He lay back with an uncontainable grin. "I'm all yours."

Her eyes lit up as she focused on his cock in her hand.

She gave him a few strokes, not quite hard enough for his

liking, but that only made him want more. He'd take great pleasure in teaching her how to touch him. Right now, he wanted to let her play. And play she did, giving him a few more strokes, then tentatively cupping his balls and rolling them in her hand.

Juliette's little tongue darted out to lick her lips, and in response, his cock hardened further. Her eyes widened in surprise, and then, without any other preliminary, she bent her head and closed her warm mouth over him.

Wet and firm, she took him deep, nearly swallowing his entire length whole.

"Jesus," he hissed as she pulled away, then swallowed him again, her throat convulsing around him.

Then she sucked, and he nearly lost his mind. He speared his hands through her thick hair, guiding, not forcing her as she drew him in and out. When she brought her tongue into play, sweeping it over and around, and nestling firmly right under the head, his eyes rolled into the back of his head.

Forget teaching her anything. She knew exactly what she was doing.

"Feels…so good," he rasped.

She mumbled something around his cock, and the vibrations only made him harder. She responded in kind, tightening her hand around his base and stroking up in time with the rhythm of her mouth and tongue.

He could barely formulate coherent thoughts, except *holy shit* and *more*.

Involuntarily, his fingers tightened in her hair, which only made her go faster and harder.

If she didn't stop soon, he was going to lose himself. Which absolutely could not happen, because he hadn't taken care of her first.

Gently, he pushed on her shoulders to indicate he'd had enough. "Tonight is supposed to be about you."

Her lips pursed. "It's supposed to be about both of us."

This is what she did. Helped him give up a little of that control. Helped him make sense of things that were senseless and ridiculous, the arbitrary lines he'd drawn for himself so long ago.

He cupped her face in his hands and kissed her wise, beautiful mouth. "You're right," he said. "It is."

This went two ways, giving and taking, speaking and listening. Trusting.

She let him push her back on the bed and spread her thighs. And when he had her positioned the way he wanted, he cupped his hands under her ass, lifted her up, and returned the favor using his mouth and tongue and fingers.

He kept working her until her breath was ragged, until her sighs turned to moans and her fingers grasped the bedsheets. He didn't stop when her thighs started quivering and when the words coming out of her mouth were gibberish. And he held on tight when she came and came hard, crying out with pleasure as she shuddered to completion.

Only then did he wrap himself with a condom, bend her knees up and out to accommodate him, and nestle himself between her thighs.

"Brody, please," she said, her arms wrapped around his back. "I need you."

Kissing her slow and deep, he slid inside.

Hot and wet and so damn tight. Nothing had ever felt this good in his life, but it was a melding that went far beyond the physical. It overwhelmed him, saturated him with pleasure and emotion. He was still scared, but he was hopeful and grateful and exhilarated, too.

Love.

He was in love, finally.

With a woman who fit him perfectly, in bed and out.

He started off slowly, smooth and sure. And then, as pleasure increased, his movements became hitched and irregular. It was too much. He wasn't going to last. But she came first, now and always.

He slipped a hand between their bodies and found that sensitive bit of flesh he knew would send her flying.

"Brody, it's—" She gasped loudly. "Oh! I'm going to— Brody!"

A second later, she came hard, gasping his name as he drove into her. And as she spasmed around him, he came, too, shouting out her name as sensation and emotion exploded within.

Immediately, his arms came around her and he held her tightly, the beat of her heart pounding against his own chest.

"I love you," he whispered into her ear.

The air in the room quieted, settled around them like a blanket. And into the stillness she said the four sweetest words he'd ever heard. "I love you, too."

CHAPTER 19

Hand in hand, Brody walked with Juliette through the parking lot at Wolfshead. Over the last couple of weeks, they'd gotten bolder about keeping company with each other. Almost every night, if he wasn't at her house, she was at his. He liked the intimacy that spending more time with her brought. Every day he learned something new about her—she loved the color green and had a penchant for emo '80s music. She collected books about wine that sat tabbed and dog-eared on her bookshelf.

He squeezed her hand to let her know she was doing great, and she squeezed back. She was getting more comfortable with PDA, but was very careful not to touch him at all if there was any chance her family might be around. Ergo, this hand-holding was a breakthrough.

So far, her family seemed to be oblivious, but his family had definitely noticed. Gabe had been annoying as crap about it, but everyone else had been fairly subtle about their approval. Like that nod Aidan had given him last week after he gave Juliette a kiss goodbye behind the distillery, or Emma's small smile when she saw them together. Even Finn, who hadn't said boo about Juliette since the day of the cruise-in, had given Brody a nod of understanding when Brody mentioned he was getting serious about her.

This was the first time Juliette was coming inside during working hours, but when they got to the front door of the brewery, she stopped short.

"Are you sure this is okay?" Her eyes were worried as they

scanned the building's exterior.

He took her face in his hands. "You're with me," he said. And that was really all there was to say. His family had to respect his claim, plain and simple.

Something in his tone must have been reassuring, because she nodded. "Okay."

"Good." He brushed his lips over hers, then ushered her inside.

"Whoa," she said, stopping just inside the door as her eyes went wide. "This place is amazing."

Brody grinned. "Thanks. We put a lot of time and energy into a redesign. And when we opened up the distillery, we did the same thing over there. I'll take you for a tour later."

"Or maybe I can." Gabe had materialized in front of the two of them. "Hello, Juliette."

"Hi, Gabe."

Brody allowed Gabe to embrace her, but when the hug lasted for a fraction too long, he cleared his throat.

Gabe didn't let go. "I'm just welcoming her to Wolfshead."

"Thanks," she said, artfully extricating herself with a little twist of her hips and a slight feint of her torso. Dazzling him with a distracting smile, she placed her hand on his biceps, keeping him at arm's length. "I truly appreciate your warm welcome."

When Gabe reached for her again, Brody wrapped an arm around her shoulder and tugged her to his side, effectively blocking him.

"Do you have a construction update for me?"

Gabe nodded. "I've been meaning to tell you that I just got word from the contractors. Construction is officially done, and they were not only on time, but under budget."

"That's amazing," Brody said, pleased. "I knew you could do it.

Aidan approached with Emma. "Morning, everyone. Hey, Juliette."

"Hi," she said back from the shelter of his arms. He squeezed to let her know she was doing great.

Aidan swung his arm out to the production floor, just beyond the glass wall that separated the tasting room from the operations side. "I can't believe you gave the okay for all of this."

"He pulled it off, didn't he?" Brody turned to Gabe. "Tell him."

Gabe's chest puffed up with pride. "We're done, just when I said we would be, and Emma and I have been busy."

"That's right," Emma said, wrapping an arm around his waist. "Hi, Juliette." Juliette gave her a smile as Emma went on. "Just to test the waters, I put up a reservation form on our website. We were sold out of all tours within a day."

"How did people find out about it?"

"Oh, I have my ways," Emma said, grinning. "We booked twenty visitors per tour at thirty dollars a ticket."

"That's six hundred dollars," Brody supplied.

Aidan gave him a repressive look. "I can multiply, you know."

"To start, we'll do four tours per day, weekends only, starting the weekend of Portland Eats," Gabe said.

"With eight tours a weekend, we'd have a two-day take at $4,800."

"I can add, too," Aidan muttered.

Emma smiled up at him. "Of course you can, honey."

Gabe nodded. "I knew there'd be interest, but frankly, I'm blown away. Once I figure out if the demand stays this high, I'll train a couple of our employees to do the tours so I can make sure I'm still doing sales full-time."

"Or your mom could do it," Emma suggested.

"Now that's a good idea," Brody mused. "Christine would be amazing."

"She's already expressed interest for when she's not traveling," Gabe said.

"I don't want Gabe to farm out all the tours, though," Emma said. "I think a Gabe-led tour at least once a weekend would showcase his brand of special."

Thoughtfully, Brody scratched his beard. Gabe, being a bro with all the guys and charming all the ladies? Sounded like a winner to him. "I'll bet visitors would pay a premium for that."

"Oh, they're already excited about it," Emma said. "I enabled comments on the tour landing page, and there's been a lot of online chatter. Apparently, everyone wants to catch a glimpse of the 'big and bearded Phelan men.'"

"I'm not a circus attraction," Aidan said, frowning.

"Don't worry. I'm sure they all want to come and gawk at Connor, anyway," Emma said.

"Some do," Gabe said, "but they're also interested in meeting Aidan because he's a baseball legend and Finn because he's a rock star, and me because, well"—he gestured at his body, as if it were obvious why people would come to Wolfshead—" and for some strange reason, Ed. For what I'm not sure because all he does is skulk and brood. Guess there's no accounting for taste."

"As long as our visitors look but don't touch," Emma said, a warning note in her voice.

"Babe." Aidan leaned down and brushed his lips against Emma's.

Gabe turned to Juliette. "Maybe you have time for that private tour now? I'd be happy to show you around."

Brody's arm tightened around her shoulders, but Juliette answered easily. "I've already got my own private tour guide, thanks."

"Are you sure?" Gabe said slyly. "Brody's such a bore. All numbers, all the time. Super dry."

"Oh, I don't know," Juliette said. "I don't think Brody's boring in the slightest. And the way he works makes me anything but dry."

Gabe just goggled at her, while Aidan coughed into his hand and Emma grinned like a maniac.

"I like her," Emma said to the group, then looked at Juliette. "Do you want to get a beer?"

"At nine in the morning?" she replied with a smile.

"Not now," Emma said, as if it were obvious. "Tonight. After work."

"Oh, I would love that, but I promised I'd hang out with my cousin Lucy."

"Bring her," Emma said, waving her hand. "We can make it a girls' night."

"That sounds great."

"Cool. What's your number?"

While the two of them swapped cell phone numbers, he and Aidan exchanged glances over the women's heads.

Clearly, Juliette had passed some sort of critical test, and he was grateful for it. If she was going to be part of his life moving forward, it would make things much smoother if she got along with his family, because Lord knew he was never going to get along with hers.

Knowing he'd been effectively shut down, Gabe smiled to show there were no hard feelings and left to get to work.

As the women kept talking, Aidan turned to Brody. "So. Gabe's tours are actually going to fly."

Brody nodded. "That's right. And what's more, they actually will help with our bottom line. I did some quick calculations, and just based off the initial construction costs, which I now know we won't go over, we'll make our initial investment back in a month. After that, it'll be pure profit."

"Will it be enough to make up for the deficit caused by the accident?" he said, his voice low.

"We're doing tours of both the brewery and the distillery, so I'll divide what we net fifty-fifty between the businesses. If all goes according to Gabe's projections and the demand keeps up, we'll have enough to cover a good chunk of those whiskey taxes within six months, even if we don't have the insurance payment to help bolster us."

"Can't believe my little brother is finally making good."

"Almost. We'll see how Portland Eats goes and take it from there. But I have high hopes."

"You always see the best in everyone, don't you?"

"I try."

"I'm just glad you're seeing the best in yourself." Aidan indicated Juliette, who was in the middle of a lively discussion with Emma. They already looked like friends. "And that you found a good woman."

"But she's a Costa," Brody said, testing him.

"So what? She loves you and puts up with your shit. She could be a Martian for all I care."

"Puts up with my shit?"

"Yeah, your shit. All that shit you've buried so deep you don't even feel it anymore. I know he fucked you up, gave you a warped sense of love. But not everyone's like that. I mean, take me."

"Your dad didn't fuck you up."

"No. My dad was great. I fucked myself up. And thank God Emma came back, gave me a second chance to make things right.

You find someone like that, you hold on and you don't let go. Ever."

Juliette was laughing now, her head thrown back with abandon, her curls streaming down her back.

"I never thought I'd fall for her," Brody said.

"Yeah, well, given what you went through, I never thought you'd fall for anyone. But you picked a good one. A really good one. And I'm happy for you."

This was Aidan, giving his explicit approval. He hadn't realized how much he'd craved it until this very moment.

His cousin and best friend stood next to him, in the building they owned for the business they ran together. And when Juliette turned to him and gave him a brilliant smile, the last piece of the puzzle fell into place. He was home. Exactly where he should be, surrounded by the people he loved and who loved him right back.

CHAPTER 20

A thrill of excitement was in the air on the day of the Portland Eats festival. Tents had been assembled early that morning over the span of two full city blocks, stretching from the Costas' property to the Phelans'. The tents were each several dozen yards apart, leaving plenty of space in between for people to move and chat, and underneath each was a different layout.

MaaMoo had set up its tent as a giant cheese display, and its employees were currently handing out samples. Ditto with Gūd, which not only had tons of chocolate samples to enjoy, but a giant blow-up chocolate bar with the company logo that it was raffling off later in the day. To show solidarity, Juliette had bought a ticket. Not that she wanted to win, because honestly, she had no room for a giant blow-up chocolate bar in her small cottage. Being a good neighbor, however, was always in fashion.

As far as the Costa Imports booth went, Juliette had personally laid everything out on two large four-by-eight tables covered with gorgeous tablecloths in blue and yellow, an Italian design that dated to the mid-sixteenth century. Atop the tables were numerous samples—olive oils, breads, cheeses, olives, almonds, and cookies, all presented in beautiful ceramic bowls. On the side were tiny cards explaining where in Italy the food and dinnerware came from. They weren't doing wine tastings, because that required a special permit, but they'd presented the very best of what they had to offer, and Juliette thought she'd done a good job showcasing their wares. Even her dad had given his nod of approval.

He stood to one side of the booth, smiling and nodding, engaging passersby in conversation and generally acting the part of benevolent king. Juliette stood at the other side, handing out postcards about the company. Her mom was behind the table with her, as were Gio and Tony. Sal was currently in the warehouse getting some extra olives because they'd run out thanks to the huge turnout.

It was only eleven thirty in the morning, but already they'd had several hundred people stop by their booth to taste samples, chat with her and her family, and most importantly, sign up for their mailing list.

She stepped out from the shelter of the booth to the middle of the sidewalk and surreptitiously peered down the block. She couldn't quite see the Phelans' booth from where she stood—the crowds were too thick—but she'd swung by before, casually of course. Gabe had given her a wink, but other than that, none of the Phelans had acknowledged her presence—purposefully, knowing the Costas were nearby and implicitly understanding the family dynamic.

Her heart throbbed with a tinge of regret, but what was she going to do? Announce that she and Brody were a thing and demand her family accept him? The fallout would be immense.

That thought did not make her happy in the slightest, but as far as she was concerned, there wasn't a huge amount of choice in the matter. Better to keep things quiet, to let the relationship run its course. When it was over, she'd pick up the pieces, mend her broken heart in Seattle where her family wouldn't be in her face about her choices and she could be left alone in peace.

Juliette was lost in thought when Tony nudged her ribs with his elbow. "So when are you gonna tell Ma?"

"Tell her what?" she asked through clenched teeth as she handed out another postcard to a passerby.

"Tell her that you're sleeping with Brody Phelan."

Juliette dropped the postcard she was holding and turned to Tony with her mouth open. "What?" she gasped.

Tony gave her an even look. "You heard me."

"How did you—" She shook her head. Reached down to grab the card and shoved it back into the stack in her hand. "Never mind. I don't want to know."

"I was at Aunt V's place last week. Saw him leaving your place."

"Who did you tell?" she demanded to know.

"No one. Look, I hate the guy, and I hate that he's with you. And I know you like to think that you can make your own decisions, but—"

"I can. I can make my own decisions," she snapped.

"A guy like that—"

"Like what, Tony? A guy devoted to his family? To his work? To his friends? That kind of guy?"

"A guy who dicks around with women. I just don't want him dicking around with you."

Tony was serious. But she needed to set the record straight. She grabbed his arm and dragged him behind the booth, where all of their additional supplies and material were stacked up. Then she whirled on him.

"He's not dicking around with me. I'm fine." Tony didn't look convinced so she kept going. "I love him, actually. A lot. And he loves me. So please keep my secret? At least for a little while longer?"

"Yeah," he said gruffly after a long pause. "I'll keep your secret."

"Thank you." She breathed a sigh of relief. "Should we go back to the front of the booth now?"

"Yeah, we better. Otherwise Ma will start worrying."

They ducked back into the booth and it might have ended there, just with her and Tony knowing and Tony keeping mum. But then something happened that blew the whole thing sky-high.

Brody strolled by and gave her a smile.

And that's when things went south in a hurry.

"You," her dad said, pointing at Brody. "What the hell are you doing smiling at my daughter?"

"Hello, Umberto," Brody said coolly. "Long time no see. I've been meaning to talk to you about the fence."

"I don't want to talk about the fence."

"Papa, please." Juliette reached out to grab his arm, but he shook her off.

Brody met her gaze and words unspoken passed between them. *Stay calm. Don't say anything.* She got it. Now was not the time or place to start up, not with hundreds of people around at a business event where they were supposed to remain professional.

"This isn't wise, Papa," Juliette whispered, but Umberto

wasn't listening.

"You think you can walk over here, strutting like a big man, owning the whole place. Well, I got news for you." He pointed at the ground. "This is my property. So get off."

Brody crossed his arms over his chest. "Actually," he said calmly, "this is the sidewalk, so by rights it's the city's property."

"Don't you smart-mouth me, Phelan. You will treat me with respect."

"You haven't earned it." His tone was mild, but the reproof was clear.

Umberto clenched his fists and stepped forward. "Why, you little—"

Tony leaped between them. "Pa, don't! They're in love!"

Juliette's mouth dropped open, and Tony shrugged as if to indicate he had no choice. Brody looked stunned. Umberto, for his part, turned tomato red.

"I'm gonna kill you." Gio rushed at Brody, but Juliette stepped in front of him before he gained too much momentum and pressed back on his chest.

"No. Stop."

If she thought his temper was bad when they believed Rudy Giaccalone had gotten her pregnant, this was a thousand times worse.

"Out of my way," Gio said, shoving her aside and knocking her tote off her shoulder with such force that papers went flying. It didn't matter. All she was focused on was preventing Gio from attacking Brody. She latched onto his elbow with both hands and dug in her heels.

"Juliette, I swear to God, if you don't get off me right now…"

"This is ridiculous," she shouted at her brother. "I'm not an object. I don't need defending."

"You sure as hell do."

"Let it go or I'll dock your pay."

"Don't give a fuck."

"I'll tell Ma you skipped out on the Fourth of July party because you went and got drunk with Vinnie Mazarelli instead of hanging out with us."

"Sal already told her."

None of her tricks were working, so she switched tacks.

"Please don't do this," she begged. "You're going to get hurt."

Gio gritted his teeth and plowed forward, dragging her along and wrenching her wrists. "He's the one who's going to be hurting."

In point of fact, it would be the other way around, but Gio was too far gone to see that.

Brody's voice cut through the mayhem. "Juliette, please let him go. I've got this."

Gio tugged again and she finally loosed her grip. Brody was taller and bigger, but that didn't stop Gio from getting right into his face. The presence of Connor, now standing behind Brody, didn't, either.

"You fucked with my sister, and now I'm gonna fuck with you," he said.

"Gio, please," she begged.

"You're hurting her," Brody said quietly. "And I can't let that stand."

"You get no say," Gio sneered, now flanked by Sal and Tony, who was looking a bit green.

"Yeah, I do," Brody told him. "Because I love her."

Gio shook his head. "Pa, you listening to this? He loves her."

But her dad wasn't listening anymore. He'd picked up the papers and was reading them intently.

"What is this?" he said quietly.

Juliette didn't answer, because she knew exactly what it was. The term sheet that Michael Sutherland had sent over. She'd printed out a copy and shoved it in her bag to review.

"Juliette?" He'd picked up his head and was staring at her intently. "Answer me." He shook the paper in her direction. "What is this?"

"Nothing, Papa. We'll talk about it later."

"It says here you're going to open up your own business. You're leaving us to open a wine bar? What wine bar?"

"It's one of those fancy bars where people drink wine," Tony supplied.

"You want to be a bartender?" her dad said, his voice shocked. "I thought I raised you better than that."

She'd never wanted to hide or lie to her parents, but for so long, it had seemed the only way to get what she wanted. Now she found she couldn't anymore. Whether her parents tried to stop her or not didn't matter. Attacking Brody—really, attacking her for being with him—was the last straw. She was done.

She forced herself to meet her father's gaze. "I'm not going to be a bartender, Papa, although if I were, there'd be nothing wrong with that. I'm going to open my own business as a high-end purveyor of wine to discriminating clientele."

"We sell wine, too!" he said, gesturing wildly. "So you're just going to open up a wine bar down the street and compete with us?"

"There won't be any competition," she informed him.

"How can you say that? This is a small town! Everyone will know that my daughter has defected. That's she's rejected the Costa name! That—"

"I'm moving to Seattle," she blurted out.

Her dad finally stopped ranting. "Why?" he breathed.

"Because that's where the money is."

Uncertainty crossed her father's face. "I don't understand."

"I have an investor willing to support my business," she explained. "But the only way I can lock down the financing is if I open up in Seattle.'

"But…why would someone invest in you?"

"Because I'm smart, Dad," she tossed back. "Really smart. And capable and good at making decisions, but you second-guess everything I do. You treat me like I'm some fragile, breakable thing without a brain in my head, but I'm doing just fine without your defense or your protection. I've been desperate for years—*years*—for you to see me as a capable woman who can get the job done. Just because you don't doesn't mean someone else can't."

She took a deep breath, ready for the hard part. "I'm not Regina, Papa. I'm not. Regina wanted to show you her strength, but she ran out on you before she could talk things through. What happened to her was an accident—an accident that we've all been paying for. Especially me. I'm not happy. I haven't been happy for a long time. Wine makes me happy." She flung an arm out at Brody. "He makes me happy. And I love you, and when you understand that I'm capable of standing on my own two feet, you will make me happy, too."

She snatched the papers from her dad's hands and shoved

them in her purse. "I have to go." She turned to Brody, expecting him to look pleased.

But the expression on his face was hard. Closed down. And then she realized what she'd said.

"Brody—"

"Not here," he bit out. Without another word, he shoved past Gio.

Juliette went to follow him, but her dad stepped in front of her. "Don't. Don't go. We have to talk about this."

She peered around her dad, where she saw Brody's head moving rapidly away. "I have to." She stepped to the side, but her dad did, too.

"You are a Costa! And you told a Phelan your plans? You went to him for help instead of coming to us? How could you?" To her father, the fact that he was kept out of the loop was the ultimate betrayal.

"He didn't know my plans, either." Not all of them. "But what he knew, I told him because I love him."

Behind her, she heard her mom's shocked cry, but her dad reared back as if she'd slapped him. "You do not love that man!" he spat.

"I do. Deeply."

"No!"

Her dad wasn't going to accept it. She could see it in his eyes. But there was nothing she could do, not now, maybe not ever, and the man she truly loved had just walked away.

She looked him dead in the eye and gripped his forearm. "We will talk. I promise. But right now I need to talk to Brody," she said, her voice quiet but firm. "You have to let me go."

Then she turned and followed the path Brody had taken. Right before the crowd closed behind her, she heard Gio and her dad yelling, but it didn't matter.

Nothing mattered, except finding him.

Reeling from Juliette's confession, Brody stalked back to Wolfshead property. Ignoring the concerned looks of his brothers and cousins, he walked directly across the lot, through the distillery, and right out the back door.

Hiding from the pain of secrets. That's what he was doing, just as he used to, a bad habit he couldn't seem to break, no matter how many years had passed.

He pressed his back up against the cool brick wall, trying to reconcile the roiling of emotions inside. All at once, he was that small, hurting little kid, desperate to slip unseen into his work shed where he could bury himself in machinery and forget about what was happening outside those four flimsy walls.

"Brody?" Her voice. Her low, sexy voice calling out for him in this moment of reckoning. She came around the corner a moment later, her heels clicking on the asphalt. "There you are. I thought I would find you here."

Of course. He'd come to their spot, after all. There was a genuinely worried look on her face as she approached. "I need to talk to you."

"You're on Wolfshead property," he bit out. "Get off."

"Brody, please. Let's talk about this."

He met her gaze, let her see his anger. Let her see that there was no way to fix what she'd done. "Did you just tell your family that you're moving to Seattle?"

"Yes, but—"

"Then there's nothing to talk about."

"I also told them I loved you."

"After everything we've shared," he said, his tone sardonic, "you think you could be honest for once?"

She looked hurt. "I've always been honest with you."

"No," he bit out. "You haven't. Not from the very beginning."

"Yes, from the very beginning. You knew who I was and I knew who you were. At least, I thought I did. I didn't know we were going to make it this far, and I swear I had no intention of moving to Seattle until Mike Sutherland made it a non-negotiable part of his offer. I needed time to think."

"And while you were thinking, you couldn't have thought to tell me what was going on? It's not like we weren't spending enough time together."

She bit her lip. "At first I didn't tell you because I was confused and scared. Then it…well, it started to get awkward that I hadn't, and I knew that when I finally did, something like this would happen. But it wasn't just that I didn't tell you. I didn't tell anyone."

Brody shook his head, unable to get past it. "Two weeks. That's how long you knew and didn't say anything. Then you go and unilaterally make a decision that is going to change both our lives?"

"I'm so sorry. I didn't think—"

"When were you going to tell me?"

Her gaze slid sideways. "Soon."

"Liar."

The word sliced through the air, opening a chasm between them.

"My feelings for you are real," Juliette said, starting to sound desperate. "Everything is real. I never lied."

"Except when it came to the one thing that counted. You kept something big from me, a huge secret that impacts both of us. I thought you respected me enough to tell me the truth."

"I do respect you." Her voice was thickening, cracking.

"If that's the case, you should have told me. Face-to-face, not letting me find out when you threw it in your dad's face when he got on your nerves." He clenched his fist. Released it. "I let you into my life, into my bed. I told you my secrets, told you about my past, connected you with Sutherland. And you didn't breathe a word of your plans to me. That's something that I can't live with."

She unclasped her hands, curled them around her upper arms, holding herself. "You've seen my family, Brody. You know how they are."

"I don't care what or when you wanted to tell your family." He jerked a thumb at his chest. "But after what we shared, *I* deserved to know. I helped you with your business plan. I—" Realization thundered through him. "Oh, shit," he breathed. "You changed the plan. After I helped you, you changed it behind my back."

She looked miserable and guilty as hell.

Her eyes were pleading. "Do you know what it's like to live a life where you have nothing of your own? Where your whole existence is fodder to be picked over, dissected and analyzed? Where everything from your job to your house to your clothes are examined and deconstructed? Where every decision you make really isn't your decision at all? This wine bar is mine. The one thing I have that no one else can touch. I had to protect it at all costs."

"You said you loved me."

"I do. And I don't want to leave things like—"

"No." He didn't want to hear it. He couldn't. This was what love did. Opened you up and left you vulnerable. Hurt. Wrecked.

He'd known about this side of love since he was a kid, and by the time his dad died, he thought he had it under control. Don't feel, only think. Don't get attached.

And for fuck's sake, don't fall in love.

Then he'd gone and done just that. And it was going to destroy him now, just as it had destroyed him then.

"Please," she whispered. "Can't we work this through? I'm sorry," but it wasn't enough. It would never be enough. Because his heart was already in pieces all over the floor.

He shook his head. "We're done." Better to end it clean, so they both know where they stood. He tried and failed to force a smile. "I gotta go. See you around, Costa."

Tears welled in her eyes and spilled down her cheeks, but she didn't speak, knowing as well as he did that it was the end. She wasn't willing to say words that she didn't mean. Even as he hated to end it, he knew that it was over.

He'd hurt her, deeply. He knew that, even if she was too proud to show it. But she'd hurt him just as badly.

The soft kiss she placed on his cheek burned like fire, but he didn't allow himself to flinch. Instead, he stood still and let the numbness wash over him.

He waited until her footsteps faded away in the distance.

Then he went back through the distillery, across the parking lot to the brewery, and directly inside, where he proceeded to get so fucking drunk on Wolfshead lager that it took both Connor and Aidan to carry him to his office later that night.

His dreams were filled with Juliette Costa…and what was never, ever going to be.

CHAPTER 21

Juliette was in hell.

Maybe it was because she hadn't woken up to a fantastic good-morning kiss from Brody, or because his beard hadn't tickled her cheeks as he wrapped himself around her in that way he did when he wanted her attention, or because he hadn't made her coffee (which he usually then proceeded to drink, sweetened or not).

Or maybe it was because at eight on a Saturday morning she was jammed inside her tiny, stuffy, doorless office trying to sort the accounts receivable spreadsheet.

It was probably all of those things.

She hadn't talked to Brody since Portland Eats. She hadn't even seen him. Which was probably for the best, because the way they ended things had her feeling pretty raw.

After she'd left him that awful afternoon, she'd holed up in her cottage and cried her eyes out for the rest of the weekend, a self-imposed exile made worse because not only was Brody not speaking to her, but neither was the rest of her family.

In times past, she would have welcomed the respite from them, but this time even Lucy stayed away, which was very, very bad.

She wished the past week was a really bad dream but unfortunately, it wasn't, because now her dad wouldn't look at her and every time she passed her mom in the hallway, Francesca would make a little sniffing sound and turn away.

On the positive side, her brothers had thrown themselves into work like men possessed. Their cars were already in the lot before she got there, and they were—shocker—actually working. Without prompting, yelling, or fighting. Sal had attacked the spreadsheet like a demon, Gio was in the middle of a complete reorganization of the warehouse, and Tony was out hustling for new clients.

She didn't miss the fighting. Not one bit. But she missed them needing her, just a little. Now it was as if she didn't exist.

She also missed Brody. Missed their banter and his teasing and the intimacy that they'd developed in such a short period of time. They weren't going to get that back, ever. They'd go back to frosty politeness and business as usual, except without the heat and definitely without the warmth. She hated that she wouldn't have that from him, especially after everything they'd shared.

And she hated that she still loved him.

She wished it would fade away, but it remained stubbornly lodged in her heart, along with the hurt that had taken up residence.

Juliette sighed and typed another number into the spreadsheet, double-checked the column, and saved it, all while invisible clamps squeezed hard around her heart.

She shouldn't be so unhappy. Her big secret was out, and while her family wasn't supportive, at least they weren't trying to talk her out of it, as she'd feared. At least she could leave Costa Imports without that hanging over her head.

A knock sounded on the doorframe. She turned, expecting one of her brothers, who, shockingly, had voluntarily come to work today even though it was a weekend. But it wasn't one of her brothers—it was her dad.

"Can I come in?" he asked.

"I'll come out. There's not much room inside."

She rose and moved to exit, but her dad peered over her shoulder at her computer and frowned. "That spreadsheet looks complicated."

"It is," she said bluntly.

He moved into the space she'd created and sat down at her desk. Then he began scrolling through the spreadsheet. "You made this? From scratch? How?"

"I took a few online business courses, and Excel 101 was one of them. It's pretty bare-bones and it's a bit finicky, but it works. You just have to be gentle. I put it into a Google Sheet and I'm teaching

Sal how to use it. He's doing okay with it so far, and I think he'll be able to handle it on his own when I leave."

Her dad turned to study her intently. "I didn't know you weren't happy."

Oh, they were going to do this now? If so, she didn't want to be boxed into this tiny room while they had it out. "Let's go for a walk, okay?"

"Okay." Her dad rose and joined her in the hallway.

On the way out, they passed her mom, who watched the two of them with red-rimmed eyes. She didn't think her mom had done anything but cry since Portland Eats.

They walked out the front to the parking lot. The day was gray, with rain threatening to fall. Across the lot, Wolfshead stood, solemn and proud.

Maybe it was because her brothers were on their best behavior, or maybe it was because nothing had cropped up that needed handling, but Brody hadn't reached out. He probably wouldn't in the future, either. Part of her knew that her family needed to learn how to handle dealing with the Phelans, but the other part of her felt guilty that she was leaving them to fend for themselves. And then there was the part of her that was just sad.

She couldn't think about that now. She had to finish this conversation with her dad, and get back to her spreadsheet, and put things in good working order for when Sal took over.

"When are you leaving?"

"Two weeks," she replied.

"Why so soon?"

"I don't want to wait to get started." The rest of her life lay before her, beckoning her to join. Since she'd signed the term sheet, it had been full speed ahead. The sooner she left her family's business, the sooner she got up to Seattle, the sooner she could find an apartment, start planning for her new place, and lay down some roots.

"If I had known you were unhappy, I could have said something, done something to make you stay."

"You weren't looking to keep me happy. You were looking to keep me stable and secure and safe. But I'm already all of those things. I have a good head on my shoulders."

"Do you?"

"I'm not rushing into anything. I spent a long time thinking and planning. I sought expert advice. I wrote a proposal and a business plan. I know what I'm doing."

Her father looked at her suspiciously. "You're not just doing this to punish me?"

"No. I would never do that. I just need my own thing. Someplace where I can make my own decisions, succeed or fail on my own merits. That just isn't happening at Costa Imports. And with you at the helm, it never will."

She swallowed, not really sure why talking to her dad like this was so hard. "I love you so much. But I need to find my own way. That's what you wanted, wasn't it?"

She looked to her dad imploringly, but her dad was looking up at the Costa Imports sign on the side of the warehouse. The family name. The family business. "My whole life, this is what I wanted. To expand Costa Imports, to be my own boss, and to work surrounded by the people I love. I wanted to pass this on to you so you'd have an easier life than I did." He shook his head. "But I find out that what I'm offering isn't good enough."

"It is good enough," Juliette said. "It's just not what I want. I want the freedom to build something from the ground up, to make my mark on the world doing what I love."

"You'll be starting with nothing."

"Not with nothing," she told him. "With every bit of knowledge you passed along to me about how to run a business. I couldn't have gotten that from anyone else but you."

"Oh, bella," he said with a sigh. "I haven't given you what you needed, have I?"

"You've given me everything I need." She looked at her father, so stubborn, so proud, and so lost. "Except one thing. Right now, I could really use your support."

He didn't hesitate. Just held out his arms. She went to him, and he embraced her. She started to cry. She was sure the Phelans could see everything on their stupid long-range cameras, but it didn't matter what the Phelans thought of her anymore. She and Brody were done. Permanently.

"I love you."

"Same."

A long pause. "Who will run the business when I'm dead?"

he moaned.

"You're not going to die," she told him confidently. "You're going to live forever. But when you decide to retire, Sal will take over. He's got the business chops and the temperament. He just has to grow up, which he hasn't really had to do because I've been here. Once I'm gone, he'll step up. You'll see. And the others will follow suit. Except maybe Gio." Her middle brother still needed to find his way.

"I don't know how we're going to deal with the Phelans."

It was on the tip of her tongue to tell him that they probably wouldn't have to, but her dad simply sighed and shook his head, signifying that was all he wanted to say about that particular topic.

Fine with her. It was enough to have the conversation about leaving. Adding Brody to the mix would just be painful…for both of them. Thankfully, her dad didn't push it with Brody. He did, however, push it with someone else.

"You know how your mother and your aunt talk?"

"Yes." Every day. For hours.

"Well, I heard from your mom who heard from Violetta, who mentioned how surprised and upset Lucy was when she heard the news that you were leaving."

Right. The grapevine—how everyone knew everyone's business in as long as it took to hit send on a text (for the younger generation) or pick up the phone and call (for the older). Lucy hadn't been responding to her texts *or* taking her calls, and she could understand why. Lucy felt betrayed. Clearly, she needed to step up her game to get her cousin talking to her again.

She flung her arms around her dad and hugged him. "Thanks, Papa. Good talk."

Then she headed for her car.

"Wait—where are you going?" her dad called out.

"To take care of something important."

An hour later, Juliette was head down, ass up on a yoga mat in a 100-degree room surrounded by thirty other sweaty bodies while her arms burned and her thighs ached.

Every time she came to one of Lucy's classes, she'd get her ass handed to her on a silver platter, and yet today had been the worst class she'd ever taken, probably because Lucy had it in for her. She went through all of the positions Juliette hated most—locust, tortoise, and worst of all, fish out of hero. Whatever that meant.

Lucy was punishing her—and honestly, she didn't blame her. She and her cousin shared everything, and the fact that she'd withheld something as important as her plans to move to a different city was something that she should have told Lucy directly instead of letting her find out through other sources.

Finally, Lucy said the words she'd been waiting for. "Lie back and close your eyes as we enter into shivasana, corpse pose, please. Breathe and relax."

Juliette shifted into position and practically collapsed on her yoga mat. She hated corpse pose, too, so nope. Relaxing was not going to happen.

It was amazing that she had so much natural padding, and yet she could not get comfortable to save her life. Her shoulder blades jabbed into the floor and her hips ached from their unnaturally tilted position and the myriad poses they'd been unwillingly coaxed into over the last half hour.

"Let go of the past and simply be in the present," Lucy continued on. "Your limbs are heavy. Feel yourself melting in the floor."

Her limbs were heavy, all right, pressing her down into the hard wooden floor under her mat. Seriously, she could feel every molecule.

"The room falls away, the universe falls away, and all that is left is your essence, floating above your body."

Where was her essence, anyway? Not floating above her body, that was for sure. Giving up on the pose, she opened her eyes at the very moment that Lucy was walking by. In times past, Lucy would have smiled and winked, but this time, all she gave her was a blank look.

By the time Lucy brought everyone up for a final meditation, Juliette's back felt as if it were about to crack in half. There was some more spiritual talk, and then Lucy finally dismissed her class with a "namaste" and a bow.

Most of the class packed up and filed out right away, but a few folks lingered, obviously wanting more time with Lucy. The next class was going to start soon—the instructor had already come in and set up his mat and turned on the music—so Juliette pulled on a hoodie, rolled up her mat and stepped into the front room to wait for Lucy to finish.

In contrast to the reverence of the inside space, the front room was much more hectic, with several people chatting or removing their shoes or getting checked in by the lithe brunette at the front desk. Juliette didn't like this room as much as the main space. It was always crowded. And it smelled like dirty socks and sweat.

The check-in woman beamed at Lucy as soon as she emerged from the studio. "You had thirty-four," she said. "Great class!"

"Nice," Lucy said, nodding. "Marco's up next for noon Bikram. He's getting set up now, so we're on schedule. I'm heading out to grab a bite, but I'll be back to teach my two p.m., cool?"

"Of course," the woman said. "Have a nice lunch."

Lucy stepped out without acknowledging her.

Quickly, Juliette scrambled to catch up, getting waylaid by three latecomers rushing through the door. By the time she caught up to Lucy, she was almost halfway down the block.

"Lucy," she said.

Lucy didn't say anything.

"Lucy, please."

"Oh, was that the wind I heard?" Lucy said, her voice sarcastic. "Must have been, since I don't hear squat from my cousin Juliette anymore."

"Come on, Lucy, I—"

"There it is again! You never know what the weather in Portland will be. Yep. Definitely the wind. An ill wind that blows no good."

Juliette grabbed her arm, stopping Lucy. "I'm sorry."

Lucy turned on her. "Oh, you're sorry? Well, so am I! Sorry that I had to hear from Angelina who heard it from her mom who heard it from *my* mom that you had a showdown with your parents at Portland Eats and that you're planning to move to Seattle!"

"Why didn't your mom just tell you?"

"She called and left a voice mail, but Angelina got to me first, probably just so she could gloat about it, but that's beside the point. I had to hear thirdhand that you're moving! That is just not cool! I tell you everything—literally everything—about my life! Not only did you not tell me about the most important parts of yours, but you didn't even call me after it all came out to give me a heads-up. My mom gave me the third degree, trying to figure out what I knew and when, and let me tell you, it was awkward when it came out that I knew you were dating Brody weeks ago. Now *I'm* in the doghouse, too!"

"I have no excuses for not calling you right away." Other than the fact that she'd been completely overwhelmed after her talk with Brody and all she'd wanted to do was lock herself in her cottage and eat salted caramel ice cream straight out of the carton.

"You hurt me. I'm angry."

"I know," she said. "I'm so sorry. And I'm sorry you're angry and hurt."

Lucy shook her head. "I just don't get you. You're always complaining about how your family doesn't support you, but I think it's because you don't even give them a chance to try! I'm not angry just because you didn't tell me. I'm angry because I've always supported you, and I always will. But you didn't let me."

Lucy's words struck her as hard as any blow because she was right. Juliette had always thought of her family as completely unsupportive, but when push came to shove, not only had Tony stepped up to the plate, but so had her dad. She just needed to give them an in.

"I'm an idiot," she told her cousin.

"Yeah, you are."

"I won't do it again."

Lucy narrowed her eyes. "What, exactly are you not going to do again?"

Juliette took a big breath. "I swear I'll never lie to you again or not tell you stuff that's important, and if I do not, may the package delivery guys never come to my house when I'm home, leaving that stupid little slip stuck to my front door and thereby forcing me to take the aforementioned stupid little slip to the delivery service office and wait in line for forty-five minutes, and when I get to the front of the line, they then tell me that sorry, the package is out for redelivery and I have missed it yet again?"

"I shouldn't accept your apology," Lucy said, then sniffed. "You made me feel so bad."

"I know. I suck."

"Yes. You do suck. You suck a lot." Lucy's expression softened. "But I love you anyway."

Juliette held out her arms and thankfully, Lucy allowed herself to be embraced this time.

"Have you punished me enough, or do I have to work through another one of your Saturday classes?"

"I know how much you hate tortoise," Lucy said with a not-so-secret smirk.

"I do. I really do. But maybe I could grovel some more and buy you lunch and then you could forgive me and we can try to put this behind us?" she asked hopefully.

"An expensive lunch?"

"Whatever you want."

"Really, I just want a sandwich from Laurelhurst Market."

"Then I will buy you a sandwich from Laurelhurst Market."

Lucy smiled at her—really smiled at her—and she knew their fight was over. Thank God. Having Lucy angry at her was too much to bear.

She linked her arm in Lucy's and the two of them continued down the block until they reached the place. Juliette chose smoked turkey with Gouda, and Lucy got a vegetarian piled high with peppers and goat cheese.

They walked the couple of blocks to Laurelhurst Park and found a shady spot on the grass under a large tree.

"So are you really leaving?" Lucy asked.

"It's the only way I can get funding. Michael Sutherland—the guy I'm partnering with—offered all the start-up costs for forty percent of the business. It's a good deal with one of the best in the business, and I'd be a fool not to take it."

"Too bad you have to go almost two hundred miles away to make it happen."

"Yeah." She took a bite of her sandwich.

Lucy gave her an appraising look. "For a woman who's got a ton of money in her pocket, you don't sound so happy."

"I still want my own thing, and I think taking this deal is the way to go. But…for the last couple of days, I've been having second thoughts about Seattle."

"It's hard to start over in a new place. Maybe you'll miss your family?" Juliette just gave her a look. "Jerk," Lucy said, elbowing her in the side. "That family includes me."

"Of course I'll miss you, but that's not it, either."

"Maybe you'll miss Brody? Or will you be doing the long-distance relationship thing?"

Her chest started to ache. "We're not together anymore."

"What? Why?"

"I didn't tell him I was leaving, either."

"Oh, no, Juliette. He took it badly?"

"That would be an understatement," she said miserably. "The thing is, I'm genuinely sorry it ended. I really liked him." More than liked him. "I just never expected things to get this far."

"Maybe he felt the same way. Maybe he's just as sorry as you are."

"I don't think so," she whispered.

Lucy must have realized that Juliette was about to lose it, because she set down her sandwich and wrapped her arm around Juliette's shoulder.

To her mortification, a tear squeezed from her eye and slipped down her cheek. Quickly, she wiped it away.

"I'm so sorry, honey."

"It's okay. I'm okay." She pressed her palms against her eyes, as if willing the tears to stop. After a long moment, she composed herself. "Tell me something happy."

Lucy nodded. "I don't know about happy, but I have some news on the expansion front."

"Good news, I hope."

"Sort of. The building next door to my studio is for sale."

Juliette knew that building—it was a decent size, two stories that included retail space on the bottom and a couple of apartments on top.

"That's great! Are you going to buy it?" She knew Lucy had the money—her studio raked it in hand over fist.

"I can't beat the location," Lucy said. "I love my neighborhood, and the building has great bones, but it's literally twice the size of what I need. In fact, the bottom floor is divided up into two separate spaces, but the whole thing is sold as one unit. I guess I could hire someone to knock down walls, but that seems like an awful lot of work, especially since what I'd hoped to do was to use the new space as my meditation and workshopping space." She stopped and shook her head. "Eh, it'll be okay. Something will crop up that'll make sense."

"But how can you be sure? The opportunity is right there for the taking. Don't you want to take advantage of that?"

Lucy shrugged. "Other stuff will come along, I'm sure. It might not be as perfect, but I'll be able to make something work."

She was so calm, so unconcerned. "You're so Zen about it."

"Life's too short to stress about little stuff like this."

"This is big stuff!" Juliette said.

But Lucy only shook her head. "Nah. The big stuff, the really important stuff? That has nothing to do with work or money or real estate. But I think you already knew that."

"Right," Juliette said slowly.

They ate the rest of their sandwiches and talked, about Angelina's upcoming wedding all the family crazy that had ensued over the past week. Finally, after they'd talked for a good, long time, Lucy rose gracefully.

"I'd better be getting back. I've got a class in half an hour." She reached out to grasp Juliette's wrist and gave it a squeeze. "Thank you for coming today. I've missed you terribly."

"Same."

"Aw, c'mere." Lucy embraced her and held her close. "Love you, Juliette. Never forget that."

The inside of her eyelids prickled. "Thanks. And ditto."

When they separated, Juliette held out her hand for the pinkie link. Lucy took it, squeezed, and gave her a tearful smile. Then, with one last look, she pulled away and walked briskly down the block, her long ponytail swaying with her movements.

Juliette stayed for another moment, then started walking in the opposite direction, towards home.

She'd miss having lunch with Lucy when she was gone. Miss seeing her smiling face, and getting her ass kicked in yoga and then heading home to her tiny cottage afterward and having Aunt Violetta come knocking, and oh, hell, she'd miss everything about living here, really. Powell's and her podcast and food carts and all of the little pockets of the city that were unique and weird and so very Portland. Her life was here, her family, too, and yes, while she wanted to stand on her own two feet and have her own business, the idea of moving away from them wasn't something that she'd ever wished for. Despite all the flak they gave her, they loved her and she loved them.

There was someone else she loved, too. Brody Phelan, with

his intelligence and his beard and his obsession with old cars and his family that was just as crazy as hers and the smile in his eyes when he looked at her.

She loved him, only she'd been too scared to see how much. Pushing him away was the biggest mistake she'd ever made. But it didn't matter because she was leaving…

She stopped stock still on the street where she stood. One breath later she pivoted, then started walking back the way Lucy had gone. She had to reach her cousin, right now. Had to tell her. Yes. This is what she needed to be doing. Moving towards her destiny, the one she'd been too afraid to reach out and take because of fears that she wasn't strong enough. But she was, absolutely. She only had to have faith in herself to see this through. She walked faster and faster, barely seeing the streets.

At some point, she must have started running, and her sharp bursts of breath only made her think more clearly. Her thoughts solidified, formed into a plan that made so much sense she couldn't understand why she hadn't thought of it before. This was real. This was right. She pounded down the pavement even faster.

She caught up to Lucy just outside her studio.

"Lucy!" she shouted. "Lucy!"

Lucy swung around. "Juliette?" She blinked. "Are you okay?"

"No," she said, pinching the stitch in her side and forcing deep breaths into her lungs. "I mean, yes. I just need to talk to you."

"About what?" Lucy asked, her brows going together. "Angelina? Aunt Mattea? You do *not* need to lose three pounds before the wedding, so ignore the insanity."

"No, no, not them." She waved her hand to signify that wasn't it at all. "About a plan that will make both of us happy. But I'm going to need your help."

"Of course. You can count on me for anything.

CHAPTER 22

Brody slid out from underneath his jacked-up Camaro and eyed the drain pan as oil dripped down. With the ventilation fan and the stereo on, it was plenty loud in his garage, but he wanted it louder. Doing an ab curl, he sat up, then dragged himself to standing and increased the volume until the strains of Finn's bass guitar pouring from the speakers rattled the windows.

Business as usual.

Yesterday as he was going for his run, Juliette's podcast had toggled into rotation. She must have recorded the episode weeks ago, and her thick, rich voice washing over him in a wave almost brought him to his knees.

Forget her. Forget everything.

Not fucking likely.

The old oil had stopped running out of the crankcase, so he dropped back down to the creeper and slid back under the vehicle. Running on muscle memory, he cleaned and replaced the drain plug and replaced the filter—the latter without spilling a single drop of oil outside the drain pan.

As he slid back out from under the car, a pair of steel-toed work boots came into his line of sight. Moving the creeper back, he stared up a pair of long legs until he reached Ed's face.

"Hey," Ed yelled. "Can I turn off the music?"

"Okay."

Ed flipped off the stereo, then turned back. "I got a couple of questions, but if you're in the middle of something, I can wait."

"I'm just finishing up an oil change."

"Take your time," Ed said, and moseyed over to a utilitarian chair in the corner.

Ed was a patient man, so Brody took the few minutes to pour in the new oil and check the engine. Satisfied that everything was running smoothly, he turned off the car. When he was done, he lifted his gaze to find Ed sitting on the chair, back ramrod straight, eyes glued to his phone.

"What's up?" he asked.

Ed shoved his phone in his back pocket. "I want to install another set of railings, cordoning off the vats from the rest of the production floor."

That was Ed. Straight to the point.

"Why? What happened?" Brody queried. "Did someone get hurt?"

"No."

"A close shave, then?"

"Nope. We haven't had any safety incidents since Gabe started doing those fucking tours. Not even close shaves."

"Got it," Brody said. It took a lot of balls for Ed to admit that Gabe did something right, so he didn't push it. "Just let me know which vats you want me to cordon off, so I can get an estimate as to cost."

"Already done. Sent it to you by email while you were working."

"Great. I'll look at it tomorrow," he said, then sighed. "I know you didn't come here just to ask me about installing guard railings, and you're not one to beat around the bush. So why don't you tell me what you're really here for?"

Ed's mouth got tight. "Fine. You want me to be blunt? I'll be blunt. When are you going to get your head out of your ass and get your woman back?"

Brody blinked. "Excuse me?"

"You heard me. You're the smartest guy I know, but you are an idiot when it comes to women."

He hadn't discussed his breakup with his family. Not only had no one asked, but it wasn't the kind of thing he talked about, anyway. "Not that it's any of your business, but if you know that

Juliette and I aren't together, you probably also know the reason why."

"The reason is bullshit. When Sienna left, I didn't have a choice. We were young, and we both thought we were doing the right thing. But you're an adult with means and money and opportunity. Don't throw away what you have because of a little distance. You can still make it work."

Brody sighed and crossed the room to dump the old oil into the catch jar. He really didn't want to get into it with Ed. Not about this. But Ed with a problem to solve was like a dog with a bone. He wouldn't let go until he'd gnawed the fucking thing to death. "I appreciate what you're trying to do," he said over his shoulder, "but you're missing a critical piece of information in this scenario."

"What's that?"

"Simple." He put the pan down and turned back to Ed. "Sienna was always honest with you about the fact that she wanted to leave. Juliette wasn't."

"So?"

"So I can't be in a relationship with a woman who withholds critical information about her life that affects both of us."

"What the hell are you talking about? So you date the woman for a few weeks and all of a sudden she's supposed to be spilling her guts to you? Let her have some fucking time to learn to trust you."

Brody peeled off his latex work gloves one by one and tossed them in the trash. "She kept a secret from me."

"Who cares? Hell, I keep secrets from you all the time!"

"Name one."

Ed thought for a moment. "Remember when I told you I was going up to Mount Hood for the long weekend in spring?"

"Yeah?"

"I didn't go."

"Where did you go? Don't tell me you just stayed in your house."

"Nope. I drove out to the coast to see the ocean and slept on the beach."

Brody frowned. "Why the hell did you do that? It's cold and dangerous, not to mention illegal in some places. Did you have a tent? Did you have a permit? And why didn't you tell me the truth?"

"Because I didn't want to answer stupid questions like those.

What I'm saying is that sometimes people have good reasons for keeping secrets, and not all of them are bad."

"There's never a good reason to keep a secret. Not if you really love someone."

"No offense, cousin, but I don't think you know what real love is."

"Says the man who hasn't gone on a date in years."

Ed gave him an even look. "Loving someone is like riding a bike. Once you understand that, you never forget how to do it. I had a woman once. A good woman. But she wanted to fly, and I set her free because I loved her too much to make her stay. So yeah, you're right. I haven't been on a date in years, but that doesn't matter because I've loved, and I've loved deep, and I don't need to fuck my way through Portland to prove that I'm over it."

Ouch.

Ed went on. "But this isn't about me. It was never about me. This is about you. You don't trust her because you don't trust yourself, but deep in your heart, you must know that's complete bullshit. Your dad was a jackass. We all know that. But what he did does not reflect on you in any way, shape, or form. You're your own man. You're a smart guy, a driven guy. You turned your talents to Wolfshead, and we've never been doing better. You can make cars purr like nothing I've ever seen. But what you don't get is that you're worthy of love. I can see it your eyes that you don't think that's true, but you are. You always have been. Accept it."

"It's not that simple." Even if he could get over the years of doubt, of what he'd seen of "true" love in the fucked-up relationship his father had with his mother, of the women using him for what he could give them, not for who he was, it took two to tango and he didn't have a dancing partner.

"It is." Ed jerked his finger to the garage door. "Out there, there is a woman who loves you because of your flaws, not despite them. So get over yourself and whatever shit you're harboring inside and go make her yours."

"Juliette's gone, Ed," he said flatly. "For good. It's over." Because she definitely didn't love him. How could she after the way he ended things?

"I have one question for you: Do you still love her?"

Brody couldn't lie. Not about this. "Yes."

"Then it isn't over." His cousin rose and walked to the door. "Thanks again for approving the guardrails."

Ed disappeared, the door slammed shut, and an engine roared to life. Slowly, the sound faded away.

Brody finished cleaning his work space, then clicked off the garage light. Silently, he made his way through the house and out to the back porch. The nights were getting cooler, the days wetter. Soon, the days would be even rainier, the evenings longer.

And he'd be spending them without Juliette.

God, he missed her. Over the past couple of months, once he'd gotten past that saucy tongue and her attitude, he'd found a woman he couldn't live without. He loved her. And the more he thought about it, the more he could not imagine his future without her.

Damn it, Ed was right. He'd been such an ass. He'd let his past define his present and affect what was to come. He'd been so wrapped up in his own head that he couldn't see the truth staring at him for so long. He could choose not to be defined by his father's actions. Love was giving and taking. Not every part of a relationship was black or white. And what he felt for Juliette was love. Real, messy, difficult, beautiful love.

Brody pulled out his cell phone, his fingers hovering over the keypad the way they'd done so many times before. He'd wanted to call, text, email, anything to let her know that he was thinking about her and that he still loved her, but he'd been too angry. Or so he'd thought. Now, what he realized was that he'd been too scared that she'd reject him. But he wasn't, not anymore. He needed to let her know how he felt. They could figure this out. They had to. She was probably already in Seattle, but that didn't matter. He let his fingers fly over her familiar number. Her voice mail picked up. His message was simple: call me.

As soon as he hung up, he started planning. Crap, he'd wasted a week without her, time he'd never get back, but damned if he wasn't going to spend the rest of his life trying.

If she'd have him back.

She *had* to have him back. She had to forgive him because he loved her. That was how it was supposed to work, right? Love always won?

Dark thoughts pushed in from the recesses of his mind—it

didn't work for you before, it didn't work for Mom—but he pushed them back, focusing only on the here and now.

He called Aidan and left a message, telling him he wouldn't be at work tomorrow. Same with his mom. They could handle things without him for once.

Tossing on a jacket, he thought through his next steps: Get on a plane to Seattle. Find Juliette. Tell her he was sorry. Confess his undying love.

It was a shit plan, but he'd done well before with less.

He had just grabbed his car keys from the kitchen counter when he heard a car's engine outside. Ed returning for another set-down? He'd been pretty effective the first time.

He peered out the front window, only to see Juliette's beaten-up Toyota, complete with one brand-spanking-new automotive belt.

He opened his front door as she got out of the car. She was dressed in a pair of stretchy pants and an off-the-shoulder T-shirt that read "Laurelhurst Yoga" in script on the front. Her hair was up in a messy bun. He'd never seen her look more beautiful. Or more nervous.

"Hi," she said.

All the breath left his lungs. She was here. She hadn't left yet.

When he didn't immediately speak, she visibly swallowed. "Okay, well, I came because I was thinking, well, not just thinking, but talking. To my dad and Lucy and, I had this plan, you see, I—" She stopped. "I'm babbling. I do that when I get nervous, because I'm really, really nervous, here." She twisted her hands together and frowned. "But I can see that I'm too late. You're done and you don't want to see me. I've made a terrible mistake. I'm so sorry to have bothered you." She started to turn away.

He finally got his mouth to work. "Juliette, wait. I—I'm just in shock because I thought you'd already left for Seattle. And I didn't really have a good plan, but I wanted to see you. I was just heading to the airport."

She turned back. "You were?" The look of hope in her eyes blew him away. "That's why I came…because I wanted to see you, too."

"Juliette, I—"

"I'm not moving to Seattle!" she blurted out.

The whole world went completely, utterly still. "What?"

"I'm not moving," she repeated. "I'm staying in Portland."

"Why?" he croaked. He needed to know.

"For so long, I'd wanted to open my own business. And then the Michael Sutherland deal dropped in my lap and working with him was so tempting, and I honestly thought it was the only way to get what I wanted. I was so committed to doing things solo, protecting my business from my family, being strong without them to prove that I could do things my own way. But I forgot something important— it's not weak to ask for help."

That's right. He'd helped her. And he'd felt good about it. It had made him feel needed. Wanted.

She was still talking. "I realized that that was true, even if the help came from my own family. Take my cousin Lucy. All she wanted was for me to share my story and be open with her so we could talk things through, like we always did, but I hid from her, too, because I was certain that no one could get it. Until I realized that *everyone* got it. Everyone except me." She took a breath. "But I finally got wise. Asked her to go in with me. I turned down the Sutherland deal," she told him. "I'm going to open my wine bar here, in Portland. I'll take out a bank loan, and Lucy and I are going to go in together to buy the building next door to her studio. She'll take half of the ground floor, and I'll take the other half to open my wine bar. Sure, it'll require some renovations, but I'm up for the challenge. And I'm going to live upstairs in one of the apartments. But that's not the most important reason I'm staying."

"What is?" The words came out low and rough.

Juliette looked straight at him. "You. All along, I kept telling myself that you were the one allergic to commitment, that you could never be serious about me, and I used that as an excuse to push you away, even as I fell in love with you. But really, I was just afraid— afraid of showing how weak I was that I wanted you so badly. You're it for me, Brody. I think I've known that forever. You're a good man."

He shook his head. No, he wasn't. Not even close.

"You are," she insisted. "Whether you see it or not, it's true. And I want you, Brody. I've never stopped wanting you. Please tell me you want me, too."

"God, yes," he rasped.

He didn't know who made the first move. All he knew was

that one moment they were apart and the next they were together, her wrapped in his arms, her face buried in his chest.

"I missed you so much," she sobbed as he stroked her hair. "I'm so sorry I didn't tell you."

"I should be the one apologizing to you." He pulled back. Wiped her tears away with his thumbs. "I was coming to you to tell you that I was a colossal ass for overreacting. I get why you wanted to keep your plans to yourself."

"I still should have told you."

"You were doing what you thought was right."

"I was protecting myself."

"So was I, always looking for the escape hatch in relationships, believing they couldn't last. I wanted so badly to protect myself that I closed myself off. And then you came along and blew my world wide open." He cupped her face in his hands and tipped it up to his. "Let me be completely clear. I don't just want part of you, I want all of you. I want to wake up next to you every morning. I want to share my life and my business with you. I want to go to work, knowing you'll be waiting for me when I get home. I want to sleep with you curled up next to me. I want your secrets. I want everything because I love you. Most of all, I want to be where you are."

"Here," she said.

"Here. So let's make a deal. Right now, we move forward, and we're going to work through our trust issues together."

"What if I have more secrets? Secrets I don't even know I'm holding?"

"Then we will deal with them." He pushed a strand of hair back from her beautiful face. "I'm not perfect. Not even close. But if you believe that I'm a good man, then I'm going to damn sure spend every day living up to that expectation. It'll take time to work through all my shit, but I know you'll tell me when I fuck up."

She nodded. "Only if you promise to do the same for me."

God, he loved this woman, body and soul. He crushed her to his body, kissed her mouth, tasting the sweetness and the tears.

This was what it was like to be in love. To trust that his partner was strong and confident, that she'd chosen him because she'd seen something in him he couldn't even see in himself. That he was worthy of her love.

"Oh, Costa," he said, his lips playing over hers. "We're going to be amazing together, aren't we?"

She looked up at him and flashed a brilliant smile. "Yeah, Phelan. We sure are."

EPILOGUE

Three weeks later…

Impatiently, Brody tapped his foot. "Come on, Costa! We're going to be late for the wedding!"

"Just one more minute," Juliette called out from the bedroom. There was the sound of something dropping on the floor, then some frantic muttering. A moment later she emerged looking unbelievably gorgeous despite the form-fitting, shiny turquoise-blue dress that hugged every one of her decadent curves. Her eyelids were highlighted with some of that colored stuff, her lips were red, and her hair was a mass of barely-tamed curls.

"Don't laugh," she told him sternly.

"Why would I laugh at you?" She was a dream. *His* dream, and he thanked his lucky stars every day that she was his.

"Because the dress is ridiculous and I look ridiculous in it. I mean, I know it's Angelina's wedding day and all, but I should get a medal for having to wear this."

He looked at it with a critical eye. "It's not that bad. I don't mind the…what do you call it?"

"A ruffle," she said through clenched teeth.

"Yeah. It's cute."

She looked at him in disbelief. "It's on my ass."

"That's why I don't mind it."

"Seriously, Brody, I—"

But he'd crossed the room, taken her in his arms, and kissing the ever-living hell out of her.

"Brody!" She batted at him ineffectually. "You're going to mess me up."

"That's the idea," he murmured before going in for another kiss. He kept kissing her until she went boneless. When he finally pulled away, her expression was relaxed, her eyes glassy.

"You're beautiful," he told her. "With or without a ruffle. In whatever you're wearing."

"You're sweet," she said, blushing.

"I speak the truth. But if I was being really honest, I'd tell you I liked you better wearing nothing at all."

She laughed. "Not going to happen right now, because we're going to be late if we don't leave now."

He nibbled at her neck. "Angelina will understand."

"No," she said, ducking out of his hold, taking him in hand and pulling him toward the door. "She will not. She will hunt me down and she will kill me with her bare hands because she is crazy." She grabbed his car keys from the entranceway table and threw them in a graceful arc. He caught them one-handed and opened the door for her.

"My family's crazy, too." Though they'd all been thrilled for him when he'd told them he'd gotten back together with Juliette— even Finn. To their credit, the Costas had also stepped up. Gio still stared daggers at him, but the rest of Juliette's family seemed to accept him. Probably because she'd told them the chief reason she was staying in Portland was for him.

She ran a hand down his lapel as he locked his front door. "Yeah, they are. And you're the craziest one of all."

He grinned. "Sure, I'm crazy. Crazy for you."

That got him another soft kiss and a meltingly sweet sigh. She finally pulled away with obvious reluctance. "We really can't be late."

"Taskmaster," he grumbled, following her to his car.

"I'll make it up to you later," she tossed over her shoulder.

"Promise?"

She stopped on the driveway and turned, then whispered in his ear. "Promise."

"Tell me you are bringing extra lipstick."

"Yes, why?"

"Because as soon as the reception is underway and your

toasts are over, I'm going to escape with you into the coatroom, kiss you senseless, and then give you the best orgasm of your life."

"That's not possible," she teased. "Because I already had the best orgasm of my life this morning."

His eyes almost crossed, remembering the scene. They'd been in the shower. Juliette had started out on her knees, taking him to completion in her mouth. Then he'd returned the favor as hot water sluiced over them both. She'd grabbed his head and screamed out his name. "I'm going to put that one to shame," he said with a grin.

She arched a brow. "You talk the talk, Phelan, but can you walk the walk?"

"Oh yeah," he said, pulling her close and kissing her again.

For her, he would. Anywhere, anytime. Because Juliette Costa was it for him. Tart, sweet, and everything in between. He saw things so clearly, the beginning of an amazing life, filled with laughter and arguments and warmth and love and children—lots of them—maybe with sparkling brown eyes and curly brown hair, just like hers. They could overcome any obstacles in their path—her family, his family, their work—because they had each other. Forever with her was most definitely in his future.

She smiled at him, and he smiled back.

He couldn't wait.

ABOUT THE AUTHOR

Elisabeth Barrett lives in the San Francisco Bay Area and spends her days teaching, editing, writing sexy contemporary romance, and enjoying time with her sometimes-bearded husband and three spirited children. She is constantly perfecting her home-work-writing juggling act, but in her free time she loves to hike open space preserves, grow orchids, bake sweet things her husband won't eat, and sing in grand choruses.

www.elisabethbarrett.com